I0647157

Battle Orders

a docu-drama of a young Lancaster crew's experiences in 1945

Following RAF service as a navigator, **George Culling** was successively a teacher, head teacher, principal lecturer in a polytechnic and director of the Schools and Teacher Training Dept of the British Council. He has been married to Maureen for seventy years and they have three sons, six grandchildren and one great grandson. 'Battle Orders: a docu-drama of a young Lancaster crew's experiencies in 1945' is a fact-based work of fiction, which includes dramatic incidents in the skies over Germany, the fears, hopes and aspirations of the seven nineteen-year-old airmen, and progress in the closing stages of the Second World War. George is also the author of *Tales of Lancasters and Other Aircraft*.

By the same Author –

Tales of Lancasters and other Aircraft

Battle Orders

a docu-drama of a young Lancaster crew's experiences in 1945

George Culling

Arena Books

Copyright © George Culling 2020

The right of George Culling to be identified as author of this book
has been asserted in accordance with the Copyright, Designs and
Patents Act 1988. All characters and events described in this book are
fictional and any resemblance to actual persons, living or dead, is
purely coincidental.

First published in 2020 by Arena Books

Arena Books
6 Southgate Green
Bury St. Edmunds
IP33 2BL

www.arenabooks.co.uk

Distributed in America by Ingram International, One Ingram Blvd., P.O. Box 3006, La
Vergne, TN 37086-1985, USA.

All rights reserved. Except for the quotation of short passages for the
purposes of criticism and review, no part of this publication may be
reproduced, stored in a retrieval system, or transmitted, in any form or
by any means, electronic, mechanical, photocopying, recording or
otherwise, without the prior permission of the author or the publisher
acting as his agent.

George Culling
Battle Orders *a docu-drama of a young Lancaster crew's experiences in 1945*

British Library cataloguing in Publication Data. A Catalogue record
for this book is available from the British Library.

ISBN-13   978-1-911593-77-5

BIC classifications:- FA, BGH, BTM, BM.

Cover design
By Anna Gatt

Typeset in
Times New Roman

I dedicate this book to members of the

Air Crew Association

many of whom completed more than thirty operations over Germany (the standard 'tour') and experienced many of the life-threatening incidents described in this book.

ACKNOWLEDGEMENTS

I am very conscious of my debt to Maureen, my wife, whose support for my writing has always been wholehearted and generous.

Our sons, Stephen, Clive and John, have also made useful contributions, especially the former, who has always been ready to solve the many computer problems which tend to accumulate following 'updates.'

I am also very grateful to the following, whose suggestions have been useful: Gill Aslett, Ian Cameron, Halina S., Virginia Brinton.

George Culling and his wife, Maureen, in a Lancaster bomber

At Duxford IWM, 74 years after his last

Navigation of one

CHAPTER 1

Sgt. Jack Rogers,

RAF Coningsby,

Nr. Horncastle,

Lincolnshire

March 9th, 1945

Dear Maurice,

Great to hear from you! Yes, I'm now the wireless operator of a Lancaster, one of a crew of seven, all of us around nineteen. We're still getting to know one another as we were strangers not long ago, but I can tell you a little bit about the others.

Our skipper, John Mason, is first rate, both as a pilot and a leader. He's calm, takes sensible decisions, and I'm sure he'll hold us together when we're at risk of being blown out of the sky by ack – ack fire or the cannon or machine guns of night fighters. And he's a very nice chap.

I don't know much about our navigator, Reg Atkins, a dark-haired little fellow who's always busy at his desk, behind a black curtain to shade the light he needs. He uses radar but I think he loves to use the stars. I see him when he gets under the astrodome with his sextant to take shots of stars. So far, he's navigated the kite without any problems.

You'd like Freddie Jones, our bomb-aimer, who joined the RAF straight from school. He's baby-faced and always looks about to break into laughter. He loves jokes and larking about (probably a handful at school), but he's very serious about playing his part in shortening the war by bombing war factories, airfields, etc.

Sam Bunting, our rear gunner, is big and muscular, and I don't know how he manages to squeeze into his turret. I wonder if he's a bit short of confidence, and unsure of the future — but aren't we all?

Scotty McDowell, our ginger-haired mid-upper gunner, was a coal miner in Scotland. A pleasant chap, he seems to get on well with everyone.

Arthur Jenkins, our flight engineer, is lanky, slow-speaking, and a man of few words. Looking after our four Rolls-Royce Merlin engines is his passion.

Well, that's us. We're all pretty new to our jobs, but I'm hopeful we'll work together well and make a nuisance of ourselves to Jerry!

You've asked me how we came together. Well, that was unbelievable. Imagine a large hall, full of navigators, pilots, gunners, wireless operators and bomb-aimers. They're drinking tea, nibbling biscuits and the noise is deafening. Recent training experiences -some of dubious validity- are related, followed by sudden loud eruptions of laughter. Some airmen circulate; others stay put. Slowly, groups consolidate and crews are formed.

Within a few weeks each crew is flying in a Wellington bomber. I'm sure you'll think that's a very odd and inefficient way of forming a crew, but it seems to work well in general.

Anyway, after a few months, we were moved to a 'Heavy Conversion Unit' at Swinderby, to crew a Lancaster. We then received a mid-upper gunner (Scotty) and a flight engineer (Arthur) to make us seven strong. I think we're a friendly crew, and each of us is keen to be good at his job. Only time will tell whether we make the grade, but I'm optimistic.

What wonderful news it was in November about the sinking of the battleship Tirpitz. German battleships have sunk so many of our merchant ships, with a huge loss of life.

Please write again soon.

Your very good friend,

Jack

***

It was an awe-inspiring sight, but also chaotic and frightening. The sky was crowded with Lancasters, with a few Halifaxes and Stirlings. Green and red flares marked out the target area, fired by the pathfinders a few minutes before the arrival of the main bomber force; puffs of black smoke, following explosions of anti-aircraft shells were everywhere; and the probing fingers of searchlights waved about the sky threateningly.

BATTLE ORDERS

There was a huge flash as a Lancaster about fifty yards away, exploded, following a direct hit from a shell, on its bomb bay. There was no chance of any of the crew surviving.

'My God, this is hell! shouted Scotty McDowell, as he swivelled his turret, with its two machine guns, from side to side, while taking in the threatening scene.

Freddie Jones, bomb-aimer, and youngest of the crew, also saw it happen. It filled him with a deep sadness; and a nagging fear that made his whole body shake uncontrollably and tightened his stomach.

Sam Bunting, rear-gunner, saw another Lancaster on fire but still flying. He noted that only four parachute canopies opened up just below the stricken aircraft. Soon afterwards, it spiralled to the ground. Three airmen had *got the chop*. He fervently hoped that one of them was not his very close friend, Bill Irons, a pilot, whose Lancaster was also on 'Battle Orders' for this operation.

Sam thought of the difficulties when baling out of a Lancaster.

All the crew are supposed to leave through the exit in the floor, but doing that quickly with bulky gear and parachutes is very difficult. No wonder some chaps can't get out in time.

Jack Rogers, sitting before his radio equipment, could not see out, though the thumps and flashes conveyed to him some idea of the reality. It wasn't enough. Anxious to see for himself what was actually happening around them, he stood up to take a quick look through the astrodome.

'Yes, it's hell alright,' he thought. *'I hope we'll soon get to the marshalling yards at Remsheid so we can get on with the bombing.'*

There was now a pungent smell of cordite, as anti-aircraft shells burst perilously close, but their Lancaster, P - Peter, battled through the barrage as they approached the target.

Some pilots nearby were manoeuvring desperately to avoid complete destruction, while others were trying to fly straight and level on the bombing run.

John Mason sometimes jigged his Lancaster a little, to make it as difficult a target as possible for the gunners on the ground, but in general he now worked hard to maintain straight and level flight as they approached the target area.

The control column he held was wet from the perspiration of his palms.

During those crucial minutes before 'bombs gone' the Lancasters were extremely vulnerable. There could be little variation of height or speed to evade the gunfire, for the bomb-aimer's calculations depended on a stable run.

Meanwhile, the dangers were many. A red-hot splinter from a bursting shell could ignite the five tons of high explosive under the fuselage. There were also the twin dangers of collisions with other aircraft and being under one that had just released its bombs. It was the most menacing and frightening period of the whole operation.

Most of the crew, especially those looking out, were tense and fearful, but determined to fulfil their tasks. Reg Atkins, calculating in front of his Mercator chart, hardly ever looked out. He was always too busy.

Freddie Jones now broke in excitedly –

'Bomb-aimer here, Skip. Target ahead!' He was gripped by nervous excitement and shaking with fear, but ready to do everything required of him.

'Skip here. That's great, Freddie. I'm in your hands.'

'Bomb doors open, Skip.'

Arthur Jenkins, the flight engineer, who worked closely with John, immediately operated them.

'Bomb doors open, Freddie.' John announced. Freddie's eyes were now glued to his bomb site in rapt concentration. Now carrying out his main task, he felt calmer. He knew his role was vitally important.

'OK. Skip. Five degrees to port... that's it... keep her steady ... shade more to port... I can see the railway marshalling yards clearly now... left... left... steady.'

The Lancaster was being tossed about by the slipstream of an aircraft in front as well as by shells exploding nearby as John struggled to keep it steady. Another Lancaster, immediately behind, was closing the gap, and that worried him, too, as he certainly couldn't get any closer to the one in front. Freddie 's voice returned.

'Steady, Skip, steady...little left...steady...steady...steady... bombs gone.'

P-Peter was too high for the crew to see the full results of the bombing. The operation, involving forty Lancasters, had largely achieved its objective. It would be some considerable time before the battered marshalling yards could be used again for the transport of troops and war materials.

Many railway sheds and other buildings had been reduced to piles of rubble, in which a few jagged wall remnants stood defiantly upright. Locomotives lay broken on their sides. Twisted railway lines were strewn on the walls of bomb craters, while carriages lay smashed and useless amidst the carnage.

Suddenly freed of its heavy bomb load, the huge aircraft shot several hundred feet into the air, then wobbled as it adjusted to flying without its deadly cargo.

There remained important unfinished business.

'Bomb aimer here, Skip. Keep her steady for a good photo.'

That required more straight and level flight, with the aircraft still exposed to a fierce battery of anti-aircraft guns, extending the tension felt by the crew. To them, the few minutes before the photograph was taken seemed agonisingly long.

'Skip here. All done. Good. Now, let's get the hell out of here - fast!'

'Skip to Navigator, give me a course for our first leg home'

' 240 degrees, Skip.'

'Thanks, Reg. Here we go.'

***

For the early part of the homeward flight, only the four Rolls Royce engines could be heard - loud, insistent and monotonous.

John thought they might be sleep-inducing, and warned against any relaxation of alertness. It was, after all, the middle of the night.

'Skip here for all crew. It was pretty dicey near the target, but well done, Freddie. You did a good job.'

'Thanks, Skip, but we all did our bit. Reg navigated us to the target, Jack gave me an accurate wind velocity for the bomb sight, and you kept the kite steady at the right time.'

'True, Freddie, but we depend on you to make the whole op worthwhile by hitting the target.'

'Skip, mid-upper gunner here. Don't you think we sometimes see more of the damage than you can see in a photo?'

'Sometimes we do, Scotty, but the photo is evidence that we really have bombed the target. Now...we have a long way to go over Germany, so expect more flak - perhaps much more. Night fighters will have a go at us, too, so Sam and Scotty, keep your eyes skinned, especially when the flak goes quiet, as now.'

'Scotty here, Skip. Sam and I have had our amphetamine tablets.' He laughed. 'And we've never been more awake, have we Sam?' He sounded extraordinarily bright and cheerful.

Sam responded in a quieter voice, close to a grumble.

'It's the flak that keeps me wide awake, and the thump of the shrapnel hitting the fuselage.'

As they spoke, John was thinking about the pressures to which his crew were exposed.

'The first few ops will test their calibre: their abilities, their characters and their courage. I must try to weld them into a high-performing crew, working well together, and building up camaraderie and team-work. Both gunners had high scores at their gunnery schools and should do well when the night fighters attack.

Scotty clearly has resilience and a nice sense of humour. He's lively and has just the right temperament for these ops. Sam seems rather moody and lacking in confidence, and might need a few words of support from time to time. But it's early days, and they'll probably both turn out alright.'

Suddenly the relative silence was shattered. There was a very loud bang, followed by a deafening sound like the crash of heavy hailstorm pellets rattling on a corrugated roof. It was both alarming and ominous.

' My God,' shouted Jack Porter, 'what was that?'

No-one answered because no-one knew. They had been hit, but the aircraft still responded to the controls. They would discover later how much damage had been done to P-Peter.

John hoped the damage would prove to be superficial. He raised the aircraft's nose, managed to climb to 20,000 feet, and settled the speed around 220 mph. So far, so good.

'Perhaps,' he thought, *' the German gunners will be confused by the sudden change of altitude.'* But soon afterwards, they had adjusted their settings to the new height, and the flak continued.

About ten minutes later, however, the guns were silent, and once again, it was only the loud, monotonous drone of the four Rolls-Royce Merlin engines that filled the aircraft.

'They've all stopped firing,' John noted. *'The night fighters can't be far away.'* A 'new' enemy would confront them at any moment. At least, they would be able to fight back with their Browning machine guns. The tired eyes of Sam and Scotty scanned the sky. And Freddie, his main task over, peered out, his own two machine guns at the ready. All three had a single thought.

From which direction would an air attack come?

***

Sam was cold and uncomfortable, with icicles sprouting on his oxygen mask. His isolated turret, at the rear of the aircraft, was only just large enough to accommodate his six foot, two inch frame. Built like a rugby prop, with his head pressed against the roof of the turret, and his shoulders nudging the sides, he was virtually trapped in one position. He hadn't even been able to climb in wearing his flying boots so he'd had to throw them in first.

He needed the clearest possible view through the perspex turret, to spot enemy fighters before they were close enough to attack. The turret tended to frost up at their normal operational height of 20,000 feet, so Sam had the panel at eye level completely removed, following the example of many other rear gunners. That meant that his face was now fully exposed to the freezing slipstream, with a serious risk of frostbite. Sam, though, had smeared vaseline on those exposed parts of his face that were not protected by either his helmet or his oxygen mask. He knew some rear gunners who had suffered from frostbitten faces, hands and feet.

All rear gunners wore an electrically- heated suit to compensate for the lack of heating in their turret. But Sam's was unreliable, and tonight it was not working at all. His turret had a temperature of -38 degrees Celsius.

He noticed that all four of his machine-guns, which he would need at any minute, were now icing-up! Without hesitation, he opened his thermos flask and poured hot, steaming coffee over them until he was satisfied that they had defrozen and were ready for use.

For the time being, however, nothing seemed to be happening, and Sam, feeling the loneliness of his physical isolation from the rest of the crew, indulged in a little reflection

'When I volunteered for Bomber Command, I didn't realise how dangerous it could be. Still, we got back safely after our first op, to the Schweinfurt ball-bearing factory so, with luck, perhaps we'll get back from this one.

It's sad that four of the Lancs on that op weren't so lucky. Curly Brown, the squadron's comedian was on one of them. I can still hear him laughing and telling jokes. Poor old Curly.

If any of our Lancs get the chop this time, I hope the crews manage to bail out and parachute to safety. Especially if Bill Irons is the pilot of one of them.'

Sam was suddenly brought back to the present reality.

An abrupt crackle on the intercom was followed by John's voice.

'Skip here. Sam, Scotty and Freddie, keep your eyes peeled! We're bang in the middle of where we're expecting night fighters!'

CHAPTER 2

S am peered into the semi-darkness of the night. There was no moon, but millions of bright, sparkling stars, which were sometimes obscured by wisps of cirrus cloud, delicate strands of ice crystals. The stars provided an ethereal light which illuminated the rolling tops of stratocumulus clouds below. On another occasion he would have enjoyed their beauty at this height.

Suddenly, he stiffened. Was that tiny spot in the distance a night fighter, or was he imagining it? Sometimes it disappeared, obscured by cloud. It was getting clearer. Now he was almost certain it was an enemy aircraft and that it was approaching rapidly. Time to report it.

'Skip, rear gunner here. Enemy aircraft astern - 500 yards.'

'OK, Sam, 'Keep your eyes on it. Is there more than one? Are they Messerschmitts or what?'

Every fibre of Sam's body was taut and he trembled, but he spoke with a calmness he didn't feel.

' Only one so far, Skip... probably a Focke-Wulf 190, but I can't be sure.'

This was Sam's first big test, his first confrontation with an enemy aircraft, and he was desperately anxious to come through it successfully. He felt his stomach tighten and he began to tremble again, which annoyed him. He had to be sure he gave Skip the right information and the right call for action. He screwed his eyes to focus on the vague shape that was definitely approaching. Suddenly he could see clearly the outline of a Focke Wulf. Again, he felt the shivering and tightening of his body and he could feel perspiration running down his spine.

'Skip, rear gunner again. It *is* a Focke-Wulf 190 ... 400 yards away and closing in fast. '

'Too fast,' he thought   Immediate action was needed.

'Skip, corkscrew right!' he shouted, his voice rather croaky, and higher-pitched than usual.

John spoke rapidly. 'Skip to all crew.   Hold on tight... ready for a corkscrew!'

He put the Lancaster into a steep, diving turn of 30 degrees to starboard for about 500 feet, as violent as the aircraft could take - the speed accelerating to 390 mph - followed by a steep climbing turn, also of about 30 degrees, for another 500 feet.

Following the speed of the dive, the control column was hard to pull forward for the climb. John then began a second corkscrew before speaking again.

'Skip to gunners. I hope Jerry's finding it hard to get into a firing position. Get him while he's wondering what the hell we're up to.'

Sam was doing his best, swivelling his power-operated turret almost continuously to keep the enemy in his sights, and firing all four machine guns in a series of brief bursts.

Scotty also kept the night fighter in his sights whenever possible, taking full advantage of his ability to swivel his two Browning machine guns 360 degrees.

The diving of the Lancaster was fierce enough to tumble the crew from their seats. Most of them, however, had either braced themselves for it or, like Sam, had limited room for movement.

Reg Atkins was not so lucky and could not prevent himself, and most of the accoutrements of his trade, from floating upwards towards the roof, and later crashing to the floor of the fuselage. Square protractor, pencils, ruler, Dalton computer and compasses made a clatter as they littered the floor. Reg, discomforted but uninjured, scrambled to his feet, hurriedly picked up his equipment, and re-arranged it on his desk.

The Focke -Wulf pilot fired a short burst of cannon whenever there was a change of direction at the top and bottom of each corkscrew, though he had to be quick to take advantage of those brief opportunities.

On one occasion, a canon shell crashed through the side of the fuselage, two metres behind the wireless operator. Jack was left shocked and pale. The others felt the rush of cold air that burst through the jagged hole and along the length of the fuselage.

'Skip here for wireless operator. Are you OK, Jack?'

'Yes, Skip. I'm OK...a bit shaken, but I'll get over it.'

At the lower point of a third corkscrew, John saw a cloud nearby, slipped his Lancaster into it and began to lose height. After a few minutes he spoke again to the crew.

'Skip here to all crew. Sorry to shake you up with those corkscrews. The hole in the fuselage is making it damn cold. We'll fix that later. I'll stay in this cloud a bit longer.'

But some minutes later the cloud dispersed.

'Skip to rear gunner. We're coming out of the cloud. Have we lost that Focke-Wulf ?'

'I think so, Skip. I can't see it. We've given it the slip.'

'Thanks, Sam.'

'Skip here for wireless op.   Take a look at the hole in the fuselage and see what we can do about it.'

A few minutes later Jack reported back.

'Wireless op here Skip.   It's a jagged hole about three inches across, halfway up the fuselage, and a couple of metres behind me.   I think I can plug it with my kapok suit.   It won't take much.   The rest will just hang down.'

'Jack, you need your kapok suit.   You can't do that.'

'No, Skip, I don't need it.   I'm warmer than anyone else, with the heater near me.   Leave it to me.'

Jack went ahead; later he reported back.

'Skip, wireless op here.   It's done.   It looks horrible' - he laughed – 'but I think it'll work.   We're warming up already.'

'Jack, you're a wonder!'

***

Scotty spotted two Messerschmitt 110s, emerging from the clouds above him.   Instinctively, he fired a short burst; then shouted,

'Skip, Mid-upper gunner here.   Two Messerschmitt 110s, above... a little to port...and diving towards us!'

John immediately began a steep diving turn but he was too late. The attack was swift and deadly.   There was the crash of cannon shells hitting the port wing, which dipped violently under the impact, shaking the crew and throwing them to one side.

John began a second corkscrew, and as one of the Messerschmitts swept past, Scotty Sam and Freddie all fired at it, but without success.

When the attackers were both at a distance, probably positioning to finish off their quarry, John managed to get the Lancaster on to an even keel. Scotty's voice expressed his concern.

'Mid-upper gunner here, Skip. There's damage to the port inner engine nacelle. Some of it's come away and it's hanging loose.'

'Skip here. Flight engineer, what do you think?'

Arthur's reply confirmed John's worst fear.

'It's not just the nacelles, Skip. The port inner's had a direct hit and it's useless. I'm glad it's not the port outer which drives a pump operating the rear turret.

'So am I,' Sam thought. He would otherwise have been unable to swivel his guns.

'In that inboard engine,' Arthur added, 'was a pump charging an accumulator operating our undercarriage, flaps, and a few other things. We've got another pump and accumulator in the starboard inner engine. When we lose an engine we lose much more besides.'

'Skip here. OK, Arthur. We seem to be alright at the moment.'

'Yes, Skip, but there may be other damage that we'll discover later. We should be prepared for that.'

'OK, Arthur, and thanks for the warning.'

'Skip to all crew. Our port inner engine is kaput, but we can manage with three engines We're badly damaged so we've got to keep out of trouble! I'll have to go down to 10,000 feet and our speed will be cut to around 145 mph. Maybe we'll be able to shelter in cloud before Jerry returns.'

He soon had an opportunity to do that, as the cloud was increasing at the lower altitude, but the Messerschmitts appeared to have gone. Perhaps they had noticed other Lancasters and moved to attack them.

Jack Rogers now expressed what was on everyone's mind.

'Wireless operator to Skip. Do you think we can make it? On three engines?'

'Yes, Jack, but we'll need a slice of luck. We can fly quite well on three engines, but we'll be both slower and lower. Attacking us will be *a piece of cake*. P-Peter is a wounded beast and Jerry will try everything to finish us off. But if we all stay very alert, especially the gunners, we have a good chance.'

***

Skip to navigator, 'Any change of airspeed or direction after all that tossing about?'

'Not yet, Skip. Carry on at 145 mph on 240 degrees.'

'Thanks, Reg.'

Jack took a look through the astrodome. Anti-aircraft fire had resumed, and he was surprised that it seemed almost as fierce as over the target. There were again puffs of smoke, searchlight beams, and aircraft weaving, climbing and diving. He saw two of their aircraft collide when taking evasive action. Both exploded and disintegrated, and he saw pieces of aircraft falling, but no sign of parachutes.

BATTLE ORDERS

Fourteen airmen had just died. A brief feeling of melancholy, tinged with fear, swept through him, but he shook it off. They must all stay positive. He knew they must now be dangerously vulnerable. *'My God,'* he thought, *'war is horrible.'*

He felt that their situation was now perilous. They could only limp along with their three engines, and they would probably face further night fighter attacks.

Freddie Jones had similar concerns, but he was pleased that his bombs had scored some direct hits on the marshalling yards and was proud that his skill as a bomb aimer had contributed to the success of the operation.

Scotty shared the doubts about their chance of survival, but such thoughts were temporarily overlaid by his hopes for the next evening. Unless they were on 'Battle Orders' for another op, he hoped he would see his very attractive girl friend, Lucy.

'Perhaps we'll see a film and visit a pub afterwards. She is a really lovely girl and I'd like to marry her as soon as possible.'

But while he enjoyed such escapist thoughts, he kept his eyes focused on the scene before him, as he constantly swung his turret from side to side. The survival of them all might well depend on the alertness of the gunners.

Arthur, with his background in engineering, was sensitive to any change in the tone or rhythm of the engines which might indicate a weakness. He was anxious to get the best possible performance from the three remaining engines.

Reg prepared to fix their position, so that he could work out the latest wind velocity and, if necessary, modify their course.

He took up his sextant, stood under the astrodome and studied the night sky. Millions of glittering stars surrounded him. There was now very little cloud and excellent visibility. He identified a particular star, 'captured' it in the sextant's bubble, and 'shot' it with a gentle squeeze of the trigger, taking the time to the nearest second. Observing the star's angle, he consulted the Air Navigation Tables and was finally able to draw a line on his Mercator Chart, somewhere along which they had been flying - a 'position line.'

He 'shot' two more stars, and when he had three 'position lines' on his chart, adjusted to the same time, and intersecting, he had fixed the aircraft's position. Quickly he calculated the latest wind velocity and a new course for the pilot. He loved the stars and was fascinated by astro-navigation.

Sam was still very tense. It wasn't fear, but he had a nagging worry that he might have let down his crew mates.

'Perhaps,' he thought, *'I should have shot down that Focke-Wulf.'*

He also thought about their future prospects.

'There'll be another twenty-eight operations, some even more dangerous than this one: to the Ruhr valley or to Berlin. I know I'm a skilled gunner and I can focus my four guns very quickly on an approaching aircraft. I must prove that I can be effective under fire. I need to shoot down an enemy aircraft.'

Sometimes he thought about Bill Irons, flying in his Lancaster on the present operation. He'd never before had such a good friend, and desperately hoped Bill would return safely.

John was acutely aware of the dangers they faced but determined to strike an optimistic note and lead his crew homeward, whatever the dangers they had yet to face. They had a long way to go, and he knew that they would be lucky to get back safely.

BATTLE ORDERS

After a few miles of flight, with danger never far away, and tension remaining high, a layer of stratus cloud began to spread everywhere, and soon there was a continuous grey blanket below.

John decided to keep the Lancaster tucked just under the cloud's upper surface, always prepared to dip down further at any hint of danger. Cocooned thus, to everyone's immense relief, they reached the French coast unmolested, with all the crew feeling much more relaxed and beginning to think there was a reasonable chance they might, after all, get back home.

However, the cloud now began to disintegrate and fade away, leaving P-Peter clearly visible from the ground. Although the crew had completed most of their journey and had only to cross the Channel, the loss of cloud cover meant they were now exposed and vulnerable, especially in the golden light of dawn that was now breaking over them.

John desperately needed a little more power to speed up their passage across the Channel, but there was no hope of that on three engines. He reminded all the crew to stay alert. There was often increased air activity along the coast and an attack by a group of fighters on their crippled aircraft could hardly fail to finish them off.

The attack did not come until they were about a fifth of the way across the Channel, and it was by a single aircraft, a Junkers 88. Sam spotted it, to the rear. It had been flying a few miles from the French coast, and was heading rapidly towards them. He spoke urgently to John.

'Skip, Rear gunner here. A Junkers 88 is coming up from behind. Three hundred yards away, and gaining on us fast!'

Sam was much calmer than he had been earlier. As soon as the enemy aircraft was in range, he fired several bursts from his four machine guns, one of which, he believed, destroyed the tip of its port wing. He was elated and prepared to continue the battle as the Junkers closed in on them, firing at every opportunity, while John made it as difficult as possible for the fighter to settle its guns in a position for firing.

Sam then had a shock. His guns were suddenly silent. He had no more ammunition.   P-Peter had now lost its main defence from a rear attack and the Junkers 88 was coming inexorably closer.   Suddenly finding himself unable to continue defending his comrades, Sam found his voice choking with emotion as he reported the bad news.

'Skip, Rear gunner here. I've clipped one wing of the Junkers but it's still coming nearer, and I have no more ammo.'

John responded in his usual calm and measured manner.

'OK, Sam. You've inflicted damage on Jerry which must slow him down. Good work.'

While Scotty, in the mid-upper turret, brought his two machine guns into action, he could not make up for the loss of superior fire power from the rear turret. John feared that, after reaching the Channel with rising hope, they might yet *get the chop*.

Then the situation took a dramatic turn. The Junkers 88 was itself suddenly attacked. Canon shells were being fired from a different part of the sky. Scotty was the first one to see them, and he reported the development excitedly.

'Skip, Jerry is being attacked from above.

'Yes, Scotty, you're right.   Amazing! But who's attacking? Where's it coming from?'

'From two Spitfires, Skip.'

 They had been on a dawn patrol along the Channel, and were now diving on the German fighter with guns blazing.

The Junkers' pilot was quick to react. Fortunately for him, the first bursts from the Spitfires were not well targeted and caused only superficial damage. But with one of his wings slightly shortened, and against two of the fastest fighters in the world, he was at a distinct disadvantage. He decided it was time to withdraw.

He dipped the nose of the Junkers, and put it into an extremely steep dive. It screamed at the unaccustomed high speed that caused, and, at a much lower altitude, he turned his aircraft away from P-Peter and towards the French coast.

The Spitfire pilots chose not to follow the Junkers to the lower altitude. They had achieved the objective of chasing it away from a disabled Lancaster, and perhaps their fuel reserves would be at risk if they diverted towards the Continent.

There was a period of uncanny silence in the Lancaster. The crew, all weak with fatigue, were quite stunned by the rapid turn of events. But a cheer erupted from them as the Spitfires flew past and their pilots waved. They seemed to realise that P-Peter was struggling, because they escorted the aircraft to the English coast, one on each side, before raising a hand in farewell, and returning to their airfield in Kent.

An almost palpable sense of relief flooded through the Lancaster as they continued on their way. The only sound was the constant, almost comforting roar of the three surviving engines. No-one spoke until they saw the familiar pattern of runways, hangars and Nissen huts of RAF Coningsby. Although most of the buildings, like the Nissen huts in which the crews lived, were primitive constructions, they were a very welcome sight. They would soon be home. Wonderful!

CHAPTER 3

John's crew were not the only ones glad to be home. At least half a dozen other Lancasters, were still in the air, awaiting instructions to land. Some were severely battle-damaged, with fuselages peppered with holes, others had hardly any fuel left, and yet others had wounded on board. The latter had top priority.

Each pilot had to explain his situation to Flying Control so that a decision on his priority for landing could be taken. Whatever their degree of urgency, all the aircraft were instructed to circuit at various heights until they received clearance to come in.

John cursed the need for stacking, though he knew that this was to be expected following every operation. He expressed his frustration to his fellow-airmen, always his main concern.

'Skip to all crew. I know you're all as knackered as I am, but we've got to hang about a bit before we land. We've lost an engine, but some kites are much worse off. And at least none of us is injured.'

Jack spoke for all the crew as he sought to reassure John

'Skip, the important thing is you've brought us back safely, and that's great. We can all put up with a little wait after what we've been through.'

'Thanks, Jack, and thank you all. You're a great crew.'

Finally, John obtained clearance to come in, and he took the Lancaster on a final circuit. He had never before landed a four-engined aircraft on three engines, and listened carefully to the advice from Flying Control. He realised that the landing would require some tricky handling.

Then he had a shock. The undercarriage would not budge. The hydraulics must have been damaged. He groaned. Landing on three engines with no undercarriage would mean a crash landing with all its dangers. He wasn't at all sure that he would be able to get P-Peter down safely. Seven lives were at stake.

The calm voice of Arthur Jenkins interrupted his thoughts.

'Skip, flight engineer here. I believe we might get the undercarriage down using high pressure air. 'It should work, though I've never tried it.'

'Go ahead, Arthur. It's well worth a try.'

Skip had no doubts about Arthur's expertise, though, since neither of them had any experience of what he was trying to do, they couldn't be confident that it would work. Arthur used high pressure air kept in a large container. After a few moments, when time seemed to drag for the anxious pilot, the undercarriage responded. It was lowered and locked in place, to John's profound relief.

With the undercarriage down, he could concentrate on keeping the Lancaster as steady as possible during the circuit and the landing approach. Lowering the flaps, he noticed there was a tendency for the port wing, with its one working engine, to drop, so he kept the starboard engines subdued and made every effort to keep the aircraft straight and level, lowering the flaps further during the final approach.

His nerves were taut as his Lancaster descended to a few feet above the runway.

Then, with the speed cut down to around 85 mph, and with very little power, he touched down. To his delight, he was able to bring down the Lancaster in a near-perfect landing. 'Good old Peter', he breathed.

As soon as their aircraft came to a halt, all the crew cheered and shouted with uninhibited relief and joy. They were euphoric. It was over! They had completed a second operation and it had been a success. Although it had been pretty *dicey* at times, they were back and all in one piece. All was well!

In spite of the crews' exhaustion, de-briefing had to be carried out soon after their landing. Here there was another queue, for several aircraft had recently landed and there was only one Intelligence Officer on duty.

Finally, all seven airmen literally staggered into the Debriefing Room, still wearing most of their bulky flying kit and carrying 'Mae West' life jackets, parachutes and other gear. The Intelligence Office greeted them with cups of rum-laced tea and they collapsed into chairs arranged in a circle. Physical and emotional fatigue combined to make them completely exhausted and struggling to keep their eyes open. But they did their best to co-operate. Perhaps the information they gave might make crews a little safer on subsequent ops.

They all knew the kinds of question to expect and were ready with their answers.

'What sort of weather did you have? And coming back?'

'Where was the flak especially heavy?'

'Were you attacked by night fighters? Where? How many?'

'What happened on each occasion?'

'Did you see of the effect of the bombing?'

'Tell me about when one of your engines was put out of action.'

'Did you sustain any other damage? Is there anything you would especially like to report? Something unexpected perhaps? Do you think that anything important was left out in your briefing?' And so on.

BATTLE ORDERS

When it was over, and before they ate a huge breakfast of eggs, bacon, tomatoes and fried bread, John wanted to have a quiet word with Sam so they went together to the bar of the Sergeants' Mess.

'I just wanted to say, Sam, that we all owe a lot to your alertness and quick reactions on that op. You did well to spot the Focke-Wulf, and then you hit the Junkers 88 and probably came close to downing it. It's good to have gunners like you and Scotty, and I'm very glad you're both in my crew.'

He knew that Sam had been under enormous strain, and noticed the dampness around his eyes, and though his face now lit up with pleasure, he choked with emotion as he replied.

'Thanks, John, I think all the crew were great, and where would we be now if our Skipper hadn't kept his nerve? Well, thank God we made it again, but I'm anxious to know if Bill Irons and his crew got back safely. Do you know?'

'I'm afraid not. We'll find out quite soon, but some planes have not yet returned so the info' about our losses hasn't yet been posted up. Don't give up hope.'

***

When all the crew had showered, eaten, and slept like babies, they decided to visit one of their locals, The Pig and Whistle. It was a pleasant, 16th century pub, with a wealth of oak beams, very near RAF Coningsby, and they knew the friendly publican who always greeted them warmly. They sat in the Saloon Bar and relaxed. It was good to have a free evening. Tomorrow they might again be putting their lives in jeopardy.

Scotty, freckled, with short and bristly ginger hair, was well settled in a corner armchair.   Lucy had not been able to see him this evening, but he had not minded much; it was good to be relaxing with all the crew after facing death together.   Always very friendly, he was keen to find out more about his fellow crew members, who had been together such a short time, and were now utterly dependent on one another for their survival.

'Arthur, what made you volunteer for aircrew?' he asked.

Arthur, always rather shy, looked surprised to find himself the centre of attention. 'Well, he began, 'I was involved in engineering and I heard that the RAF had a shortage of flight engineers.   We were all going to be called up anyway, so I knew I had to do something in the War. What about you?'

Scotty grinned. 'Mine's an escape story,' he began. 'I was a coal miner in Lanarkshire, following in my father's footsteps. I hated it. I was keen to do my bit for the War effort, but I was stuck in a 'reserved occupation' which meant I couldn't leave.   Then someone told me that if I volunteered for aircrew I might be accepted as a gunner. So, I volunteered, and was accepted.'

'Yes,' Reg put in, 'we all had to do something in the War. Either you volunteered for something or you'd be called up and pitchforked into any branch of the Services. I joined the Air Training Corps, and learned about navigation, which really interested me. Before I was 18, I enlisted in the RAF in the PNB (*pilot, navigator, bomb-aimer*) category and was finally selected for navigation training.'

They all listened with particular attention to Reg. Not only was he normally very reserved in his speech, but his work as a navigator kept him so occupied during a flight that usually he spoke only to give new courses or speeds to John.

John was enjoying the conversation among his crew, the first one of its kind they had managed. He was convinced he'd been lucky. Although they had all come together casually - they had virtually chosen one another - it was working out very well.

'I was in the ATC, too, he said. 'I wasn't especially interested in either flying or aircraft. But like the rest of you, I had to do something and I decided to try for aircrew.'

'But you're a very good pilot,' Jack said.

'Thanks, Jack. I think I made the right choice for me.'

'I can tell you quite quickly how I became a bomb-aimer,' Freddie said. 'I, too, was recruited in the PNB category. My efforts at piloting a Tiger Moth were pathetic, though it was fun, and I loved sitting in an open cockpit. But when the time came to land, I was always too high. I would 'land' a yard or two above the grass. Then the undercarriage - the two pram wheels - would crash down, followed by the tail, causing the lift to suddenly increase, and we'd be back in the air. My Tiger Moth would do that four or five times, so that it bounced across the meadow, and I couldn't do anything about it. It was hilarious, though my pilot trainer was not amused.'

But Freddie's fellow crew-members were, and they laughed uproariously.

John thought, *'It's great to hear them all laughing, after what they've been through.'*

Freddie grinned and continued, 'When I put it into a spin, it hurtled towards the earth. I saw the countryside spinning round the nose and was terrified. The instructor shouted - and I think he was scared to death of what I might do next - 'Push the other pedal and open the throttle fully - now!'

And I thought, 'Oh blimey, I should have done that earlier. Anyway, I managed to pull out of the spin, and climb back to our previous height. The instructor gave me a good old roasting when we landed.

I was hopeless at navigation, too. Somehow, I always managed to get lost, so I became a bomb-aimer.'

Freddie was only a little younger than the others but, apart from when he was behind his bomb sight, he was always boyish and fun-loving.

'And you do that very well,' Scotty said. 'The photos make that clear.

Jack was smiling. Small, wiry, and alert, with versatile skills, he would often, in the coming months, make a unique, and sometimes courageous contribution to the success of the crew. He now joined in. 'I've always been interested in wireless sets, so I naturally volunteered to become a wireless operator,' he began. Then he paused and suddenly looked thoughtful.

'This morning,' he continued, 'after a hair-raising experience over Germany, we have this evening free, and we' re enjoying ourselves. I wonder whether that's a regular pattern; an op every other day.'

'Not necessarily,' John smiled. 'It often happens that way, but not always. The other day I spoke to a pilot who told me that he and his crew finally got into their beds at around 7.30 am, after a particularly long op - about eight hours - and they were woken at 12. 50 and told that they were on 'Battle Orders' for that evening.'

'I'm not keen on that,' Jack said. 'We all need a proper rest after an op, to relax our bodies and our nervous systems.'

John agreed, and added, 'but I think it's exceptional when crews are pushed as much as that...perhaps only when a squadron has just had very heavy losses.'

Sam said, 'I wonder whether we'd have volunteered for aircrew had we known how often we would have to face death.'

'Well,' John said, it's hard to say, but submariners are often blown out of the water by depth charges, and merchant seamen are in ships that may be torpedoed. Our generation couldn't avoid facing danger and sometimes death. I think most of us preferred the RAF to the other Services. How did you get into aircrew, Sam?'

'I volunteered for aircrew at a time when there was a shortage of rear gunners.' Sam answered. 'I realised, much later, that the shortage was because so many gunners had been killed.'

That was followed by a short period of uneasy silence. Sam had only been talking in a matter-of-fact way, but now was not the time to talk about death. Rear gunners had a very high death rate, as night fighters would often concentrate their fire on the tail of an aircraft. John decided it was time to change the focus of the conversation.

'It's great to chat about ourselves like this. You're all very good at what you do - and I'm very glad you're all in my crew. Now... I'd like to get you all a pint of mild and bitter.'

After he had returned with a tray full of beers, John asked-

'Scotty, how's your romance with Lucy going?'

While Scotty gave a characteristically optimistic reply, Sam looked very thoughtful and even perplexed.

'I'd like to have a girlfriend,' he said. 'How do you go about finding one?'

'In my case,' Scotty replied, 'I went to a village dance. I could just about cope with a waltz, a foxtrot or a quickstep. There was *a ladies' excuse me waltz,* and while I was dancing with someone else, Lucy came up and said, 'Excuse me,' and took over. Well, one or two other girls came up and did the same - I can't help being irresistible!' - he grinned - 'but Lucy returned about three times before the waltz ended. We've never looked back. '

There was laughter all round, but Sam looked nonplussed. He said he'd never danced a step, but he would love to know a really nice girl.

'You'll meet someone soon who's just right for you, Sam,' John assured him. 'I bet some of the Station WAAFs have already got their eyes on you.'

Sam beamed. 'I'd like to know who they are,' he said.

'You'll soon know,' John assured him, 'because they'll make themselves known, as Lucy did with Scotty.'

'That would be wonderful,' Sam said, with a broad smile. 'I can hardly wait!' Then he suddenly frowned and looked worried.

'We're all OK,' he said, 'but what about all our friends in the squadron who were on the same op. They must all be back now unless they've been shot down. I'm especially worried about Bill.'

John turned to him and patted him sympathetically on the back.

'Our losses haven't yet been posted up. It's expected that a few other aircraft will come in late. Don't worry about it too much, Sam.'

***

Sam had remained hopeful until he read the following morning an announcement about losses on the Remsheid raid. Then his hopes were shattered, and he was immediately plunged into despair. Fifteen aircraft had not returned from the raid on the railway marshalling yards, and one of them had been piloted by Bill Irons.

John comforted him and pointed out that Bill might have parachuted to safety.

'If Bill did manage to bail out, he would probably have landed in a rural area. In that case, his first task would be to bury his parachute, and then he would try to stay free for as long as he could, making good use of his silk map and the issue of German currency. I believe he has some knowledge of German, too. Some airmen who have baled out have made their way to an occupied country, and then, helped by the Resistance Movement, have got back to England. Or he may be able to reach an Allied-occupied area.'

'Well, his German is much better than mine,' Sam confirmed. 'He'd be able to get around the country without difficulty. But Remsheid is a large town and it's not far from Dusseldorf, which is an important city in the industrial Ruhr. If Bill has baled out and lands in an urban area, he could come face to face with some furious people and have the sort of unpleasant experience some others have had.'

'I agree,' John said, 'but there are extensive farms not far away, and anyone parachuting on that raid is much more likely to land in a field than, for instance, a city centre or someone's garden.

If Bill is finally captured, he will first be interrogated by local police, then by Luftwaffe officers, and sometimes the Gestapo, so there will be some delay before he is sent to a POW camp, and a further delay before we learn about it. I'm afraid we just have to wait, Sam. There are others in our squadron who had close friends among the crews of those fifteen aircraft. Fifteen Lancasters means 105 airmen. We're all anxious to learn what happened to them; how many died in the raid and how many survived.'

'Of course, you're right,' Sam responded with a rueful smile, 'and I know we must all just carry on doing our job, whatever happens. I expect we'll be on 'Battle Orders' for tonight.'

'Yes, I think we will,' John said, 'It will be our third op. I wonder where we'll be sent?'

CHAPTER 4

Sgt Jack Rogers,

RAF, Coningsby,

Nr. Horncastle,

Lincolnshire.

March 13th.,1945

Dear Maurice,

Following our second op, I must say I'm very glad to be in this crew. We're a good, effective team. The dangers we face test our characters as well as our skills, and we soon learn about one another when we're under fire from ack-ack guns or night fighters.

You'll remember that I specially mentioned Sam, our beefy rear gunner. He's actually a very sensitive, emotional chap. He was in tears when he heard about our losses, and kept thinking about our friends who'd got the chop. I think he's going to be great. At first, he seemed over-anxious and lacking in confidence, but after firing at attacking aircraft, with some success, he's much more confident. He's proving to himself that he is up to the job.

In the evening we got together in a lovely old local pub, so had the chance to unwind. It was lovely to sit on cosy chairs, sipping a pint of beer, chatting and laughing. That was just what we needed.

I'm glad to hear that, although you have to put up with the stingy amount of rationed food, you're still able to buy fresh fish from the local fishmonger. You've mentioned cod, haddock and herrings, and even kippers and bloaters. And there's always whiting for Tiger, the cat! That's amazing, really. The fishermen often have to put up with terrible weather, with mountainous seas, as well as German U-Boats and bombers. They're as heroic as anyone in the Armed Services, don't you think?

Your letters with all the family news give me a lot of pleasure. Keep writing!

BATTLE ORDERS

Your very good friend,

Jack

The ground staff had been working tirelessly from 8 am. Take-off was planned for the early evening so that aircraft might return before any early morning fog. Many aircraft parts had to be checked, and replaced if deficient. Replacements affecting the aircraft's ability to fly had to be flight-tested. It was often a race against time.

The Lancasters stood waiting at dispersal. They were going to be flown past Berlin, 590 miles away, to attack a number of aircraft factories, several miles outside the city.

John's crew were on 'Battle Orders' and they listened attentively to the briefing.

On the outward flight their route would not reveal the ultimate target to the Germans until the later stages. They would fly north east over the North Sea, and cross over Schleswig Holstein towards the Baltic Sea. East of Rostock, they would head straight for Berlin.

All the crews studied where dense anti-aircraft fire was to be expected. Anti-aircraft fire was more feared than night fighters.

Stumbling through a dense concentration of exploding shells could be a terrifying experience. At least, when attacked by night fighters, there was a foe they could confront, attack, perhaps fight off, and sometimes destroy.

Following their briefing, the airmen dressed ready for the flight in the crew room, and collected all their gear, including helmets, Mae Wests and parachutes. Pilots and navigators collected maps; and they all picked up escape kits, including German currency and silk maps, along with sandwiches, flasks of coffee, chocolate and barley sugar sweets.

John's crew could hardly wait to discuss the planned operation.

'We've been issued with amphetamine tablets again,' Scotty said. I hate taking pills. 'Do we *have* to take them?'

'Yes, we are strongly advised to,' John replied. 'This is going to be a long op, probably about eight hours, and that's after all our work preparing for it. The amphetamine tablets will keep you awake and alert for the whole period, throughout the night. You know how important that is.'

'Yes, I can see that, though I detest all pills.'

'Well,' Sam said, 'so do I, unless I'm ill, but amphetamines might make all the difference between bagging a Jerry and not seeing him in time.'

'Who can argue with that?' was Jack's comment. No-one did.

Sam wanted to know how the others felt about flying to Berlin.

'Did you notice,' he said, 'the reactions of some airmen when we heard that Berlin is the target for tonight? There were quickly-stifled groans, long faces and worried looks.'

Scotty turned to face him 'That's not surprising, is it, Sam? It's the furthest we can fly with a full bomb load, and we'll all be knackered when we get back.'

'Yes, but the real reason isn't that, Scotty,' Sam responded. 'The city's defended like no other. It has three lines of defence and masses of ack-ack guns. Bombing Berlin is the toughest op of all.'

'That's right. Our losses over Berlin have been very high,' Freddie added. Let's not kid ourselves. Sam is right. Berlin's going to be really tough. Hasn't it been a graveyard for our bombers?'

John wasn't happy about the way the discussion was going.

'I wouldn't put it like that,' he said. 'Sometimes, when the losses are heavy, it's been down to the weather or some other factors.'

'Yes,' Arthur said, 'and one of those factors is patching up badly-damaged aircraft so you can fly them soon afterwards. You can't then expect them to be 100% reliable. Many aircraft have problems *en route* and have to turn back.'

'That's true,' John said. ' Dozens of aircraft have sometimes had to turn back long before they reach enemy-held areas. But a kite has many thousands of components and most of the time they all function well...And abortive ops aren't always to do with technical failures. The problem might be severe icing or fog. On one operation to Berlin, more aircraft failed to return because of the weather than because of enemy action!

'Anyway,' he finished, looking much more cheerful, 'I think P-Peter is being repaired very well. Wouldn't you agree, Arthur?'

'Yes, John, I'm very happy about the work that's been done so far. In fact, I'm amazed that two of the ground staff were able to fit a new engine today in two hours! And it didn't take them long to fit new metal plates on the fuselage, either.'

'I think the ground staff - especially the fitters - do a wonderful job,' Jack said, and the others agreed.

'Well,' John continued, 'with P-Peter restored to its best, we're going to bomb some very important aircraft factories. For me, that makes it a worthwhile op.'

'Yes, you're right,' Freddie agreed, 'and I want to see those aircraft factories blown to bits.'

'Don't we all,' Jack agreed. 'It's one way we can help shorten the war.' The others nodded.

***

Soon afterwards, John's crew were bussed to dispersal along the perimeter track, where, at intervals, all the Lancasters, including P-Peter, stood waiting. They jumped out when their aircraft's letter was called out by a corporal at the door of the bus.

For much of the day, when they were relatively inactive, all the crews had felt their nerves stretched, with a tautness in their stomachs. Some thought about how little opportunity they'd had to accomplish anything in their lives, or about the possibility of an early death. A few nursed a secret hope that, at the last minute, the raid would be cancelled, rather forced jokes helping them to reveal little of their inner feelings to one another. Their concerns increased steadily as take-off drew near.

But once each airman was in his own part of the aircraft, they were very busy, and their nerves soon settled down. They chatted to one another about various aspects of the operation and their minds were entirely focused on the job ahead.

John had to be satisfied that every part of the aircraft was in good working order. Arthur had a close interest in the quantity and distribution of fuel. He sat near John, and they worked together very closely.

All four Rolls Royce engines were now brought to life, each one spluttering and coughing, before settling into a steady, throbbing rhythm.

BATTLE ORDERS

The crew looked out and saw a group of ground staff, including WAAFs, waiting to see them off. They were waving and the crew waved back, glad to see the airmen and WAAFs who had worked all day on P-Peter.

Taking off with a heavy load of bombs and petrol was always potentially hazardous. There was the possibility of an engine failure or a burst tyre causing a crash and a horrific explosion, before the wheels had left the tarmac.

Once John had received clearance, he released the brakes, gradually opened the throttles, and accelerated rapidly, juggling the throttles to keep the aircraft straight and in the centre of the runway, before raising the tailplane. He then brought up the control column and, at about 110 mph, the Lancaster rose majestically. Their third operation had begun.

With a heavy load, it was vitally important to keep the Lancaster low for a longer time than usual. Time was needed, to build up enough power for even a shallow climb.

John was aware that low-flying aircraft had sometimes crashed into power lines or low hills so as he built up speed he kept a close eye on his surroundings.

When he pulled back the control column, the speed was 165 mph and P-Peter climbed steadily.

CHAPTER 5

O ver Britain and much of the North Sea, Reg used his two radar aids to fix their position. Even when flying above complete cloud cover, his H2S screen showed up all cities and towns as patches of light whose shape revealed their identities, while rivers and coastlines appeared as meandering, illuminated lines, and were also easily identified.

The other radar aid, Gee, fixed their position fairly precisely, and Reg used it every ten minutes until they were about 350 miles from base, when it was out of range.

The stars, however, were always there, and Reg used them whenever possible, the sextant being his most valued instrument. He loved the brilliance and beauty of the night sky and was fascinated by astro-navigation.

John broke into his thoughts.

'Navigator, Skip here. It'll be muggy for much of this flight, won't it? What did you get from your Met briefing?'

(Reg had attended a Navigators' briefing some time before the general one)

'Well, Skip, we'll probably meet some whacking great cumulonimbus clouds. They often have a base of 3,000 feet, rise up to 40,000 feet or more, and extend horizontally for many miles.'

'O, my God, with ice building up all over the kite and freezing the instruments?'

'Yes, Skip. And sometimes static electricity in the airframe, interference with the radio and the disruption of electrical circuits. Then...'

'OK, Reg, don't go on... I'm terrified!' John joked. He laughed, a little uneasily.

Reg laughed, too. Arthur, as concerned as anyone else, added his own sober thoughts:

'Well, Skip -flight engineer here - in a cumulonimbus cloud, ice may form up to six inches thick on the wings, which is obviously really dangerous. But we're as protected as we can be. There are de-icers for the propellers and the leading edges of our wings and tail plane have been smeared with anti-ice paste. But can't we just keep well away from those clouds. Give them a wide berth?'

' Hope so, Arthur.'

'Skip, navigator here. We can keep clear of them, but we must spot them early. If anyone sees a cumulonimbus cloud, I'll give you course changes so that we fly two sides of an equilateral triangle, to by-pass it. That way, we'll keep on track.'

'Skip to all crew. Keep your eyes skinned for cumulonimbus clouds.'

'Skip. Rear gunner here. I've heard they can be a worse danger than night fighters.'

'Possibly, Sam, but if there are lots of cumulonimbus clouds, night fighters may be grounded. Don't count on it, but it's possible.'

When they had been flying for about an hour, Scotty reported on cloud developments he'd observed during a sweep of his capsule.

'Mid-upper gunner here, Skip. We're definitely close to some pretty big cumulus clouds. If they continue billowing out at this rate, they'll become cumulonimbus clouds pretty soon.'

'OK Scotty.'

'Bomb-aimer here, Skip. It's happening already. There's a massive cumulonimbus on our port side, about a mile ahead.' In his forward, bomb-aiming position, Freddie could see further ahead than anyone else.

'OK. Thanks, Freddie. Got that, Reg?'

'Yes, Skip. We should act on that pretty soon. I'll take a look at it through the astrodome.'

Shortly afterwards, he decided it was time to take action.

'Navigator here, Skip. Change course 60 degrees to starboard... Good... Stay on that course for three minutes.'

'Skip here. Glad to know we're moving away from it, Reg. It's a monster!'

A little later, Reg broke in again.

'Navigator here, Skip. Change 120 degrees to port, for three minutes.'

'Good. I can still see it on our port side. I hope we're doing enough to bypass it.'

'Yes, we don't know the size of this cloud, or how much it's shifting position.'

'I think we'll miss it - just. I'll alter course 60 degrees starboard now, and bring us back on course. OK Reg?'

'That's fine, Skip. We'd better look out for others. Sometimes there's a line of them - it's called a 'squall line.'

John gave a forced laugh.

'Oh, no, Reg, one's enough.'

Arthur now decided to unload the *window*. *Window* consisted of hundreds of strips of foil which were kept in bundles. It was discharged through a chute in the aircraft's nose, often by the bomb-aimer, but sometimes by the flight engineer. Its effect was to interfere with German radar, and it had proved to be very effective, though sometimes it showed up the presence of the bombers.

Meanwhile Scotty had been taken by surprise by the sudden appearance of another cumulonimbus cloud.

'Mid-upper gunner here, Skip. Another one has come up quickly on the port side and it's only about thirty yards away.'

Reg responded immediately, his voice loud and urgent -

'60 degrees to starboard. Now, Skip!'

But they were too late. The cloud was moving rapidly towards them. A very heavy shower of hail crashed against the fuselage, with such a loud rattle that it drowned the engine noise. The Lancaster rocked under the heavy, noisy bombardment which, combined with the force of powerful and erratic air movements, tossed the huge aircraft about. At one time they were swept up several hundred feet. Ice was now forming all over the aircraft. Pieces of ice whipped off the propellers and crashed against the fuselage. John was worried about parts of the aircraft icing up, and constantly tested moving parts. Scotty kept looking at the wings. He was better placed than the others to see how much ice was forming there.

'Mid-upper gunner here to Skip. There is quite a lot of ice on the wings,' he reported, 'two or three inches at least.'

'OK, Scotty, let me know if it gets worse.'

Fortunately, their Lancaster had only been caught a short way into the cloud, and P-Peter soon emerged from its roaring turbulence to fly in relatively peaceful air. The four engines became once again the dominant source of noise. They were flying at an altitude of 19,000 feet.

'Skip here. Well, it wasn't very nice, was it? Thank God we're out of it. We must spot these thunder clouds earlier. I don't suppose we've seen the last of them. Keep scanning the sky for night fighters, too.'

***

But the next threat did not come from either cumulonimbus clouds or night fighters.

The pilot's cabin was suddenly flooded with light as they were coned by dozens of searchlights. John was temporarily blinded by their glare, and could only read his dials with difficulty. Recovering, quickly, he put the aircraft into a sudden diving turn, then jigged it about. Shells exploded on every side. A shell splinter crashed under the bomb bay and set off one of the incendiary bombs which glowed red in contrast to the whitish glow of the searchlights. Had it struck in a slightly different position, their bombs might have exploded, with disastrous effect.

Scotty swivelled his turret to maximise his overview of the scene. On his port side were two Lancasters, one above them, one below.

BATTLE ORDERS

Each one was *coned* by ten to twenty searchlights, and was the focus of fierce anti-aircraft fire. Shells were exploding around them, and enveloping them in a dense cloud of black smoke. On the starboard side he saw another Lancaster that had just been hit, but was nevertheless battling on towards the target minus its outer port engine.

John continued to twist and turn P-Peter constantly to change its height and the aspect it presented to the ground. Again, the shells began to get closer, some exploding loudly near the starboard inner engine, pounding the wing and rocking the aircraft. Scotty felt very vulnerable, and looked out helplessly. His heart was pumping furiously and he was badly shaken.

'Mid-upper gunner here, Skip. That shell was just outside the starboard inner engine.' he managed to gasp. 'Amazingly, it's still working.'

'Flight engineer here. Yes, it's still working, but the prop's bent. It must have lost some pulling power.'

Reg, as usual, was bent over his chart, and taking little notice of matters not concerned with navigation. They were getting closer to Berlin. Time for a progress report.

'Navigator to Skip, we're on track and about ten miles from the target.'

'Skip here. Thanks, Reg. Glad to hear we haven't far to go now.'

'Skip to all crew. The bent prop means we'll have to reduce speed and get down to around 15,000 feet. There's no ack-ack fire now, so keep a sharp look-out for night fighters.'

But though the crew could see them attacking other bombers less than a mile away, no night fighters confronted them, which was a blessing, as the bent propeller would limit their manoeuvrability in combat.

An excited shout from Freddie Jones now gave the others the news they were expecting. They were desperate to get the bombing done, and get away from the menacing situation around them.

'Bomb-aimer here, Skip. I can see the factories about a mile ahead. They cover several square miles. I want to place our bombs in the middle of them. Some of them are already alight.'

'That's great, Freddie.'

Fierce anti-aircraft fire now resumed, as the crew pressed on towards the target area, and it seemed to intensify with every mile.

Sam saw three parachutes descending not far away, through the forest of searchlight beams and shell explosions, but he did not see the aircraft that had been hit, or the parachutes of the other four crew members.

'Poor devils,' he thought. *'I expect they couldn't get out in time. Will it soon be our turn?'*

As they approached the target, John was acutely aware that while many aircraft were engaged in evasive manoeuvres, his aircraft, now on an even keel, was more exposed to the guns below than they were. He could hardly wait for the bomb-aimer to complete his task.

The words he was waiting for came in a few minutes -

'Bomb-aimer to Skip. Open bomb doors.'

'Skip to Freddie. Bomb doors open.'

'Bomb-aimer to Skip. 'Five degrees right....OK ...steady...steady... shade more right.'

John noticed that the explosive puffs on his right were creeping nearer so, instinctively, he moved the aircraft a little further to the left. Freddie's frustrated outburst was immediate.

'Right!.. Right!.. That's better!..steady..steady.' Fortunately, they had not quite reached the target.

'Little more left now...good...steady...steady... bombs gone... Now a photo... Good.'

High explosives and incendiary bombs were released from the bomb bays, the majority landing on the acres of factory buildings, many of which were soon engulfed in flames.

Some of the crew looked down on the conflagration and shuddered. Their overwhelming thought was that war was a nasty business. They had completed their task successfully and destroyed factories and equipment with huge war-making potential. But even at night there would be some factory workers down there. Some would have died; others would be seriously injured. But this was war and there were no holds barred. They had to do their job.

John interrupted their thoughts.

'Skip here. Job's done. Course to take us back, navigator. Let's get out of here!'

'Navigator here. Course 220 degrees, Skip. '

'Ok, Reg, we're on our way. I'll have to carry on jigging and diving while this ack-ack fire continues Freddie, sorry I had to take evasive action on the bombing run, against your call.'

'That's OK, Skip, it just upset me for the moment, but it worked out alright

CHAPTER 6

O ne of John's worries now was the sheer number of aircraft in the sky. There were Lancasters, Halifaxes and Stirlings at different altitudes. John's Lancaster, at 15,000 feet was now below most of the four-engined bombers and in constant danger of being at the receiving end of bombs dropped from above. The second worry was the danger from collisions, as aircraft dived, turned and corkscrewed in various directions, trying desperately to escape the flak.

About a hundred yards away, Scotty saw two Lancasters collide. One must have still had its bomb load under the fuselage because there was a huge explosion. There was no hope for the fourteen airmen. He saw hundreds of pieces of flaming debris falling to the ground. He grimaced and trembled and fervently hoped they would soon be clear of the area. Other crew members had also seen the collision. Sam was one of them.

'My God,' he shouted. The poor devils didn't stand a chance. I'm glad we've got rid of our bombs.'

'I'm always glad to see them land on the target,' Freddie said, and that we're now on our way back.'

He was pleased that he had completed his task successfully. Every member of the crew had a vital task, but without his careful sighting and bombing over the target area, this highly dangerous operation would be pointless.

'If only we could now go a little faster, and escape from this ghastly scene,' he thought.

A tremendous crash was now heard on the port side, as a bomb struck the wing, and passed through it, rocking the aircraft on its axis and causing some of the crew to be almost thrown from their seats.

They were all too stunned to react for a few moments. Then Scotty, who was once again, the nearest to the crash, and had hardly recovered from the last shock, shouted,

'Skip, a bomb has crashed through the port wing and there's a large, gaping, jagged hole in the middle of it.' He knew that they had all just escaped death, and found himself shaking. He managed to gasp out in a quieter voice,

'It must have been quite a small bomb: otherwise, we'd have all had our chips.' He was almost breathless. John certainly thought the end had come and was both shaken and furious.

'Skip here to all crew, 'That must have scared the living daylights out of all of you. Being bombed by your own aircraft is a type of so-called 'friendly fire' that makes me livid. We all have our nerves shattered, and our lives hanging by a thread because some idiot above us hasn't done his job properly. Believe me, I'm going to go for him when we get back.'

'Skip, Mid-upper gunner here.' Scotty was still breathing hard. 'Just after the bomb crashed on us, I had a good look at the Lancaster responsible. I know it well because my friend Matt is its wireless op.'

'That could be very helpful, Scotty. I'm very angry and I'll deal with it as soon as possible after we land. '

'Flight engineer, what d'you think of the damage?'

'It's a jagged hole...about six inches in diameter, Skip. It'll interrupt the air flow and slow us down. It just missed the fuel tanks. It's a wonder we're still here!'

'It is. Thanks, Arthur.'

'Skip for Scotty. Are you OK? You've had another nasty shock. You're in the thick of it tonight.'

'I'm OK, Skip, I'm just 'all aquiver,' but I'll be alright. '

'Good... It may have been smaller than a 250 pounder. But now, with a bent prop on the starboard side and a jagged hole in the port wing, we're going to limp along, and the German gunners haven't finished with us yet.'

But five minutes later the ground attacks abruptly ended, and only the noisy engines broke the peace.

'Skip here. Stay alert! The night fighters won't let us get away. We're slower, and we can't manoeuvre easily.'

They hadn't long to wait. There was a shout from Freddie who was amazed to see a Junkers 88 heading straight for them. Head-on attacks were rare.

'Skip, Bomb-aimer here. There's a Junkers 88 heading towards us and closing rapidly. About 800 yards away.'

'OK, Freddie. Skip to all crew. Ready for a very steep dive Scotty, here's your chance!'

John's dive, at over 350mph. probably took the Junkers' pilot by surprise. Scotty, seeing the fighter now almost above him, fired a short burst from his two machine guns. The combined speed of the opposing aircraft made for only a fleeting opportunity, but Scotty thought he might have clipped the enemy's tail plane. In any event, the Junkers 88 made no further attacks and soon disappeared.

'Skip to Scotty, Well done. I think you've damaged it. Anyway, you've frightened off the pilot.'

'Skip to all gunners. 'That was an odd form of attack. Perhaps he was a novice? I don't suppose we'll have another one quite like that.'

P-Peter continued on its way, with Sam, Scotty and Freddie, all swivelling their turrets around - a total of eight machine guns at the ready - and straining their eyes for any sign of an enemy aircraft. Freddie lay on his stomach in the forward turret, bending his head downwards, striving to search the area below and astern. With all three working together there was less chance that an enemy aircraft would be able to creep up on them unnoticed.

A single Messerschmitt 110 now emerged from the clouds just above them, near the point where Scotty's attention happened to be focused at that moment. His instinctive reaction was almost instantaneous. He fired a short burst from his two machine guns. In a few moments, something exploded in the fighter and it began to fall to the ground in a glowing, red ball, turning over and over in the sky, and leaving a long trail of fire and smoke behind it.

At first Scotty could hardly believe his eyes. The incident had lasted only a fraction of a minute Then he shouted 'I've got it! My first! Wow! I can't believe it.'

He was overjoyed, but trembled from both the brush with death and the excitement of the kill.

'Skip here. That's terrific, Scotty. Well done! We can still dish it out. Great!'

All the crew felt elated by the success. It was a very timely event, coming just when most of them were in need of something to raise their spirits.

***

BATTLE ORDERS

Reg Atkins needed to fix their position in preparation for a new course, and prepared to use his sextant. They were still flying at about 15,000 feet and John was managing to keep the aircraft a little steadier. That would help Reg use his sextant effectively, as would also the full panorama of twinkling stars that now lit up the heavens.

He rose to his feet, stood under the astrodome, identified his first star, and raised the sextant to capture it in the sextant's bubble. He was having difficulty standing upright as the aircraft was being buffeted by the wind, but he was happy to be involved again in astro-navigation. He was just completing the work of following up his first star shot when John announced the bad news.

'Skip here, to all crew. Our heating system is kaput. Arthur's been trying to fix it but no luck. I'm afraid it might get colder and there's nothing we can do about it. If you can, stand up and move about.'

Reg's involvement with the stars made him quite unaware, at first, of the tumbling temperature. Some of the others, too, being immersed in their work, had hardly noticed it.

But soon they all began to feel the freezing temperature penetrating every part of their bodies, causing them to shiver, with icicles growing ever longer on their oxygen masks.

Then Reg made a worrying discovery. There was a hard layer of ice covering his Mercator chart. Would that make normal navigation impossible? He thought for a moment and then reported the problem.

'Skip, there's a hard layer of ice covering my chart so I can't draw any lines with my normal 2H pencils. I'm going to try a 4H, which much is harder, and very sharp, and see if that will cut through the ice.'

'OK, Reg. Let me know how that works out.'

Reg took a 4H pencil and began to move it firmly again his steel ruler on the ice. It made a noisy scraping sound and a shower of tiny ice particles rose up and then settled on his chart. He blew them away, delighted that he had cut right through the ice and actually drawn a line. He then continued star shooting, though handling the sextant with numb fingers was difficult, and he was soon able to fix their position. Then, having calculated a new wind speed and direction and finally a new course in the worst of circumstances, he was as pleased as Punch and grinned like a Cheshire cat as he reported his achievement to John.

'Skip. Navigator here. It worked, and everything's OK. I've got a new course - 270 degrees. Yes, due West. That'll take us clear of most of the Ruhr, and heading for Ostend. I'll give you another course when we've crossed the coast.'

'Skip here. Well done, Reg. To all crew - I'm sure the temperature is now as low as it will get. Don't forget to move about whenever you can.'

'Rear gunner to Skip. Move? If only I could! It's pretty cold here in the fag-end. My guns have iced up and I'm de-freezing them with all the very hot coffee from my flask. As you know, I've had to do that before.' He managed a short, forced laugh. 'I don't know why I don't bring at least two thermos flasks; one for the guns and one for me!' He laughed again.

'Skip here. Poor old Sam is probably suffering more than the rest of us. Has anyone got some spare coffee for him - not for his guns?'

'Wireless Operator here. Yes. I'll take some along now. Good to move around a bit.'

'Thanks, Jack.'

Their Lancaster took them over Ostend, as planned, and without further incident, except for some random anti-aircraft fire, and soon they were over the North Sea. Reg now fixed their position, and gave Skip a new course for home.

In the hope of becoming a little less cold, they now flew at only 5,000 feet, but the Lancaster's temperature remained very low, and all the crew still had icicles on their oxygen masks, which dripped under the warmth of their breath.

CHAPTER 7

Enduring Arctic-like conditions, after a long, tiring and highly dangerous operation over enemy territory was a great strain on all the crew. As P-Peter finally crossed the coast, and was flying over England, the crew were pale, dishevelled and dog-tired. Or, as Scotty put it 'whacked.'

But they were also elated that, after a near disaster or two, and the constant threat of death, they had helped not only to destroy some German war factories, but had also downed a Messerschmitt 110, and then returned safely again.

As they approached RAF Coningsby, the crew gazed down at the runways, hangars, Nissen huts and other buildings with an affection they never experienced on the ground.

John was by now quite used to handling his damaged aircraft in the air, though not at all sure he would manage the landing. He had landed it on three engines, and that had given him confidence in both his expertise, and in the tolerance of P-Peter, but getting the kite back safely on the deck with a gaping hole in the port wing, and a bent propeller, was problematical.

The main difficulty he experienced as he began his approach was how to keep the aircraft stable. It sometimes wobbled alarmingly. He lowered the undercarriage later than usual, and had it locked down well before the final approach, at a speed of about 130 miles per hour, He reduced speed further as he approached the runway, and when he was about to touch down, at around ninety miles per hour, he used little power. He was tremendously relieved when the undercarriage wheels contacted the tarmac, albeit with a heavy bump, and further down the runway than he had intended. But he managed to keep P-Peter in the centre of it as he gradually slowed it down, and finally brought it to a standstill. The crew cheered lustily.

After scrambling out, they chatted for a few minutes, while getting used to standing on solid ground, after nearly eight uncomfortable hours in the air. Still feeling cold, they stamped their feet while walking up and down.

'It's wonderful to be back on *terra firma'*, Sam grinned. He was stretching his long legs thankfully, after they had been trapped for so long in his cramped turret. 'I've never before felt quite so cold.'

'I can well believe that,' Arthur said. 'It was bitterly cold, and you must have felt it more than the rest of us.'

'I'm a bit better off than you, Sam,' Scotty observed, 'but it's no joke spending every op suspended on a canvas sling sheet, with your head stuck in the dome of a turret, and this time it was much worse. I was frozen meat! I'm still pretty cold, but it's great to be standing here at last.'

'Yes, it is,' Freddie agreed. 'but why do return flights always seem longer than outgoing ones?'

Reg laughed. 'They always do, but sometimes they really are longer, either because we've taken a different route back to try to mislead Jerry, or we're going slower to economise on fuel.'

John noticed that a WAAF driver was standing nearby.

'Time to move off' he said. 'There's an attractive young lady waiting patiently to drive us to the debriefing. We mustn't keep her waiting.'

The crew waddled towards the bus in their heavy, cumbersome clothing, with arms full of Mae Wests, parachutes and other gear. In their present weary condition, even a walk of twenty yards towards the bus was a physical effort.

They were nearly there when Sam rushed forward, leaving the others behind and, to their amazement, embraced the WAAF, who was smiling with delight. As the others arrived, Sam introduced her.

'This is my friend Jenny. We met when having a cup of tea in the NAAFI canteen.'

'Crikey,' Scotty whispered to Reg. He's a fast worker!'

They all exchanged pleasantries with Jenny before entering the bus and being driven round the perimeter track.

At the debriefing, John explained how a bomb dropped from a Lancaster flying above them had crashed through their port wing, and the problems and dangers they experienced because of it. The Intelligence Officer listened carefully, while making notes.

They were given the usual cup of tea or coffee laced with rum and mercifully, the interrogation was a short one. They had yet to return parachutes and other gear.

In the Sergeants' Mess, six of them clutched pints of mild and bitter. They took turns to use the telephone, which was standing on a table in a corner of the room. None of them mentioned on the phone any of the ghastly experiences they had endured in the past eight hours.

Scotty phoned his girl friend Lucy.

'Hello, love. Are you OK?... Good, I'm glad to hear you haven't had any more bombs falling nearby.'

'Me? I'm fine. I've been thinking, if I'm free tonight, perhaps we could go to the pictures. What do you think...?'

'Well, at the Odeon, there's Tyrone Power in 'Blood and Sand....'

'Too violent?   Then what about Bing Crosby in 'Holiday Inn?' That's at the Gaumont....'

'You'd like that. That's great. Well, I'll phone you later today to confirm that I'm free, and then we'll decide where to meet. OK...? Good...Till later, then, sweetheart.. Bye.'

Arthur phoned his parents.

'Hello, Dad. How are you getting on...? Houses nearby were bombed last night...? What happened...? A land mine...Are you and Mum OK...? Some windows were blown out and tiles blasted away...? Is someone coming to do the repairs....? Good.'

'Oh, I'm alright.   I'm in a good crew, and we get on very well. Good camaraderie' ....'Yes, we'll all have some leave but it's not due yet.'...

'Has Mum's arthritis troubled her recently...?'

'How do you get on with the food rationing..?   Won't it be nice when you no longer have powdered eggs but the real thing....? No, you won't see any bananas until after the war......'

'I'd better ring off now, Dad, as some of my friends are waiting to use the phone. Look after yourselves. I'll ring again in a day or two. Goodbye.'

John now came in and the crew gathered round him.

'I've had words with the pilot of the aircraft that bombed us.'

'What did he say?' Scotty asked.

'He said that he knew that we were below his aircraft, but his bomb-aimer assured him that he could drop his bombs without hitting us.   He added that if his bombs hadn't been released then, he would have had to fly round again to begin a new bombing run, and that would have exposed his crew to extra danger. I could hardly believe what he was saying, and implying - that his aircraft and crew had to be protected even if our lives were put in jeopardy.'

'It's almost unbelievable,' Arthur commented.

John grimaced. 'I told him that, as captain of his aircraft, he was fully responsible for putting all our lives at risk, and crippling our aircraft, and that he had made a criminally irresponsible decision.'

'Good,' Scotty said. 'You told him a few home truths.'

'Oh, I said quite a lot more, but I'd rather not repeat it all,' John replied. 'I left him in no doubt about my absolute disgust.'

'And what did he say to all that?' Jack asked.

'He said that he had made a regrettable mistake, and he wanted to shake my hand. I refused.'

'Is he an officer?' Scotty wanted to know.

'Yes. He's a Flight Lieutenant, but to me his rank was irrelevant. I spoke to him as one pilot and captain to another.'

The crew were delighted that John had spoken for them all. Then Jack remembered a similar incident.

'John, did you hear about when Bill Reid's aircraft was bombed from above by one of our own aircraft? He's the chap who was awarded the Victoria Cross.'

'Oh, yes. Bill Reid, VC, is a pilot of enormous courage. On an op to Dusseldorf, his aircraft was attacked by night fighters. His windshield was shattered, he was wounded in three places, and his navigator was killed by a bullet in the head. To cap it all, the oxygen system was kaput. Amazingly, Bill carried on to the target, navigating by the stars and the moon. It was successfully bombed. Bitterly cold air poured over Bill, and the blood from a head wound froze. He was unconscious from time to time during the homeward flight, when another member of the crew took over the controls. But Bill successfully landed his badly-damaged aircraft. He was awarded the VC for his astonishing bravery.'

'He must have spent a long time in hospital after that.'

'Oh yes. He took some time to recover.'

'Yet he went back on operations. I think that's tremendous after what he'd been through.'

John agreed. 'I don't know how many ops he did after that, but on one of them a 1,000 pound bomb dropped on his aircraft and made a huge hole in it.'

'My God! And he survived that?'

'He did, but five of the crew died immediately. Apparently, the nose of the aircraft broke off and spun away. Bill and his Flight engineer were in that part, and amazingly they managed to bale out. They were then captured and were sent to a POW camp.'

'It's incredible and almost unbelievable,' Sam commented, 'that so much happened to one pilot.'

'And weren't we lucky?' John added. 'The 'friendly' bomb that landed on Bill's kite killed five of his crew immediately, but we all survived a similar incident.'

' I wonder how many other aircraft have been bombed?' Sam asked.

'We'll never know the full answer to that' Jack answered, 'because often there are no survivors. The aircraft just doesn't return, and naturally, everyone thinks it was shot down by ack-ack fire or night fighters. '

CHAPTER 8

Sgt. Jack Rogers

March 17th. 1945
RAF Coningsby

Dear Maurice,

I was very sorry to hear about the bomb damage to your parents' house in Bromley. Thank heaven their injuries are not serious, but the explosion must have shaken them up. I'm also glad that the bomb actually fell about fifty yards away from their house and that the damage -mainly to roof tiles and windows- will be soon repaired. It's good that you live not far away so you're there to help them when you can.

Someone here told me that Bromley has often been bombed when Jerry was actually trying to bomb Biggin Hill fighter station, which I believe is not far away.

How are you all managing with rationing? I experienced it before I joined the RAF. I remember that a week's ration for one person includes only 4 ounces of bacon or ham, 2 ounces of butter, 4 ounces of margarine, 2 ounces of tea, and one fresh egg. I particularly remember the powdered eggs, and there were never any bananas, oranges, etc. I wonder how much imported food lies at the bottom of the ocean, following the torpedoing of merchant ships by U-Boats?

You write about how fed up you are with the War. Aren't we all? But the end can't be far away. When large numbers of Allied troops cross the Rhine, which must happen soon, it will strike fear into German hearts.

On our third op we got caught up in a cumulonimbus cloud. We were tossed up and down, while ice formed on the wings, and we were battered by hailstones which even drowned the sound of our noisy Rolls Royce engines. Never a dull moment!

Coming back, a bomb from one of our own Lancs hit our port wing. Thank God it was only a small one but it made a nasty jagged hole. Yet, after that, Scotty managed to shoot down an *attacking Messerschmitt. How we cheered his success!*

More trouble on the way back. Our heating system failed.   We had icicles on our oxygen masks, and poor old Reg had an ice-covered chart. I don't know how he managed to navigate, but he got us back.

After that long -about 8 hours- flight, we were really knackered, and glad to relax in the evening in The Pig and Whistle

It's always good to hear from you, Maurice.

Your very good friend,

Jack

O n June 6th., 1944, Allied soldiers had crossed the English Channel to invade Normandy, France, on what came to be known as D-Day. While battles raged in Normandy, Hitler pinned his hopes on new terror weapons to be directed against England.

The first such attack was on June 12th, 1944 and it involved a new type of bomb which did not require manned aircraft.

The weapons, called V1s, and popularly known as 'doodlebugs' had been designed and manufactured at Peenamünde, and then delivered to launching pads in France, from where they were aimed at London and other urban areas, mainly in Southern England.

'Doodlebugs' were streamlined bombs with wings, attached to small petrol engines. They normally carried just enough fuel to take them to the London area. Where they finally landed would depend partly on the wind velocity. They could be clearly heard and seen, even at night, as there was always a light, and they could come at any time, day or night.

When the fuel ran out and the engine stopped, people living directly below knew that, this time, they would be safe. The bomb's trajectory would ensure that 'some other poor devils would get it.' Doodlebugs could not be targeted, their purpose being indiscriminate killing and destruction, in order to lower the morale of the civilian population.

During the daytime, some Spitfire and Hurricane pilots flew dangerously close to the doodlebugs to try to turn them back by nudging their wings against the tiny wings of the bombs, sometimes very successfully. Such courageous action required cool nerves and great skill.

Freddie's uncle, and all his family, had been killed when their house, among many others, was destroyed by a single 'doodlebug.' He was now determined to do his best to help destroy the V1 factories, should the crew be on 'battle orders' for an operation to Peenamunde.

Most of the V1 sites had now been overrun by the Allied armies. But the V2s, launched mainly from Holland, remained a menace. They were rocket-propelled bombs which travelled very high so that they were neither seen nor heard. Without warning, there would be an enormous explosion, many deaths, and extensive damage.

The parents of Arthur Jenkins had had a narrow escape when a V2 rocket exploded in an adjoining street. It completely destroyed six houses, killing all their occupants, and damaged many others, causing a range of injuries. That had happened only a few days after their ordeal following the landmine explosion.

It left them in shock. It shattered most of their windows and only a few tiles remained on their roof. They had been temporarily evacuated to a nearby hostel whilst emergency repairs were carried out to their house.

Many British people had an Anderson air raid shelter in their garden. Made of large curved sections of corrugated steel bolted together and semi-submerged in back gardens, they contained four bunks. Some families would go to them every time the wail of an air-raid siren was heard. Children often spent night after night in them.

Other families had a Morrison shelter (both shelters were named after Government Ministers) which was a large sturdy steel table in the house, under which people could shelter.

Both kinds of shelter had saved many people from death or injury. But since the attacks by rockets occurred without warning, people had little opportunity to seek protection.

The Nazis were placing increasing faith in their secret weapons, of which the doodlebugs and V2s were only the beginning, especially as their fortunes in the war began to turn, and they were in retreat on more than one front. New weapons were in the pipeline, including a super-gun to fire across the Channel.

The Cabinet and the Air Ministry wanted the destruction of Peenamünde to have a high priority. Otherwise the frequency of V2 bombing would, as Germany planned, escalate to an alarming level.

***

A number of crews assembled in the Briefing Room including John's. There was a noisy, vibrant atmosphere, punctuated by occasional explosions of laughter as airmen drifted in. But beneath the banter there was the usual degree of tension. All the air crews had been listed on 'Battle Orders' for the next operation, and they were anxious to know what was in store for them. Two questions dominated their thoughts-

What is the target for tonight?

Will it be an especially dangerous operation?

Suddenly the Intelligence Officer, who had been chatting to the Station Commander, stood up and walked towards the curtained board. In a flash, all conversations dried up and silence reigned. He pulled aside the curtain to reveal a map of North Germany and announced -

'The target for tonight will be Peenamünde.'

There was an immediate bubble of excited comment from the audience. It was quickly silenced as the I.O. had a number of points to make in a limited time. Several others, too, including the Squadron Commander, the Met Officer, the Section Leaders and the Station Commander were awaiting their turn.

The bombers would concentrate on the buildings used by scientists, the research laboratories, and the factories. There would be a diversionary attack, or spoof raid, on Essen, also by Lancasters.

The briefing was wound up by the Station Commander, who outlined the progress of previous attacks on Peenamünde, and concluded with a pep talk.

The first attack by the RAF, on August 17th, 1943, well before the weapons were ready to be fired, was largely successful, and German plans were set back by at least two months. However, destroyed buildings were feverishly rebuilt and facilities replaced. The bombing had to be repeated again and again. Both the RAF and the US Army Air Force took part in subsequent raids.

Reg took a special interest in the forecast wind velocities at various stages of the flight.

Freddie was glad that it would be a moonlit night with little cloud, so that their target should show up clearly.

John and his crew discussed the raid when they were 'dressing up' in their flying kit, and when each one collected silk maps and deutchmarks, which would be essential if they had to bail out over Germany.

Sam sought reassurance.

'We're in the first of three waves. With a diversionary attack over Essen, and the Jerries concentrating their night fighters there, we shouldn't meet so many of them, should we?'

'I hope not,' John responded. 'Diversionary attacks have often worked well. They fool the Germans for a while, so that night fighters assemble in the wrong place. But Jerry will soon realise what is actually happening and redirect the fighters. Yes, it may not be too bad in the first wave, but don't count on it.'

'A moonlit night is expected over Peenamünde,' Scotty recalled, 'so Freddie should have a clear view of our target, and Sam and I should be able to spot any night fighters.'

'True,' Jack responded, ' but in moonlight our Lancaster will also be a very large target for night fighters. On a clear night, they'll see us well before we see them.'

'Well,' put in John, 'Scotty and Sam have shown us what they can achieve on moonlit nights, and what they've done before, I'm sure they can do again.'

Scotty chuckled. 'We'll do our best, won't we Sam.'

Sam smiled. 'We're ready for Jerry,' he said.

On this occasion, John's crew used bicycles to get to dispersal. They reached P-Peter, and all the crew were soon sitting in their own part of the aircraft and busily carrying out their specialist tasks.

Following John's pre-flight tests, involving especially components that had been repaired or replaced, and when all his crew had carried out their own checks, John awaited a signal to move. Then he taxied the aircraft around the perimeter track, and was soon queuing behind other aircraft, and waiting his turn to take off.

Cleared for take-off, John gave all four engines enough throttle to have them noisily pressing forward against the brakes which stubbornly held the aircraft back. Then he released them and steadily increased the throttle so that the aircraft accelerated forward.

The Lancaster rose slowly into the air at just over 115mph. John kept it low until the power increased significantly. Then he climbed at 165 mph, P-Peter, accepting her burden with apparent determination.

**

They flew northwards in the direction of Denmark. They didn't expect to encounter much enemy action until they were well over half way towards that country. However, it was always wise to be prepared for the unexpected, especially as they would not be very far from enemy-occupied coast for a large part of the route.

BATTLE ORDERS

John's crew now regarded themselves seasoned warriors. This was their fourth operation and they felt they had already become a closely-knit unit, with a good understanding of one another. They knew that the fate of all of them could well depend on the skill and courage of each of them, and they prided themselves on their team work. Both camaraderie and confidence had developed rapidly since their first operation.

The gunners had been warned that German fighters had increasingly been using their new Schlage Musik weapon, with its twin, upward-firing, canon. They had been fitted into the cockpits of Messerschmitt 110s and some Heinkels, and had caused havoc. Lancasters were not well protected from attacks from below. Freddie, when not bomb-aiming, had the task of operating the two machine guns in his forward turret. He had quite a good field of vision, but that did not extend to directly underneath the aircraft.

This new weapon had become a regular talking point among all airmen, not only the gunners.

Scotty was convinced that they would meet Messerschmitts equipped with the dreaded weapon, and he wasn't at all sure how they would cope with a sudden attack from below. Nevertheless, by almost continuously swivelling his turret, he scrutinized every part of the sky above, and his vigilance never wavered.

It soon paid off when he spotted two Messerscmitt 110s. They were probably carrying out a coastal patrol in which they were flying between the coast and a point several miles out to sea. Observing the Lancaster, they had turned to engage it. Scotty announced their presence in an urgent tone.

'Skip, two Messerschmitts to the east, approaching rapidly. 500 yards away.'

Shutting out his fears of the Schlage Musik weapon, he was ready for action.

'OK, Scotty,' Skip replied. ' I can see them now.   All crew stand by for an extended corkscrew. Hold on tight.'

Judging the right moment to move was critically important. There was going to be a battle, and he wanted his gunners to have plenty of opportunities to fight back, while he made the situation as difficult as possible for the fighter planes.

He throttled back and dived steeply, turning thirty degrees for 1,000 feet, and continued with another steep diving turn for a further 1,000 feet, the airspeed reaching nearly 400 mph. He then pulled out and carried out a steep climbing turn through sixty degrees in the opposite direction, with the speed dropping to 140 mph. He marvelled, as he had before, that the P-Peter could manoeuvre through the air with such a heavy load.   'Lancasters,' he mused, 'are amazingly tolerant.'

The climb continued until P-Peter recovered its original height and course.

The Messerschmitts had only brief opportunities to focus their cannon on P-Peter, but they made the most of them, one raking the Lancaster from one end to the other.   John was immediately anxious for his crew.

'Skip here to all crew. Is everyone OK?'

'Wireless op. here. I'm OK but there's a short row of three or four holes high up along the port side of the fuselage...well above our heads!'

'Thanks, Jack. A lucky escape.'

During these violent manoeuvres the gunners sat with eyes glued on one or other of the enemy aircraft, sometimes swivelling their turrets rapidly, and were poised to attack whenever an opportunity, however short, presented itself.

Sam had the first opportunity and he took it immediately, bringing all four guns to bear on one of the Messerschmitts and firing a short burst as the fighter swept past. Not expecting immediate success, he was momentarily stunned to see his bullets smash squarely into the enemy aircraft and to witness the immediate effect as some of them penetrated the petrol tank. There was a huge explosion and the Messerschmitt disintegrated in a ball of fire, pieces of the aircraft falling nearby. Sam could hardly believe his eyes and was dumbstruck for several seconds.

His fellow crew members were jubilant and shouted with unalloyed triumph. Then Sam, still breathing deeply with nervous tension, recovered his tongue.

'Marvellous. I've bagged my first Jerry! I didn't expect'...he stuttered for a few seconds... 'anything like that would happen at this stage of the raid.'

'I didn't either,' Scotty said. 'but that was an amazing bit of shooting.' He shared Sam's pleasure. At no time had the Messerschmitts been in a position to attack them from below, so they had no chance to use their secret weapon, and he was delighted that Sam had succeeded in destroying one of them. So was John.

'Wonderful, Sam. You and Scotty did very well. It's great that you've both had a kill, now. The good news, too, is that the other kite has disappeared. Perhaps it was a long way from its base and worried about running out of fuel.'

The morale of the crew was now high as they continued their flight. They felt ready for anything.

As they approached the Danish coast, a few anti-aircraft batteries opened up. John planned to cross the peninsular in the north of the country, and pressed on, weaving and twisting P-Peter, while varying the Lancaster's height almost continuously, but keeping as close as possible to their agreed course in order not to create problems for Reg's navigation.

Over Denmark they were relieved to meet only sporadic anti-aircraft fire, which was not particularly accurate, and John felt it hardly warranted modification of either course or height.

When they had crossed the peninsular, Reg gave John a new course, largely in a south-east direction.

They had passed an area full of lakes of all sizes and were soon flying along the Kattergat, and then over the Baltic Sea, with its many German-occupied islands. Over some of them they met no opposition, but over others, the anti-aircraft fire was as intense as they had previously experienced. They continued over the Baltic and past the island of Rügen until, just ahead, was Peenamünde.

The crew were now charged with both excitement and fear. This was it, one of the most highly defended of all German targets. A great deal depended on the result of this attack.

No-one in the crew doubted that this was going to be a particularly dangerous operation. Many aircraft would not return. Each one felt the tension in his body. For the present, though, their objective was to seek their target and bomb it successfully, and at the moment, that was all that mattered.

CHAPTER 9

The scene over Peenamünde was both spectacular and menacing. Group Captain Bannister was in a Master bomber controlling the entire attack. The Pathfinders had done their job effectively, and illuminated with flares the buildings that were to be attacked. The anti-aircraft fire was fierce, accurate and deadly, and, as on earlier operations, John's crew smelt the cordite of close-exploding shells which shook their aircraft as it progressed towards the target. And all the time the searchlights waved threateningly.

Their specific target would be the factories manufacturing 'doodlebugs' and V2s. Other aircraft would concentrate on the research areas or the scientists' quarters.

John steered P-Peter towards the bombing run. Freddie had requested that the bomb doors be opened. He had set the wind velocity very carefully on the bombsight, incorrect winds being a common cause of bombing errors. The bombsight was calibrated for various types of bomb, and Freddie had to press the appropriate selector switch.

He then began to guide John in the usual way, while the latter struggled to keep the Lancaster straight and level as it was rocked by exploding shells.

Freddie now held the stage.

'Three or four degrees to starboard, Skip... steady..steady...little more to starboard...good...steady...steady...bombs gone.'

As forecast, the visibility was excellent and John watched the bombs falling, most of them exploding on factory buildings, some of which burst into flames, while others were flattened. He kept the

Lancaster on an even keel with difficulty, while a photograph was taken, and then turned on to the course Reg had given him.

'Good work, Freddie,' John said. 'We've done our bit to destroy the factories and rockets.'

At that moment they were hit by flak in three places and immediately the Lancaster began to lose height. The outer starboard engine had been largely destroyed, the inner starboard propeller was bent and there was a gaping hole in the floor of the fuselage, not far from Scotty's turret and behind Jack Porter. John feared there might be other damage that they would discover later.

The temperature in the Lancaster fell rapidly as a powerful draught of ice-cold air swept through the aircraft. Arthur shut off the outer starboard engine and switched some of the fuel from one tank to another, while John lowered the aircraft from 20,000 to 14,000 feet and cut back the speed from 220 to 130 mph.

'Skip. Mid-upper gunner here My turret won't move at all. I just can't swivel it,' Scotty almost shouted. He was very upset.

'Flight engineer here for Scotty. The outer starboard engine is kaput. That engine normally drives a pump which operates your turret. That's why it won't move. '

'Skip here, Scotty. I'm afraid that puts you out of action. It's a blow. We'll miss your gunnery skills but just keeping your eyes peeled will be very helpful. '

'OK Skip, but I feel I've been disarmed.'

John steered the crippled aircraft with difficulty. The power and performance of the aircraft had been severely impaired. It was very difficult to keep it straight and level as he strove to escape from the turmoil around Peenamunde.

'There must be night fighters waiting to finish us off,' John thought. They were still in the most exposed and precarious zone, and all the crew were very aware of their vulnerability.

The hole in the fuselage was a worry, but John's main concern was that either Jack or Scotty, might have been injured. He contacted them on the intercom.

'Skip here for Jack and Scotty. You must have been pretty near when the shrapnel crashed in. Are you both OK?'

'Wireless Op. here, Skip. I'm OK, but a bit shaken up. A piece of red hot shrapnel crashed through about two metres behind me. Had that happened while the bombs were still in the bay, we'd have all been blown to Kingdom Come.'

'And Skip, Mid-upper gunner here. I'm OK, too. Like Jack, I'm a bit shaken, but glad to be alive.'

'That's great. Jack, take a look at the hole. See if you think we can do something about it. He gave a short laugh. 'I seem to remember that you plugged a hole for us on an earlier op. '

'Yes, I did, and it worked. I'll take a look at this one.'

'Thanks, Jack.' A minute or two later Jack reported back.

'Wireless Op. here Skip. The hole is about four inches in diameter and has very jagged edges. My solution is to stuff it with my kapok suit. Only a small part of the suit will do the trick, and I think I can anchor the rest by placing various heavy items on it.'

'O.K., Jack, though it will be the second time you've ruined a kapok suit!'

'They're expendable, Skip. We're not. Anyway, I'll go ahead and let you know how it works out.'

Jack lost no time. He took off his kapok suit, and plugged part of it in the hole, while ensuring that its jagged edges were all projected into the suit, to help to hold it in place. Then he spread the remainder of the suit as flat as possible over the floor and placed several heavy objects on it. Finally, he stood back to examine his work while putting on his flying jacket. Back in his normal place, he reported to John.

'Skip, wireless op. here. I've plugged the hole, and, so far, it's working. There's little, if any, air coming through. Fingers crossed, the problem's solved.'

'Skip here. Jack, that's terrific!'

'Thanks, Skip, but we still have three holes high up in the fuselage from the Messerschmitt attack, so we're not going to be very warm!'

'I know, Jack, but it would have become a lot colder without your work.'

P-Peter seemed to settle down to its restricted ability, and Arthur nursed the three functioning engines.

The propeller with the bent tip was working, though its effectiveness was clearly reduced.

They returned largely the way they had come, except that, after a brief discussion with the crew, John decided to go round the top of the Danish peninsular, not across it, and then to keep well out to sea, and to the west, to keep clear of further threats. In their weakened state, they were ill prepared for combat. Arthur was satisfied that their fuel supply was just sufficient to get them back, though there was always the uncertain factor of landing priority. He warned John.

'Skip, Flight engineer here. We won't have much fuel left when we get back...not enough if we have to mess about stacking.'

'OK, Arthur.'

BATTLE ORDERS

For the remainder of the homeward journey the gunners now kept an extra sharp look out. Though thoroughly exhausted, they were determined never to allow their attention to waver in view of the Lancaster's damage and weakened state. They had been surprised, on the outward flight, by the appearance of the two Messerschmitts, so now they would take no chances.

P-Peter met no more night fighters and the crew had begun to think that they would reach RAF Coningsby without serious incidents when Arthur reported to Skip that a new problem had suddenly arisen.

'Skip, flight engineer here. The outer port engine has just stopped, and I've no idea why.'

'That's a damn nuisance, Arthur.' John grumbled. 'Poor Sam won't be able to swivel his turret and I'll have another landing problem.' He gave a short laugh, and went on, 'One day, I hope I'll be able to carry out a normal landing of our Lanc on four engines. Earlier I had to land it on three; now it looks like two!'

'It may not come to that, Skip,' Arthur responded. I'm going to try to get that engine started again. There are several techniques I can try.'

'OK, Arthur, I'll stand by for some good news.'

About ten minutes later, the outer port engine spluttered into life.

John cheered. 'You've done it, Arthur. You're a wizard.'

'Wish I were,' Arthur retorted. 'As a matter of fact, I don't even know what the problem was. I just tried out a few possibilities to get the engine going, and one of them worked! I've just been lucky!'

'That's good news, anyway.'

'Rear gunner here for flight engineer. Thanks, Arthur. I hate it when my turret won't move. It's moving well, again.'

'That's fine, Sam.'

John was able to complete their homeward journey without further incident. and he began to think increasingly about what to expect at Coningsby.

'Arthur, Skip here. We've lost an engine and we have a bent prop and a hole in the fuselage. What sort of landing priority do you think we can expect?'

'Well, Skip, we flew a longer route back, so our fuel reserves are low. We really can't afford to hang about. And you've got to land a badly damaged kite on three engines.' He laughed. 'Perhaps I should say two and a half. I think we should be allowed to land as soon as we arrive.'

John agreed. 'I'll make our case strongly,' he said, 'but Control must have the last word. Anyway, let's wait to hear what they say.'

When they were getting quite near to Coningsby, they could see that there were many more aircraft waiting to land than they had anticipated- 30 to 40 -, but they still expected to have priority. It came as quite a shock to be told that they would have to wait for some time for their turn. When John had argued his case, he was told that five of the Lancasters had worse damage than P-Peter, including one with only two working engines. Also, three of the waiting aircraft contained wounded airmen. They must have top priority.

With the time drawing near for P-Peter to prepare to land, John found that their petrol level was extremely low, and he did what he could to conserve it, but the Lancaster is a thirsty monster, even on three engines. On the final circuit there was hardly anything left in the tanks. He straightened out and began to lose height steadily on the approach. He was almost gliding when approaching close to the runway, and the Lancaster began to wobble and was difficult to control.

John was very tense and not at all sure whether he would be able to get his aircraft down without a crash.

Finally, he touched down. The landing was a little heavier than usual, but his crew did not care in the least. John had once again landed them safely, following another very dicey operation, and there was profound relief all round and a heavy exhalation of breath.

Jenny was waiting for them by her vehicle, so they waddled over to her as soon as they had collected all their gear and equipment and were ready to be driven away. Sam sat as close as he could to Jenny and they exchanged whispers throughout the short journey. Scotty noticed, grinned, and winked at Freddie.

A later examination of the aircraft by ground staff revealed that, in addition to the destruction of one engine and the bent propeller, the starboard wing tip had been torn away. Little wonder, thought John, that the aircraft had been so difficult to keep steady during the landing. He thought about the strength, resilience, and adaptability of his Lancaster, that enabled them once again to get back safely in spite its widespread damage.

The crew of P for Peter were content. They had once again completed an operation successfully, Sam had shot down a Messerschmitt, and they were all in one piece.

Squadron Leader Lewis, their Flight Commander, who attended the de-briefing, congratulated the whole crew on their achievements. They appreciated this acknowledgement of their efforts, but were desperately anxious to get away and relax as soon as possible.

Sam was upbeat. 'With the downing of that Messerschmitt, I've broken my duck,' he chuckled. 'The fighters have the advantage of speed but their guns are fixed, while we can swivel ours freely. John, your manoeuvres make it very difficult for them to get into a firing position. They should be afraid of us. We're not afraid of them!'

***

With de-briefing over, and all their gear returned, the crew had eaten and showered and slept for many hours.

In the evening they were again in 'The Pig and Whistle.'

This time, while they sipped their beers, they were all keen to unwind their thoughts about the constant dangers they had to face, their worries and their fears about the future.

'The worst part,' Scotty suggested, 'is on the bombing run. We're flying straight and level, with aircraft in front and behind doing the same, while other Lancasters nearby are corkscrewing and diving. I'm really scared that they might crash into us, or drop their bombs on us, as happened on our third op.'

"We're all scared, I'm sure,' Sam agreed, ' I'm especially worried that some of the ack-ack shells exploding all around us, will ignite our bombs before we can get rid of them. That really would mean curtains for all of us.'

'Yes, we are all scared,' John said, 'and there's plenty to be scared about during any bombing operation, but we've now been to Berlin, the most highly-defended city in Germany, and to Peenamunde. They were both very tough assignments. It won't always be quite so bad.'

'And,' Jack added, 'we're not the crew that we were only a few weeks ago. We're now experienced, and we've learnt a tremendous amount. And best of all, we're all good at our jobs and we work together well.'

'I absolutely agree with that,' John said, 'and we're not simply at the mercy of ack-ack and night fighters; we've got two gunners who do a great job fighting back.'

'Yes,' Arthur said, 'if Sam and Scotty hadn't each downed a Jerry that was attacking us, who knows what might have happened?'

'And when they haven't been able to shoot them down,' Reg added, 'they've damaged them or scared them off.'

'John's face lit up. 'Altogether,' he added, 'we're doing pretty well, so let's sink another pint.'

'And they'll be on me,' Jack insisted.

CHAPTER 10

Sgt Jack Rogers,

RAF Coningsby

March 21st., 1945

Dear Maurice,

I hope you and your family are all keeping well.

You mention the doodlebugs and V2 rockets. I believe you can always see the doodlebugs, and hear them. too. Then the engine stops and the bomb begins to fall. That sounds terrifying, but, as you say, the V2 rockets are worse because they go very high and fall without warning so there is no time to hurry to an air-raid shelter. By the way, the doodlebugs should have stopped because of the Army's advance, but perhaps there are a few launching sites still operating.

The V2 rockets are more recent. They've been fired over England only since November 12th.,1944.

BATTLE ORDERS

They are launched mainly from bases in Holland that are still in German hands. I understand that we can thank a mysterious scientist named Doctor Werner von Braun for the V1 and V2 horrors.

Our crew is still having a pretty lively time. The good news is that Sam has shot down his first German aircraft. It was a Messerschmitt, one of two that was attacking us. That gave him a huge boost of confidence. We're lucky we have Sam and Scotty defending us when night fighters are on the attack. Scotty couldn't use his guns on the way back because our outer starboard engine, which controls the movement of his turret, was put out of action.

John did it again! This time he had to land our Lancaster with a bent propeller and three engines, and managed it without too much trouble. We all think he's terrific. At one time another engine had stopped suddenly and it looked as if John would have to land with only two engines, but Arthur managed to get it going while we were over the North Sea.

I believe you used to belong to the Home Guard, but it ended last year, didn't it? I read about King George VI taking the salute at their final parade last December. What are you doing with all the spare time you now have? I'm kidding.

So, you were caught out showing a light in your study! You'd better get some more blackout curtains! It seems that the ARP wardens are as vigilant as ever, and a good thing too. Any lights seen from the air might persuade a German pilot to release his bombs. And there are still volunteers doing fire duty. That's good because incendiary bombs can cause terrible fires.

We're all following the progress of the invasion forces. The Allies have now advanced quite a long way, but Jerry sometimes carries out sudden counter attacks. The Russians are also advancing south very rapidly. It's difficult to predict when the end will come but it must be some time this year. How we'll all cheer our heads of off!

From your good friend,

Jack

'Skip here to all crew. This is urgent! We're going to ditch! Get ready!' Then, almost shouting, his voice sounding increasingly hoarse and desperate. 'The kite may stay afloat for only a few minutes!'

'Wireless Op here, what's the problem, Skip?'

'Fuel, Jack. We're running out of it.'

The crew were prepared for the worst. It was a depressing prospect, because ditching was always dangerous and, even if it was successful, meant a hazardous future lay ahead. They would be lucky to survive the ordeal, and they all knew it.

They had heard of crews that had never been found; and of others that had not been found for two or three days, an eternity for airmen sitting in their wet clothes in a dinghy amidst billowing waves and sometimes every kind of foul weather. You could never tell what kind of weather you might have in the North Sea, but they'd heard stories of ditched airmen facing waves of up to five metres high.

At the outset, a great deal would depend on John carrying out a successful ditching, so that P-Peter might rest on the waves for a sufficient length of time for the crew to get out the dinghy, inflate it, launch it on the waves, and then get into it.

Much would depend on the swell, and on the weather. With the sea rising and falling several metres, there could be difficulties impossible to overcome.

'It's going to be very dicey,' Scotty thought. *'I should have made out my will.'*

John's mind was on the possibility of rescue.

'Navigator. Skip here. What is our exact position?'

'It's 58.21 degrees north - same as the Moray Firth - and 3.13 degrees, East, Skip.'

'Thanks, Reg. Skip to Wireless operator. Send an SOS now, with that position.'

After a few minutes -

'Wireless operator here, Skip. Our position sent.'

John dipped the nose of his Lancaster towards the sea. He looked around to assess the weather conditions, and carried out a close inspection of the waves, now not far below. It was about two thirty in the morning in the middle of winter, and they would have to ditch in fairly dark conditions, though the moon shone clearly when not obscured by cloud, and at present, he could see the surface of the water reasonably well. Otherwise, it would remain dark for a long time at that latitude.

They had carried out their second raid on Peenamünde and were sure that photographs would show, beyond doubt, that they had again hit their target - the research buildings this time.

For the most part, they had met little opposition, but there had been very concentrated anti-aircraft fire a few miles from the research area and some of the flak had caused a leak in one of their petrol tanks. Arthur had transferred as much fuel as he could to other tanks but there had been so many distractions at the time that a huge quantity of fuel had leaked before he could do so. One of the distractions had been an engine fire which had finally been put out by John, using the fire extinguisher controlled in his cabin. But the leak had been a major worry as they had a long flight home.

They had three self-sealing tanks fitted in each wing, numbered 1,2 and 3, outboard of the fuselage. Arthur had tried to keep the petrol level in tanks one and two fairly even, so that if one was punctured by enemy action, the loss would be limited. He had done that by running on each alternately for half an hour.

It was the number 1 tank, in the starboard wing, between the fuselage and the inner engine, with a capacity of 580 gallons that had been punctured. Unfortunately, it had not self-sealed. It was a flight engineer's nightmare.

The fuel levels were now very low, and they were faced with ditching in the North Sea, several hundred miles from their base in England. At least, thought John, we have enough fuel for a controlled ditching.

He approached the waves at 100 mph; then almost glided at 90 mph before attempting to land squarely on the water. To the airmen, the sea now looked like a boiling cauldron, angry and terrifying.

The nose of the Lancaster plunged into it with a shuddering thud, felt by all the tense airmen aboard, pushing up gallons of water on either side. It then rebounded to the surface, slid a short distance on its belly, and then settled unsteadily on the heaving water, the waves splashing over it relentlessly.

P-Peter, they all knew, might sink immediately.

'If it does,' Sam thought, *'it will be curtains for all of us.'*

'I hope to God it stays afloat long enough for us all to get off and into the dinghy,' Scotty was thinking.

All the crew knew the ditching drill, and had had time to rehearse in their minds how they would act when the moment came.

Jack released the dinghy by pulling the release cord running along the fuselage roof, aft of the rear spar, and all the crew were quickly out of the aircraft and on to the wings.

In a short time, the dinghy was out and inflated, but it was difficult to get it fully on to the water. It seemed to have got caught up with some part of the fuselage because the aircraft was slightly askew in the water. As P-Peter was filling rapidly with water, there was a general fear that the dinghy would sink before they could get into it. And perhaps aircraft and dinghy would sink together beneath the waves. The sea, working its way into the fuselage, and settling in some parts more than in others, was increasing the lop-sidedness of its settlement. Some quick and decisive action was urgent.

Jack Rogers immediately volunteered to jump into the sea to try to free the dinghy and get it floated. Ignoring objections, he dived into the freezing cold water and spent some minutes pushing the dinghy, sometimes diving under it, and trying to push it from underneath. At last, following his heroic and patient efforts, he managed to get the dinghy floating, free of impediments and ready for the crew. He was blue in the face and shivering with cold as he summoned all his strength to clamber into it.

'That was terrific,' John said. 'The sea must be freezing cold.'

With teeth chattering and his bluish body trembling with cold, Jack could not reply for some time, but he managed a grin, and a wave to dismiss any notion that he had done something special.

All the crew succeeded in clambering into the dinghy, though some of them had to swim to it, and then scramble in, their clothes dripping wet. Half the crew were therefore soaked and rather miserable as they sat around the dinghy and began their wait to be rescued, their only consolation being that at least it contained a good supply of water and emergency rations, a Very Light pistol and about twenty red flares. Jack had recovered his voice

'They'll be very useful,' he said, 'when we want to contact any would-be rescuers in ships or aircraft.'

'Would-be rescuers will have the helluva job finding us, won't they?' Sam suggested.

'Yes, they will, ' John answered, 'but at least we'll be able to make good use of the flares whenever we see or hear a ship or aircraft. They give us hope.'

They put out the sea anchor and prepared for a long wait. Their Lancaster, which had been sinking for some time, now slid into the waves and sank. Watching it sink until there was only a final sucking noise and then a cluster of bubbles on the surface of the sea, was a sad sight for all of them, for P-Peter had served them well. It was their kite, and they had always felt more secure in it than they would have felt in any other Lancaster, however illogical that might seem. Put simply, they felt closely attached to it.

It was now a little after three in the morning. The crew looked around at the vast expanse of sea stretching in all directions up to the horizon. How long would they remain before being rescued? Would they ever be rescued? As a tiny object in a vast sea, their dinghy would be extremely difficult to spot from the air.

Suddenly they all felt very lonely and isolated.

***

It was not until six o' clock in the morning that the crew heard the sound of an aircraft. Their hopes rose. But being some distance away, it sounded very remote, and there was a morning mist swirling about, so the visibility was poor. The crew fired two of their red flares, more in hope than expectation. Then they waited, hoping for a response. There was none, and, to their dismay, they heard the aircraft flying away, and soon the sound of its engines began to fade, until they could no longer be heard.

'Don't worry,' John assured his crew. 'I'm sure there'll be others. Any aircraft looking for us would find it an almost impossible task in these misty conditions, and it's too much to expect a passing aircraft to notice us.'

At eighty thirty, they heard another aircraft, and its engines sounded loud, positive and familiar.

'I'm hearing Rolls Royce Merlin engines,' Arthur told the others.

'Yes, I'm sure you're right,' John said.

'And there it is, coming in this direction,' Freddie shouted, excitedly.

'They may not have seen us, ' Jack said. 'It's still foggy. Let's fire another couple of flares.'

They did so, and were rewarded when the Lancaster dropped a white flare which lit up the dinghy. It then flashed OK on its downward identification light, and circled once more before flying away.

'Do you think their crew will report our position to Air/Sea Rescue?' Sam asked, of no-one in particular.

'Well, we've been spotted,' Arthur replied, 'and I expect our position has been sent, but it will take a long time for their aircraft to find us. We're drifting all the time. When they arrive, we'll probably be somewhere else!' John agreed.

'But it's good that we now have reason to hope.'

He looked round at his comrades, some of whom were looking anything but hopeful. How long, they were thinking, would they have to wait for help. They knew that they could survive in their exposed state, with a minimum of food and water, for only a very limited time. They were feeling the cold increasingly, especially when the wind became gusty, and penetrated their wet clothing.

'I think it's colder than when our heating failed in P-Peter, and we had Arctic conditions in the aircraft,' Scotty remarked.

'We're feeling it more,' Jack pointed out, 'Because all our clothes are soaking wet. It wouldn't be so bad if the sea were a little calmer.'

The dinghy was not suitable for mountainous seas, should they develop, and even the present choppy waves regularly splashed icy-cold water over them.

At present it appeared to be waterproof, but dinghies had been known to develop leaks. It was round, and they knew that if they tried to paddle it towards England, they would only go in circles. There was, in fact, very little they could do to help themselves. Had they been able to do something to keep them busy, their morale might have been a little higher.

The sea was becoming rougher, with large waves sometimes breaking over into the dinghy, so that they had to bail out the water desperately in order to stay afloat. Having no tool for that purpose, they had to use their hands.

Many hours passed, with their hopes of a rescue steadily diminishing. Even if an Air/Sea Rescue boat were to reach them, they were thinking, would it be before some of them had succumbed to their long exposure to the icy winds, combined with the constant splashing of the waves.

Inevitably their morale had been sinking as they shivered in their wet clothing. They cursed the long delay in their rescue, but were fully aware of the difficulties to be expected in locating them in poor visibility, and they knew they had drifted significantly since they were first spotted.

It was fourteen hours after their ditching, at five o'clock in the afternoon, before they heard another aircraft. There were two Air/Sea Rescue Hudson aircraft, that had been searching for them for many hours, their crews constantly peering, with tired eyes, through the mist or fog.

One of the Hudsons now lowered an airborne lifeboat by parachute. It had previously dropped a flare to see the direction of drift, and had descended to about 700 feet to drop the lifeboat. To the beleaguered crew, the falling lifeboat, attached to a parachute, was a wonderful sight. They managed to cheer.

Unfortunately, it landed some yards from their dinghy, and was about to drift away. The crew were desperate to get to it, and paddled furiously with their hands, until they were able to grab the ropes hanging from it. Then they abandoned the dinghy and scrambled into the lifeboat.

There were waterproof suits in the boat's lockers, enough for each member of the crew to discard his soaking-wet clothing and change into the dry suits. All the wet flying gear they had been wearing was now thrown into the sea. There was no room for it.

Changing into waterproof suits, after sitting for many hours in wet flying gear, was much appreciated by them all. It gave their morale a boost, albeit a temporary one. In dry clothing they felt infinitely more comfortable, and the waves splashed into the lifeboat less frequently than they had into the dinghy.

Arthur started the four-horsepower outboard engine, and, full of hope, but not over-optimistic, because there was a long way to go, the crew pointed the little craft towards England, to the South, and began their journey.

'It's nice to be wearing dry clothing,' Sam remarked, 'but this little lifeboat is quite flimsy. It's not robust enough to get us to England, is it?'

The others were silent for a few moments as they digested Sam's fears, and one or two turned to examine the little craft on which their survival depended.

'That's probably true,' John conceded, 'but hopefully it will stay afloat until we're rescued.'

'But we don't know, John, whether we will be rescued, do we?' Scotty said. 'I'm sure the Air/Sea Rescue people will do their best. They've provided this lifeboat - obviously the best they could do at the time - but what else can they do? We're a long way from England and our position is constantly changing. We're steering this little boat, hopefully towards England, but the waves and the wind are constantly shifting our position. If and when they set out to find us, it'll be like looking for a needle in a haystack. We're a tiny dot in a massive sea stretching to the horizon and beyond.'

Scotty's sober assessment of their perilous situation set them all thinking.

Would they ever be rescued? If so, how long might they have to wait? Were they going to die, one after the other?

CHAPTER 11

They had been travelling for about half an hour, most of the time in silence, when suddenly, above the sound of the splashing waves and the outboard engine, one of them began to sing. It was so extraordinary and unexpected that the others could hardly believe their ears. For a fleeting moment it must have sounded to them rather eerie, as if it came from somewhere else.

The singer was Jack Rogers, who had decided that he must do something to keep up the spirits of the crew, and he thought he might try to do that by starting a sing-song. He had been a choirboy for a time and when his voice had broken, had joined a local amateur choir - as a tenor - that sang major classical works such as Bach's B Minor Mass. He also knew many popular songs from the 1920's to the Second World War.

In a good, clear voice, he began, without any introduction, to sing the first verse of 'O My Darling Clementine' -

> *In a cavern, in a canyon,*
> *Excavating for a mine,*
> *Dwelt a miner forty niner,*
> *And his daughter Clementine,*

To Jack's delight, the whole crew joined in singing the chorus.

> *Oh! my darling, Oh! my darling,*
> *Oh! my darling Clementine,*
> *You are lost and gone forever,*
> *Dreadful sorry, Clementine.*

Jack knew the words of two other verses and he sang them so that the crew could again join in the chorus, which they did. He grinned,

'That was great. And now I'm going to test your sense of humour. We're surrounded by water so we're going to sing, 'I Do Like to Be Beside the Seaside.'

There were a few rueful grins. This time there was no chorus but Jack hoped that the crew would join in if they knew the words. Most of them did.

> *Oh, I do like to be beside the seaside,*
> *I do like to be beside the sea,*
> *I do like to stroll along the Prom, Prom, Prom,*
> *Where the brass bands play*
> *Tid-de-ly om pom pom!*
> *So just let me be beside the seaside,*
> *I'll be beside myself with glee,*
> *And there's lots of girls beside,*
> *I should like to be beside,*
> *Beside the seaside, beside the sea.*

'Well done!' Jack managed to say, as he tried to recover his breath. 'Would you like another one?'

'Yes,' John replied, 'It's just what we need.'

'OK,' Jack said, 'How about 'What Shall we Do with the Drunken Sailor?' He had chosen that song because he was sure his fellow airmen would all know the words and there was plenty of repetition.

Once he had sung the first note, they belted out the words without hesitation -

> *What shall we do with the drunken sailor?*
> *What shall we do with the drunken sailor?*
> *What shall we do with the drunken sailor?*
> *Early in the morning.*

Hooray and up she rises,
Hooray and up she rises,
Hooray and up she rises,
Early in the morning.

And that was all there was to it, but they sang it twice. Then Sam said, 'Can we have another one? Do you know any other songs, Jack?'

'I do,' Jack answered with a smile, 'and I think that considering you're crammed into a tiny lifeboat, pitching and rolling its way through choppy seas' - he grinned - 'that was a great performance. But perhaps any more singing might give you dry throats, and we've got a limited supply of drinking water.'

'I agree,' John said. 'Thanks Jack,' for getting us all to sing our hearts out, but we'd better not make ourselves parched. Perhaps we might have another tune or two when we're nearer home.'

'OK by me, John. I'm always ready to sing.'

Jack looked round at his companions. There was no doubt that they looked a little more cheerful after the singing. John had noticed that too, and patted Jack on the back. He thought how lucky he was - in fact, they all were, - to have someone like their wireless operator, who could make a unique contribution to the safely or morale of the whole crew.

The singing had apparently loosened up the tongues of the crew, for they now began to talk in a lively manner and more frequently. John thought it remarkable how the singing seemed to have raised the spirits of his fellow-airmen.

Scotty spoke with unbounded enthusiasm of his love for his girlfriend Lucy, and how they hoped to get married fairly soon. He wasn't sure about how he would earn his living after the war, but he certainly would not go down the Lanarkshire pits again.

Sam explained how much the war had curtailed his education, and that he hoped to go to a university after the war rather than go back to being a clerk.

Arthur spoke about his wish to become a skilled engineer.

John definitely wanted to continue his university course, and to have an academic career.

Jack wanted to continue his medical course.

Reg thought he would probably complete his accountant's training and Freddie, who had never worked for a living, confessed that he had no idea at all what he would do when demobbed.

By singing and chatting, the crew had passed away a little time, but then they all relapsed into silent meditation as they appraised their prospects of getting to England.

They knew that they could not possibly get there in such a small and relatively flimsy craft. The sea was getting increasingly rough, and there was a very real possibility that the little lifeboat would break up. It was intended to be used only over much shorter distances.

The crew now made more use of the radio to update the authorities on their situation and on the frail condition of the boat on which their lives depended.

John swept his eyes round the crew, noting their facial expressions and general condition. They had already endured over fifteen hours at sea, from about 2.30 in the morning to 6pm in the afternoon. Their faces had now been drained of colour, their complexions being a pale blue/grey and they had very little energy. He wondered whether one or more of the crew might soon crack - though there was no sign of that at present - or perhaps they would shortly begin to suffer from exposure, which would be inevitable if their ordeal were to last much longer. They would be overwhelmed by the penetrating cold and dampness.

Always as optimistic as a situation allowed, even John began to doubt that he and his crew would survive. If death was coming, he mused, it would be either through exposure or drowning.

***

Their little lifeboat had been making slow progress for some time, through increasingly turbulent waves, when Freddie, who had been studying the horizon for some time, broke the silence.

'Look over there,' he almost shouted. 'It's a boat of some sort, and I think it's heading this way. 'What do you think?' he asked his fellow-crewmen.

Freddie, as bomb-aimer, was adept at identifying objects some distance away, and his words galvanised his companions afresh, with hope and optimism.

'You may be right,' Jack answered, 'but it's some way away, and the visibility is not good. I believe it is definitely a boat but I' m not sure it's getting any nearer to us.'

The others, who had been listening intently, were now straining their eyes in the direction of the tiny, bobbing craft on the horizon that Freddie had spotted. After a few minutes, Jack felt confident enough about the mysterious boat in the distance, to be more definite.

'I think that boat is definitely heading this way,' he announced. 'Freddie was right. And we'll soon be able to see what kind of a craft it is. I think there's a good chance we'll soon be rescued.'

Jack's opinions were highly respected among the crew, and hearing his confident prediction was a salient morale booster. There was suddenly a new spirit of hope among them.

Soon afterwards, Scotty noticed a Hudson aircraft coming towards them and then there was the unmistakable drone of the engines above the splashing of the waves on their lifeboat.

'Good,' John said. 'The Hudson is guiding a rescue launch towards us. We must still look very tiny from a distance.'

Another Hudson appeared and replaced the first one.

Meanwhile, an Air/Sea Service rescue launch was cutting its way, with apparent determination, through an increasingly angry sea, and rapidly reducing the distance between them. The crew were overjoyed.

'It's been tough, but we're going to be saved in the nick of time,' Scotty said, shouting above the noise of the waves which were now pounding the lifeboat and often splashing over it. 'Sixteen hours is long enough in these conditions.'

Soon their lifeboat was bobbing up and down alongside the launch, which now looked huge to the crew. They climbed aboard and were welcomed by a small group of smiling sailors, given hot drinks and sandwiches, and made as comfortable as possible.

Some of the airmen were soon asking the crew about their destination and what they might expect after landing.

'Where are we going to land?' Scotty enquired of one of the older crew members, who appeared to be in charge. They had all been wondering about that.

He told them that their base was near Newcastle, and that he had been in touch with a nearby hospital which had agreed to send a transport to pick them up from the dock. They expressed their gratitude to all the crew. None of them doubted that their timely rescue had definitely saved their lives.

For most of them, the next hours passed in a blur. The launch entered the Tyne Estuary and docked after about an hour. The crew disembarked and travelled by minibus to a hospital. Medical examinations there were followed by a day of rest, and then more check-ups before their rail journey back to Coningsby.

On the train, several of the crew drifted off to sleep, but some of them found time to reminisce about their recent ordeal.

'I thought we'd had it,' Scotty confessed. 'I mean, we spent many long hours, first in our dinghy and then in a lightweight lifeboat, an insignificant little object, surrounded by a very rough sea. Visibility was poor with waves breaking over the side.'

'Yes, and the time dragged,' Sam said. 'It got worse and worse the longer we were there without any sign that help was on the way.'

'It was great, though, the way you got us all to sing, Jack, ' Freddie said. 'Our spirits were getting low. Singing took our minds away from the awful prospect we faced. We just stopped thinking about it and joined in.'

Jack quickly changed the topic.

'We welcomed that little lifeboat with open arms. At least, we then had some dry clothing - marvellous.

Of course, once we were on our way, I think we all realised that heavy waves would reduce it to matchwood. I really think it would probably have broken up long before we got to England...'

CHAPTER 12

There had been much concern about John's crew at the Station, particularly among other crews and friends in the Squadron.

Soon after their return, therefore, and before they had had an opportunity to contact girl friends and family members, many airmen came along to see the crew and to express their pleasure at seeing them 'all in one piece.'

But first, John and his crew had to be debriefed by the Intelligence Officer, who promised that his interrogation would be 'short and sweet.' That met rueful grins and whispered expressions of scepticism. The crew had nothing personal against Intelligence Officers, but from their point of view, debriefings always happened at inconvenient times and this was one such.

Finally, they were very warmly welcomed by their C.O., Group Captain Bannister, who was keen to hear about the ditching. They gave him a brief account, and he responded in his usual generous, supportive manner.

'I welcome you all, as fellow members of *The Goldfish Club*, which you are entitled to join, following your ditching,' he began. 'I survived a ditching three years ago, so I'm a member, too. It demands a lot of skill from the pilot to get an aircraft to settle on the waves, especially in rough seas, and first-class team work from the whole crew. It puts a great strain on everyone. Once the aircraft settles in the water, really good dinghy drill is essential if you are all going to get clear of the aircraft before it sinks. You obviously did everything that was needed. And now, you all need a good rest, and you can begin your fourteen days survival leave.'

The last few words produced an exchange of smiles all round. The CO continued,

'I'd also like to add that I've been looking at your record as a crew since you joined the Squadron. It's very impressive. You've had some tough times, but all your ops have been very thoroughly carried out and you've shot down two enemy night fighters. And although your aircraft has been severely damaged at times, you've never aborted an operation. Well done, all of you. '

'Thank you, sir,' John said, 'but on this occasion we only managed to get back with a lot of help, and we're very grateful for that.'

The CO smiled. 'Especially for your rescue by the Air/Sea Rescue Service. Believe me, the whole Station is very grateful to them. And now I'll leave you to prepare for your leave.'

The crew were desperately anxious to be left alone, so the COs departure was followed by several expressions of relief.

'He's a nice chap,' Scotty grumbled, 'but he did go on a bit, didn't he? Lucy, will be beside herself with worry, and wondering why I haven't given her a ring. ' He looked towards the other crew members. 'I expect we all have urgent phone calls to make.'

'That's right, I must contact Jenny,' Sam smiled. 'I'm sure she has been out of her mind, too.'

'My parents will certainly be worried and waiting to hear from me, ' Arthur said.

Reg was looking very tired. 'You'd have thought,' he grumbled, 'that having experienced the ordeal of ditching himself, the CO would have kept his welcome as short as possible. He must know that we're knackered.'

114

BATTLE ORDERS

John pointed out that Group Captain Bannister was obviously very pleased with the crew and generous in his praise.

'He's a very nice chap. Don't forget that he was in the Master Bomber directing one of our ops, putting himself in the centre of danger. He's one of us, a good chap and very sincere. And isn't it marvellous that we're all going to have fourteen days survival leave?'

There was wholehearted agreement and cheers about that. John grinned. 'I've never heard of 'survival' leave, but when I think of all the times we've had a brush with death, I think that perhaps it's a little overdue.' The others laughed. He continued, 'Anyway, we're certainly all knackered. Let's have a quick drink in the bar, where we can make all our phone calls and then we can get to bed. Tomorrow we'll all go home for a well-deserved break.'

The others agreed at once, and they trooped into the Sergeants' Mess and flopped out in the armchairs there, while John arranged for each of them to enjoy their usual tipple.

***

Jenny managed to obtain five days leave to coincide with a part of Sam's survival leave, so they spent as much time as possible together. But Sam's concern about what had happened to his friend Bill never left his mind, so when he returned to RAF Coningsby, the first thing he wanted to know was whether information about survivors of the Remsheid raid had come through. It had.

Eight of the fifteen Lancasters and Halifaxes that had failed to return, had probably been completely destroyed. Fifty-six airmen had suddenly lost their lives; probably, in some cases, so suddenly that they would have known little or nothing of what had happened.

Of the other seven aircraft that had not returned, thirty, of the forty-nine airmen, had successfully parachuted from their doomed aircraft and the other nineteen may have died in their aircraft.

Sam scanned, with some desperation, the list of POWs reported by the German authorities, and was tremendously relieved to see Bill's name on the list. Thank God he was alive. He turned away and then, for a few moments, stood stock still while tears rolled down his cheeks. Bill was safe and well, but he would remain incarcerated until the end of the War and no-one knew when that would be.

Then a hand was placed on Sam's shoulder and he turned to see Scotty. The two gunners were close friends and Scotty wanted to express his warm sympathy, support and understanding.

'It's good to know, at last,' he said, 'that Bill is safe and well. The Red Cross will be sending him parcels and he'll be able to receive letters from us. I'm really pleased that you've had some good news. You must be very relieved.'

'I am,' Sam replied, 'but my emotions are a bit mixed up at the moment. I won't see my friend again until after the War, if we're both still alive then. But life must go on. I'm glad to see you again, Scotty. Did you enjoy your leave?'

'I did, Sam,' Scotty replied, 'Lucy and I spent a lot of time together planning our future. I can tell you what we discussed: that we're going to have a pretty cottage in a beautiful part of the country, and that we'll have four children...and we'll live happily ever after.' He laughed. 'It's just a dream, Sam, but what else can we do? The reality is that I still don't know how I'm going to earn my living after the War.'

'Oh, you'll be alright,' Scotty. I believe there'll be a number of opportunities for ex-servicemen after the War, such as courses in Technical Colleges and special concessions for those wanting to go to a university. That's where I want to go. We'll all have to acquire new skills and knowledge after the War if we want to get on.'

'You're right, Sam. Anyway, here we are back at Coningsby. We'll all be together again at 'The Pig and Whistle' this evening. It'll be good to meet up again. Tomorrow we may be on 'Battle Orders.'

Sam nodded. 'I'm sure we will.'

CHAPTER 13

Sgt. Jack Rogers,

RAF Coningsby,

Nr. Horncastle,

Lincolnshire,

March 27th., 1945

Dear Maurice,

I've written my full address this time. I don't always, as you have used it several times and must know it well.

I happened to see some newspapers today and two items caught my eye. One was the death of Lloyd George, Prime Minister in the First World War, on March 26th. What a shame he didn't live long enough to see the end of this awful war!

The other was the good news that Allied armies, who are making good progress, will soon be crossing the Rhine and fighting on German soil.

But the Germans still counter-attack when they can, as they did at the end of last year, when they broke through in the Ardennes with tanks and infantry, a quarter of a million men and 950 tanks. We just weren't ready for that and our forces there were overwhelmed. Thank goodness that by January we managed to push back the Germans and resumed our advance.

Our crew had to ditch in the North Sea recently. We managed to float our dinghy, but we were surrounded by a pretty rough sea and a lot of mist. We were freezing cold, wet and wondered how long before we would die of exposure. We had managed to give our location to the Air/Sea Rescue people, but wondered whether they'd ever find us, as we were drifting about and the visibility was getting worse.

Eventually a small lifeboat, suspended by a parachute, was dropped to us from an aircraft and we were glad to throw away our soaking clothes and put on some waterproof suits which were there. But that little boat would never have made it to

England in such rough weather. It was really quite flimsy.

Fortunately, we were finally rescued by an Air/Sea Rescue launch. And we were given a fortnight's 'survival leave.' Once again, Lady Luck was on our side!

Maurice, your letters are always very welcome. I want to hear more about how you and your family are coping. I read the other day that the number of rocket attacks is increasing. Is the bombing in your town getting any worse?

Best wishes, from your very good friend,

Jack

John's crew were, as expected, on Battle Orders the next day, and they met other crews in the Briefing Room, which was full of curling smoke from cigarettes and pipes.

The atmosphere there was much the same as usual. There was laughter and banter, and cheerful faces everywhere. No-one gave any sign of the inevitable underlying tension.

The briefing was short. The target would be V2 launching sites in Holland which had not yet been recaptured. It would be a daylight raid undertaken by twelve Lancasters accompanied by a Mosquito, equipped with the radar aid Oboe, which would be invaluable in identifying the target, as there was an extensive amount of cloud. The bombing operation had to be very accurate to ensure that the launches were thoroughly destroyed. The captain of the Mosquito would order when bombing was to commence.

The Lancasters were to fly in formation of threes, with one aircraft a little ahead, in the centre of each group.

That last point, coming towards the end of the briefing, was an immediate topic of conversation among the crews as they left the room.

'We've never flown as a crew in formation,' Sam remarked. 'How do you feel about that, John?'

'Well, I had to do some formation flying during training, and probably all Lancaster pilots have done a little of it with four-engined aircraft, as I have. But I don't suppose many of us expected to go on a daylight raid in formation, like the Americans with their Flying Fortresses. We're night raid specialists, used to operating individually. It will be a new experience for all of us.'

In fact, John was not at all happy about the prospect. He had been with several Lancasters in formation, a few weeks earlier. It was a training exercise, and all the aircraft had been required to keep very close together.

Everything had gone well until the three leading Lancasters were suddenly enveloped in a cloud. Then one of the pilots had apparently become disoriented and his aircraft collided with another one. He had seen both of them, falling below the cloud, one breaking up as it fell and the other disintegrating very rapidly. There had been no survivors It was fortunate that the pilots were without their crews. Fortunately, too, all the other Lancasters had managed to keep clear of the crash. They had received a message to return to base immediately.

John was well aware that close formation was not easy to maintain with four-engined aircraft, and that some pilots who were otherwise very competent, were not good in formation, which required highly skilled control and manoeuvring ability. He felt that he himself would be able to rise to the challenge but that formation flying added to the risks inherent in every operation. Determined, however, to be as upbeat as usual, he concentrated on the positive aspects.

'I'm glad the flying time for this op is much shorter than others we've had, and we're over enemy-occupied territory for a relatively short time, too,' he said.

'Good point,' Sam agreed. 'Perhaps this op will be pretty incident-free, unlike the others we've had. There'll be twelve aircraft with a total of ninety-six machine guns (including the bomb-aimer's two) to protect us, and we won't spend long flying over enemy-occupied territory.'

'Sounds alright to me,' Scotty said. 'It's a nice short op to Holland.'

But Jack sounded a word of caution.

'We may meet some fighters while we're over the North Sea,' he pointed out, 'before we get near to the Dutch coast. As we're going to fly in a fairly large bunch, the Jerries can hardly fail to see us coming.'

'Yes, their radar will spot us, anyway,' John said.

'I reckon we gunners will have to be careful when we fire at an enemy aircraft,' Sam observed. 'There's the danger that we might hit our own aircraft, don't you think, John?'

'That's true,' John agreed, 'but I'm sure that you'll be certain you only have Jerry in your sights when you fire'.

Following the loss of their faithful P-Peter somewhere in the North Sea, John's crew had been allocated T-Tommy as a permanent replacement.

T-Tommy was an aircraft that had been used on many operations, and had often been damaged and constantly repaired.

A fellow airman had told the crew that none of its engines were the original ones. Each one had been replaced at least once, following its destruction by enemy aircraft or anti-aircraft fire. 'It is,' he said, 'an old war horse.'

John was not entirely happy about having to fly what some airmen referred to as *'a clapped-out aircraft.'* He knew that the epithet was probably unmerited but he was nevertheless resolved to carry out the most stringent of tests on T-Tommy before it was airborne. He recollected Arthur's words about the large number of aircraft that had been patched up very frequently, with many parts being replaced - including new engines - often in the very short time between operations. The ground staff, Arthur thought, were too often pushed for time, and some work was inevitably rushed. On some flights this had led to far too many Lancasters having breakdowns, and aborting an operation.

John was therefore very thoughtful as he entered an aircraft that was both familiar, yet different. Every aircraft was distinctive. He wondered whether their 'new' Lancaster would prove to be as reliable as P-Peter. He would soon find out.

***

They were to leave at dawn. The weather was changeable, with some short showers between periods of sunshine. In addition to the ground staff, the Padre and the Commanding Officer stood near the runway to wave them off. The CO wanted to see for himself how the pilots coped with guiding their aircraft into position for formation flying. They were all pilots used to night flying.

Sam noticed Jenny in the group and they waved to each other.

When T-Tommy received a green light, John opened up the throttles and the aircraft accelerated along the runway. Then he raised the tail plane and pulled back the control column, the speed being about 115 mph. T-Tommy rose slowly but positively, from the tarmac. John kept it low, increasing speed and power before rising gently with his heavy cargo of a variety of large and small bombs and hundreds of gallons of petrol.

He was satisfied, so far, that it handled normally, though still concerned whether he would be able to fly it without any problems. Formation flying would challenge both the aircraft and its pilot. It would be in the second group of three Lancasters, and on the left of the aircraft in the middle.

Moving into formation as soon as all three Lancasters had reached the operational height, for this op, of 10,000 feet, John turned south, and maintained an agreed distance from the three aircraft in front, while the next three were forming up behind them. The sixth operation of John's crew had begun.

Most of them were excited, intrigued, and a little apprehensive about this op. Sam and Scotty remained concerned about firing their guns within a tight bunch of aircraft, while John and Reg felt that tight formation flying imposed a restriction on both of them. John, as pilot, normally made his own decisions about speed and movement, always working closely with Reg so as not to interfere with the navigator's calculations.

But there were advantages, too, in flying in formation, especially with a fighter escort, and one of them became evident while they were flying over The North Sea. The bomb-aimer in the leading Lancaster spotted two German aircraft, ME 262s, that had not long been in service and were extremely fast. The Lancasters were flying at about 220 mph while the approaching aircraft were diving towards them at something like 500 mph. The accompanying Mosquito could increase its speed substantially but could not quite match that of the German aircraft.

The ME 262s approached the leading group of Lancasters, and the mid-upper gunners in all three of them opened fire as soon as the enemy was in range. Freddie, too, was able to join in sometimes. Meanwhile, the pilot of the Mosquito flew rapidly above the German aircraft until he was able to attack them without risk to any of the Lancasters.

The ME 262s sprayed a short burst of canon on the Lancasters and then suddenly they turned away and flew back towards the French coast.

There was no damage to John's aircraft, but a message was received that one of the Lancasters in the first group had been raked with canon shells from one end to the other: two engines had been destroyed, and one airman had been seriously wounded. That aircraft was still airborne, however, and its pilot was instructed to abort the op and fly back to England immediately, so that the wounded airman could be hospitalised.

'Crikey, the ME 262s is very fast,' Scotty said, 'but I'm glad I was able to have a go at one of them.'

'Yes, it started with piston engines but now has jets,' John said. He chuckled. 'We Brits invented the jet engine, but Jerry has produced a very fast jet fighter. I believe it can reach 530 mph.'

'I don't know how we'll cope with fast jets,' Sam grumbled. 'We were expecting an easy op and now we have super jets attacking us.' Then, sounding much brighter-

I wonder why those two went off so suddenly?'

'Well, our Mosquito helped,' John suggested. The Jerries might have done even more damage if they'd had only our gunners firing at them, but with the Mosquito also involved it was a different cup of tea. They had bullets coming towards them from more than one direction and literally didn't know which way to turn. They may also have been damaged a little, but I didn't see any sign of that. I think they just decided it might be better to come back with reinforcements: a few more aircraft. I think we should be prepared for that.'

CHAPTER 14

The weather was still changeable, with showers from large cumulus clouds alternating with periods of sunshine.

The Lancasters encountered no more German fighters while they were flying over The North Sea, but soon after they crossed the coast into Holland there was very fierce anti-aircraft fire. A Lancaster behind them was hit, and one of its engines largely destroyed, but it continued flying in formation for a time. Then it caught fire, and as the fire spread rapidly and enveloped most of the rear of the aircraft, it moved away from its group. It was clearly doomed.

Sam saw it happen and his heart pumped rapidly, while his stomach tightened with a new tension. He feared that all seven of the crew must perish. He was pleasurably surprised, therefore, to see five parachutes billowing out under the smoke-and-flame-covered aircraft. The sight was strangely reassuring. He hoped that the brave Dutch Resistance people would help them, and that they wouldn't drift into German-held territory. They might then manage to get back to England. He had read how some airmen parachuting over France had managed to avoid capture and make contact with Allied armies advancing from the south.

And then he thought about the two who had not managed to bale out...

Suddenly, Freddie's excited shout was heard.

'Skip, the target is just a few miles ahead. I can see several launching pads for the V2 rockets.'

'Good. Carry on normally, but the bombs are not to be dropped until we receive orders from the master bomber.'

But hardly were the words out of his mouth when they were instructed to go ahead and bomb if they could see the target clearly.

The sky was now clear, with bright sunshine, and the countryside below showed up clearly.

'OK, Freddie, proceed as usual,' Skip said.

After a few minutes, Freddie decided it was time to act.

'Bomb doors open, Skip.'

'Bomb doors open, Freddie.'

'OK... Right, right, steady, steady, steady.'

John did not see a Lancaster ahead of theirs, so there was no turbulence caused by a slipstream, but a gusty wind was now making it difficult for him to hold T-Tommy steady.

'Sorry, Freddie, we're being blown off course,' he said. 'I'm afraid I'll have to go round again to begin a new bombing run.'

'OK Skip,' Freddie replied, trying not to sound too disappointed, as he was fully worked up and ready for the climax of the operation.

John carried out a circuit of the area, and approached the target a second time, adding to the period of maximum danger, although it did not take long, and they were soon back on the bombing run.

Freddie again identified the target, checked the settings on his bomb site, and spoke again.

'Bomb aimer here, Skip. Left, left, left again, steady, steady, steady, bombs gone.' He had selected the smaller bombs to go first, and then released the largest bomb.

He looked down to survey the damage as the smoke cleared. He could see that more than one launching pad had been reduced to rubble. *'Good,'* he thought, *'that's at least one less.'*

John turned T-Tommy on to Reg's new course for England.

'Skip for bomb-aimer. Well done, Freddie. Mission accomplished!'

Freddie grinned. 'Thanks, Skip. I hope we'll be back until we've destroyed all of ------' Then he almost shouted,

'Skip, one of the bombs, a 1,000 pounder didn't go. It's stuck in the bomb bay.'

'Skip here. Ok Freddie, we'll have to go round yet again and see if we can free it manually.'

The crew were becoming a little edgy. Spending much longer than usual over the target was adding to their exposure to danger. They hoped that this would be their 'third time lucky' for the bomb clinging to the bomb bay.

Unfortunately, Freddie's efforts to release the bomb were in vain.

John then moved the Lancaster about violently to shake it off, an action that had worked before, but that too was unsuccessful. He was left both annoyed and fearful, though he tried not to let the latter show.

'Skip to all crew. The 1,000 pounder won't shift. I'll try again to shake it off when we're over The Wash. Otherwise I'm afraid I'll have to land....'

Sam broke in as he had just observed four ME 262s behind them and approaching at a very rapid speed.

'Skip, four ME 262s coming up behind us. Corkscrew left.'

John paled. This is what he had dreaded - an attack by the new German fighters, capable of over 500 mph, about twice as fast as T-Tommy could manage. And their Lancaster was carrying a 1,000 pound bomb!

He immediately dived the aircraft as rapidly as possible, while turning thirty degrees, and the crew braced themselves. Sam and Scotty focused their guns on the enemy aircraft, and prepared to fire as soon as one or more was in range.

It was a fierce battle. John made T-Thomas a difficult target, but with four very fast fighter aircraft, there seemed little hope their Lancaster could avoid destruction. One flew quite close to them and raked their aircraft with cannon shells, one of which crashed close to the bomb bay. Thinking of the bomb still stuck there, not far from his turret, Freddie found himself shaking violently. Trying to sound calm, he reported the close shave to John.

But John's concern was fully on Arthur, who had a deep cut in his leg from a piece of shrapnel that had crashed through the fuselage. His seat in the aircraft was very close to John's.

'Jack, bring the first aid kit to Arthur He needs a tourniquet and morphine urgently. He's bleeding freely. See if you can help, Freddie.'

Freddie joined Jack, and together, in spite of the violent manoeuvres, they managed to carry Arthur to the rest bed. They gave him morphine, fixed a tourniquet round his leg, and succeeded in staunching the blood.

Meanwhile the battle continued, and Scotty was sure that some of his bullets had struck one of the ME 262s., especially when it began moving about erratically. He had, in fact, killed the pilot, and sooner or later the aircraft would crash. The three other enemy aircraft continued chasing the elusive T-Tommy, John continuing to carry out one corkscrew after another.

Sam, who, like Scotty, seized every opportunity to fire at the enemy, now noticed another aircraft high above, but bearing down at full speed towards them.

'Skip, rear gunner here. Our Mosquito is about to rejoin us. My God! How we need him!

'That's good news, Sam.'

Almost before the German pilots were aware of its existence - they were so fully engaged with T-Tommy - bullets from the Mosquito struck one of them. It immediately moved away from the scene of action, while the other two aircraft turned to face the 'new' enemy, and Sam and Scotty continued to fire short bursts at them.

Suddenly, one of the Mosquito's petrol tanks exploded. The pilot managed to bail out in the nick of time, as the aircraft meandered erratically for a few seconds, and burst into flames before dropping out of the sky.

The pilots of the two ME 262s now decided to leave the scene of combat. Both turned and flew away. John was both relieved and surprised to see them go. He had been expecting the worst.

'I hope our Mosquito pilot is OK,' Scotty said.

'If he lands safely, he may be able to get to the Allied armies. They're not far away,' John pointed out. 'Anyway, thank God that little battle has ended, and we're still here! I'd have been happier if we hadn't been carrying a 1,000 pound bomb while we were being attacked.'

'I'm amazed that we haven't been damaged more,' Jack said. 'I know your corkscrews are very effective, John, and Sam and Scotty give us a great defence, but I still think we've had a big slice of luck.'

'Yes, we have,' John agreed, 'but Arthur's wound is very deep, and the leg bone may have been shattered. Better take another look at him,

Jack, and see if you can loosen the tourniquet a little. And now, let's head for home.'

CHAPTER 15

It proved impossible to shake off the bomb while flying over The Wash, so, as they approached their base, John decided to put a proposal to his crew.

'Skip here to all crew. We'll shortly be faced with landing with a 1,000 pound bomb.' He forced himself to sound as calm as possible. 'You all know how dangerous that is. I don't want to put your lives at risk unnecessarily, and Flying Control says you should bale out. That would be safer than staying in the kite while it lands with a large bomb hanging down under it. It could easily explode during the landing!'

'But what about you?' Scotty protested. You're going to land the kite, and I for one want to stay with you and Arthur.'

'Yes, and that goes for me, too,' Sam said, and all the others had the same view. They were adamant that they should stay together. John had anticipated no other response.

'OK,' he said, 'I'll bring the kite down very slowly and gently; then we'll all depend on Lady Luck.'

Some of the crew looked down as their aircraft approached Coningsby. The airfield had been cleared of personnel and aircraft, and looked strangely abandoned.

'They've cleared the way for our landing,' Scotty announced.

'But the ambulances won't be far away. They'll be ready to take Arthur to the hospital as soon as we land,' John said. 'And the fire engines are also ready. I can see them near the peri track.'

John was now instructed by Flying Control to begin a circuit ready for landing. Although he realised that Arthur's condition, and carrying a 1,000 pound bomb, had given T-Tommy top priority for landing, he was still surprised to be preparing to land so soon, though also very relieved, as he was worried about Arthur, whose injury, he suspected, was very serious. They had become very close friends. The sooner Arthur was in hospital, the better.

He knew that landing with a large bomb a few feet from the surface of the runway was extremely dangerous. His crew gave little indication of their fears, but he knew that they must be gripped by an inner fear and be on tenterhooks, until they were safely down. As they neared the completion of a circuit, he spoke to all the crew again.

'Skip here. Take up emergency positions; backs to the main spar, feet braced, and hands clasped behind your heads. Be prepared to evacuate the aircraft as soon as it comes to a halt, and then get well away from it! Jack and Scotty, will you support Arthur and, as soon as we've landed, get ready to carry him out, though I suspect there'll be orderlies from the hospital to do that.'

He now turned T-Tommy towards the runway, losing height all the time. This was going to be his most testing experience so far. Everything, especially the lives and safety of his crew, depended on his skill.

John found it very hard to fly straight and level because of the damage the aircraft had sustained in combat, some of which he could only suspect. However, he had past experience to guide him, and he managed to fly on an even keel towards the centre of the runway. T-Tommy was now almost gliding.

He was breathing heavily as the undercarriage made contact with the tarmac. He had never before felt so much under strain.

Then there was a heart-stopping moment for all the crew as the tail wheel came down...

T-Tommy lurched unsteadily along the runway, the bomb still hanging close to the tarmac.   If it impacted against almost anything now, or any of the tyres were to go flat, or the undercarriage were to collapse as a result of damage, there might well be a tremendous explosion.

But, to John's enormous relief, after travelling along most of the runway, T-Tommy finally came to a standstill.

The crew's immediate reaction was to laugh almost hysterically. They had landed; and they were still alive.   Then, remembering John's advice, they scrambled to get out as quickly as possible.

There was now the noisy approach of an ambulance and two fire engines.   Most of the crew jumped out and were well away from the aircraft before they turned to watch, as Arthur was taken down, placed on a stretcher, and carried to the ambulance.   The hospital was not far away, and everything was prepared for his arrival.

***

In the afternoon, following their rest, John and his crew visited the hospital to see Arthur.   His leg wound was much more serious than most of them had suspected.   Part of his lower leg had been crushed, and the bone splintered.   He had been given pain killers and sleeping tablets, and the staff had decided to bring in a specialist doctor for advice.

Outside, John spoke to his fellow crew-members.

'I've had a word with one of the doctors who explained why they decided to bring in a specialist doctor. Evidently there is a very real possibility that Arthur's leg may have to be amputated below the knee. The doctor wants to feel certain that amputation cannot be avoided. He is anxious to have a second opinion.'

The crew were stunned, and Sam had tears in his eyes as they returned to their Nissan hut.

***

John and his crew continued to be very worried about Arthur. The following day they again visited him in the Station hospital. He managed to sound cheerful and upbeat, but his news was grim. It had been confirmed that his lower leg was irretrievably damaged. It was shattered and would have to be amputated. The news depressed all the crew. John was Arthur's special friend, but all the crew liked and respected their flight engineer, and they knew that Arthur loved the job he was now to lose.

'You know,' Sam remarked, 'dear old Arthur has saved our bacon a few times.'

'He has,' agreed Reg, 'especially when he got the undercarriage down, when it wouldn't budge, using compressed air.'

'Actually,' John pointed out, 'Arthur nursed all four engines so well that we've never had an engine failure in flight.'

But beyond all that, Arthur was one of a crew, that shared dangers had drawn together in comradeship and camaraderie. They felt both Arthur's loss, and their own loss of Arthur, very deeply. As they left the hospital, it wasn't only Sam whose eyes were moist.

CHAPTER 16

Sgt Jack Rogers,

March 29th, 1945   RAF Coningsby

Dear Maurice,

I've just seen the newsreel about Belsen concentration camp, which I found really horrible. British soldiers entered the camp and were shocked to see the huge piles of corpses and the emaciated survivors who were just skin and bones. The people running such camps are less than human and should be punished for mass torture. It's made all of us determined to do all we can to bring this ghastly war to an end as soon as possible.

The soldiers forced the guards to bury all the corpses. I'll never forget those horrible images. They confirm what a ghastly evil is Nazi Germany.

It was good, as usual, to hear all your news. I'm glad there has been no more bombing, including doodlebugs and rockets near your parents' house, and you have been OK, too.

BATTLE ORDERS

We've just had a new experience – flying in formation in the daytime. We were escorted by a Mosquito. They're very fast aircraft, and amazingly, they're made almost entirely from wood. It may be a little safer for us now that the Allies have advanced so far.

Sadly, our Flight Engineer, Arthur, was seriously wounded when a piece of shrapnel struck his leg. He may have to have the leg amputated below the knee, which would mean him leaving us.

John continues to be a wonderful skipper and pilot. He had to land our Lancaster with a 1,000 pound bomb still in the bomb bay. It hadn't been released with other bombs. It was a very dangerous landing, but John managed it wonderfully. We always trust him. We now fly in T-Tommy, P-Peter being at the bottom of the North Sea.

Best wishes from your very good friend,

Jack

BATTLE ORDERS

In the Briefing Room, the airmen sat on forms, their cigarette and pipe smoke creating a haze, spreading slowly. They gossiped, apparently without a care in the world, with occasional bursts of laughter, as apocryphal yarns were exchanged. But beneath the veneer of light-heartedness was, as always, an underlying fear.

Where would they be sent tonight? Would it be a particularly dangerous mission from which they would not return? Would they see their loved ones again?

They would soon have the answer to the first question. The others, some of them felt, might depend on Lady Luck. A few would take good-luck charms with them.

John's crew were there, Arthur's place as Flight Engineer having been taken by a Pilot Officer Terry Goodman. Short and sturdy, his face was creased with lines of humour, which might suggest that he didn't take life too seriously. In fact, although a good joke would precipitate a loud explosion of infectious laughter, he was as dedicated and serious about his engineering tasks as Arthur. He had been introduced to the crew shortly before the briefing. They had received him politely but, in a short time, they would be won over by their new comrade, by his personality, character and ability.

Although John had not been consulted about Arthur's replacement, he was very pleased it was Terry. He had met him soon after his sixth operation, when he had had a particularly traumatic experience.

His Lancaster had been struck by ack-ack shells exploding between two petrol tanks. It caught fire and six crew members were killed. Miraculously, only Terry had managed to bail out of the burning aircraft. He had landed a few miles inside the French border, and had been helped by members of the Resistance, to get back to England.

BATTLE ORDERS

The platform party, led by the Station and Squadron Commanders entered the room, and immediately, both conversations and cigarettes were quenched. A roll call was given to ensure that all squadrons and their crews were present.

The Intelligence Officer pulled aside a curtain covering an operational map of Germany, with its red ribbon outlining the route to be taken to the target - the U-Boat (submarine) pens, in Hamburg.

The IO then emphasized the vital importance of the raid. U-Boats were torpedoing large numbers of our merchant ships, with the death of thousands of sailors, and huge quantities of both food and war materials were being sent to the bottom of the ocean. He added that Hamburg, a port essential to the German economy, was also the centre of her U-Boat production.

Britain normally imported about half of her food, and Germany's aim was to sink as many merchant ships as possible to try and starve us into surrender.

We also needed to import a variety of manufactured goods, as well as many raw materials, for the successful prosecution of the war.

Germany's heavy cruisers, known as pocket battleships, such as the *Admiral Scheer,* and aircraft of the *Luftwaffe,* had sunk many of our ships, but the U-Boats were the greatest threat, especially as their numbers had increased significantly as the war had progressed. They were under the command of Admiral Doenitz.

Britain and her Allies were making every effort to sink both U-Boats and pocket battleships, and to thwart the air attacks. Winston Churchill called it *The Battle of the Atlantic,* with reference to our most vital sea lane. It was a very long battle, that swung first one way and then the other, throughout the war.

There were particularly heavy losses of ships in the early years of the war. For example, the German battleship *Graf Spee* sank nine of our merchant ships during the first three months, and from June to October, 1940, over 240 Allied ships were sunk. Apart from the huge loss of food and war materials, the loss of life was appalling.

Britain used a convoy system to try to reduce her losses. Thirty or more merchant ships would be guarded by destroyers. corvettes, or other armed ships of the Royal Navy. The Germans replied to this development by changing their attacking tactics.

From October, 1940, their U-Boats hunted in *wolf packs*. Groups of three or four U-Boats co-ordinated their attacks by radio. One group sank eleven ships in a single convoy, and damaged two others. Another convoy lost 59% of its ships, mainly to U-Boats.

The British response to such terrible losses was to hunt down and destroy the U-Boats by every available means. Coastal Command of the RAF sank 27 U-Boats in 1942. By 1945 258 U-Boats had been destroyed altogether. By that time, the battle had swung in favour of the Allies, but the losses from U-Boats continued.

The Battle of the Atlantic was grim and relentless, and continued day and night.

***

John and his crew could hardly wait to discuss the coming op.

'What exactly is a submarine pen? ' Freddy asked. 'We were shown some grainy pictures, but weren't told much about them.'

' No, we weren't,' John agreed. 'The Germans call them U-Boat bunkers. They are massive constructions of concrete and steel, the concrete being many feet thick, to harbour and protect the U-Boats from attack.'

'If they are so well protected, how can we expect to destroy them?'

'Because,' John replied, 'the Germans didn't realise, when they were built, that we would be able to use massive bombs, like the Tallboy, designed by Barnes Wallis; more than twenty feet long with 12,000 pounds of explosives. Nor did they realise that our Lancaster bombers would be able to carry such a large bomb.'

'So,' Scotty said, 'with bombs like that, can we really destroy massive concrete constructions?'

'We certainly can,' John answered. 'I believe other U-Boat bunkers have been bombed successfully. I'm not sure which ones.'

'I spoke recently with a pilot who has been on similar ops,' Jack told the crew. 'He told me that some crews have used Tallboys to bomb bunkers in Trondheim in Norway, the island of Heligoland, Bordeaux, Brest and St.Nazaire.'

'I've had a special briefing about the Tallboy,' Freddie said. 'We'll have some smaller bombs too. I must drop the smaller bombs first. Otherwise, the Tallboy might be hit by them and blown up, and us too.'

There was a stunned silence as that was digested, until Scotty broke in,

'Then please do us all a favour, Freddie, and get rid of the small bombs first.'

The others laughed.

'Trust me,' Freddie said.

'What a nice, easy op it would be if we only had to pop over to one of those French ports you mentioned,' Sam said with a grin.

'Well, perhaps we will later on,' John said, but don't forget that we've captured most of them.'

'At least, Hamburg should be easier than Berlin, Essen or Peenamunde,' Jack suggested, thoughtfully.

'That's right,' Reg agreed. 'We don't need to fly over much of Germany. We'll be mostly over the North Sea.'

'Yes, but over the North Sea we've met German night fighters before, and we'll probably meet them again,' Sam said.

When it was about twenty minutes to take-off, a bus waited outside the locker room, to take the crews to dispersal. With all the crews aboard, it was driven around the perimeter track, and stopped at each aircraft. John's crew alighted when they reached T-Tommy. Every op was a life-threatening experience, they all knew.

What would await them during this one?

CHAPTER 17

Reg now passed to John the first course on his Flight Plan, based on forecast wind velocities. For the flight over English soil and for some time after that, he would use radar aids to fix their position. Later, he would use the stars.

Eight hundred bombers would be involved in tonight's operation, and there would be no diversionary attacks.

Hamburg is some miles upstream from the mouth of the River Elbe and its latitude is some miles south of 55 degrees north.

As planned, T-Tommy did not fly directly towards the German port, John keeping his aircraft well away from enemy - occupied coast for as long as possible. Then he flew eastwards, north of the River Elbe, and finally turned towards Hamburg's U-Boat bunkers.

As their target drew nearer the crew became a little apprehensive, but, as always, maintained their self-control and even a degree of nonchalance. They knew that the city would be very well defended. Sam and Scotty searched the sky ceaselessly for signs of enemy aircraft.

So far, there had been little enemy activity, but now the bright fingers of searchlights began to pierce the darkness, waving in all directions as if trying to penetrate every inch of the sky, so that no aircraft could escape. They were almost immediately followed by the firing of anti-aircraft guns, and puffs of explosions around the aircraft. John constantly varied T-Tommy's height to make difficulties for the ground attackers, while Sam and Scotty scanned the sky for enemy night fighters.

BATTLE ORDERS

Sam saw one Lancaster that was on fire. Six of its crew-members managed to bale out. 'I'm glad they got out in time,' he said to himself, 'but one poor devil can't have made it.'

Scotty, too, saw the parachutes drifting downwards and hoped that the airmen would land well away from the U-Boat bunkers, soon to be the centre of fire and destruction, and well clear of the centre of the city of Hamburg itself. Hopefully the wind would take their parachutes towards a rural area, where their chance of survival would be better.

The visibility now deteriorated and John, not being confident that they would be able to identify a target, shrouded in mist, from 20,000 feet, descended to 15,000 feet. In fact, the Germans' submarine bunkers were so massive that the whitish concrete stood out clearly in spite of the mist, and Freddie, who had been straining his eyes to see through the murky sky, soon shouted triumphantly,

'I can see the target, Skip, five degrees to port... Open bomb doors.'

But before John could do so, a shell exploded just above one of the twin rudders, Though the damage appeared minor, T-Tommy bucked and turned, largely out of control, until John managed to fly it fairly straight and level again. He then reduced the aircraft's speed to help him keep it as stable as possible, at the risk of adding to their exposure to the anti-aircraft fire. He nodded to Terry, who opened the bomb doors.

'Bomb doors open,' John announced.

Freddie guided John towards the target and, the crew were glad to hear, after what seemed a prolonged time on the target path, with their hearts beating fast, the words 'bombs gone.'

They remained on course for a few more minutes, John flying the Lancaster as steadily as possible, and ignoring the flak, until Freddie announced that a photograph had been taken.

The Tallboy had fallen between two of the concrete bunkers housing U- Boats and appeared to have largely destroyed the U-Boats themselves as well as their bunkers. The crew had only a brief glimpse of the destruction, as a great cloud of dust and debris rose up from the bombed area, and soon blotted out the scene below.

Then John, now anxious that they should waste no time, began to climb to 20,000 feet. T-Tommy, freed from the huge weight of her cargo, responded with what John thought was like sheer enthusiasm, by climbing effortlessly to the new height, in spite of the damaged tailplane. But now, flying normally straight and level, John realised how much the damage had affected the stability of his aircraft.

He was very relieved that, contrary to their expectations, they had been able to bomb the U-boat bunkers without overwhelming opposition. His crew were very thankful, too.

Terry joked, 'I'm amazed that we haven't yet met any night fighters. Perhaps Jerry has heard about those dangerous sharpshooters, Sam and Scotty, and decided to keep out of harm's way!'

The gunners joined in the laughter that followed. Then Scotty pretended to admonish Terry.

'You should be aware, Terry, that this crew never has a dull moment. We're not yet out of the woods, and I'm sure that we'll soon meet both night fighters and more ack-ack fire.'

'Scotty's right,' Sam said, 'but thanks for the compliment, Terry.'

Now that T-Tommy had used up nearly half her fuel, and she no longer carried a heavy bomb load, John found he was able to increase her speed to about 240 mph. The damage to the tailplane would cause problems at times, he knew, but at least they still had four undamaged engines.

Suddenly there was a fierce barrage of anti-aircraft fire, which John did his best to evade. One shell burst very close to the port inner engine which immediately began to emit smoke and flames. Scotty spotted the danger and reported it immediately.

'Skip. Mid-upper gunner here. The Port inner engine is alight.

'OK Scotty,' John replied. 'I see it. I think I can put that out. On my instrument panel I can operate a fire extinguisher bottle for each engine. Here goes.' A few minutes later he noticed the flames had subsided.

'Skip here. The fire's going out, but keep an eye on it, Scotty, and let me know if it flares up again. The engine seems to be working.'

'OK Skip.'

The anti-aircraft fire suddenly ceased, and as T-Tommy droned on its way, John decided to remind his gunners to stay on maximum alert. 'Skip here for the gunners. We're still in the danger zone. I'm sure we'll soon meet some fighters.'

He had hardly finished speaking when two Junkers 88s were spotted by Sam.

'Skip. Two Junkers 88s, flying abreast, are approaching dead astern. About 600 yards. Corkscrew right!'

At one time Sam would have been agitated, even nervous, but he was now confident of his ability, calm and ready for action.

John wasted no time.

'Skip here for all crew. Hold tight for an extended corkscrew!'

The crew were now familiar with the way John could put the Lancaster into a very steep dive at about 350 mph, sometimes more, and braced themselves as best they could. After losing over a thousand feet, with a thirty-degree turn, John then repeated the process. He then pulled out and began a steep climbing turn through sixty degrees in the opposite direction, at about 140 mph, and brought T-Tommy back to its previous height and course.

The violence of these manoeuvres made it very difficult for the fighters to focus their guns on the Lancaster. They fired whenever they could but their opportunities were limited. Both Scotty and Sam managed to train their guns on one fighter or the other at various stages of the extended corkscrew, and fire short bursts, but to no avail. After some minutes, neither side having succeeded in mortally wounding the other, John sought refuge in a cloud, and the fighters broke off their chase and went on their way.

John now resumed his former course and noted that they were getting clear of the area considered to be the most dangerous. He wondered whether they would now have a problem-free flight home.

But it was not to be.

CHAPTER 18

As they approached the North Sea, several crew-members commented on the atrocious weather that was developing. Huge black clouds were massing in all directions. It looked ominous, dark and threatening. Scotty was concerned.

'Skip, Mid-upper gunner here. We're in the middle of several large cumulonimbus clouds. They've sprung up very quickly. I don't see how we can get round them.'

'I don't, either, Scotty.'

'Navigator, how do we cope with all these cumulonimbus clouds? We're only a short distance from the nearest one! I'm getting edgy.'

Reg, sitting as usual behind a black curtain to screen the light he needed for navigation, had been quite unaware of the imminent danger.

'Navigator to Skip. I'll take a look at them through the astrodome.'... He returned.

'Skip, they're enormous. We're surrounded by them!'

Reg was thinking about his navigational problems, while John was dreading the icing difficulties to be expected, should they be caught in the middle of one of the clouds.

Reg continued, 'The anvils, at the top of each one stretch for miles and often merge, blocking out the stars, so no astronavigation is possible. Jack can't help with radio bearings at the moment and we're too far from home to use radar. My next course will be based on earlier wind velocities, so we may go well off track as the winds change.'

'OK Reg. Just do your best.'

John could see that although the clouds often appeared to stretch their icy tentacles, almost to touch one another at their apexes, there was often a gap between them lower down, but, as there were so many, he would need to steer very carefully to keep clear of them. Previous experience of their destructive ferocity and of the icing dangers made him very wary of them.

Meanwhile, Jack had been trying to help discover their position using the radio, but at first, the static and other noise rendered his efforts useless.

Suddenly, his luck changed. He was now able to press his key for half a minute while three ground stations in England took a bearing on his transmission. The aircraft's position was where their reciprocal bearings, sent back to him, intersected on Reg's chart.

This procedure worked well, and Reg soon fixed their position fairly accurately, though he was dismayed to see how far they had strayed from their intended track.

'At least,' he thought, *'I now have an up-to-date fix of our position, and I can use that to calculate a new wind velocity and a new course for the pilot.'*

The radio (M/F) Stations, aware that many aircraft had lost their way in the atrocious weather, said that the procedure should be repeated every twenty minutes. Reg was very grateful for their help which, working closely with Jack, he used to good advantage, until T-Tommy was within radar range, when he was able to make use of both Gee and H2S. The latter was particularly useful when they crossed the British coast, which he could see clearly illuminated on the screen.

Over the whole of Britain, however, there was now a very dense fog, of the kind once known as *a pea souper,* and then as *smog,* (fog contaminated with pollutants), at the time a frequent phenomenon in the winter months, but which gradually disappeared with the passing of the Clean Air Act in the post-War years. It was a fog in which a person could sometimes not see his own outstretched hand.

For airmen, such fogs were extremely hazardous, and it was in fact responsible for a significant proportion of our total losses in the air during the Second World War.

A technique for dealing with fog at airfields, called FIDO (Fog Investigation and Dispersal Operation), was used. FIDO consisted of pipes on either side of a runway with burner jets at intervals. Petrol was fed through the pipes, and the vapours were lit by the burners, producing a sheet of flame on either side of the runway, keeping it well illuminated.

It had been possible at the time to equip only fifteen airfields with FIDO, and that was a very small proportion of the total, so aircraft needing to land in foggy conditions were often diverted to FIDO-equipped airfields, which were then under pressure, trying to cope with the extra demand.

John was aware that RAF Coningsby was not yet equipped with FIDO so hoped that he would hear from Flying Control that they should divert to another airfield. Terry, agreed, but was concerned that the diversion might take them too far away. Their fuel reserves were particularly low because they had flown extra miles over the North Sea.

When they were still many miles from their base, Flying Control gave them the bad news. A large number of their aircraft had already been diverted to FIDO-equipped airfields, and there was no possibility of T-Tommy joining them. Most of those Lancasters were still airborne and it would be at least an hour before any more could be sent. T-Tommy did not have sufficient fuel for a long wait. John was told unequivocally that he should land at RAF Coningsby by Standard Beam Approach, which was a blind-landing navigation system.

A second shock for John was that, even for the SBA he would have to wait. There were already a number of Lancasters waiting to land and they were being 'stacked.' Stacking, with other aircraft above and below, in a dense fog, was extremely hazardous.

John made sure that T-Tommy was well above the aircraft immediately below, while he kept his eyes skinned above, looking out for other aircraft that might collide with them. All the time, he was very conscious that, with a damaged tail plane, his control over the Lancaster was much reduced.

When it was his turn to land, he took T-Tommy down through the fog, while straining his eyes in all directions in an effort to see familiar landmarks. He knew of pilots whose aircraft had crashed into hills, hangars. petrol bowsers, churches and other buildings on the way to landing in fog. One problem was that altimeters did not give a completely reliable reading of the distance from the earth immediately beneath an aircraft. Crashed aircraft often had altimeters which might indicate 500 feet or even 750 feet above the actual elevation, at the moment of impact.

Finally, John had a brief glimpse of the faint outline of some familiar landmarks, and was able to line up his Lancaster in the centre of the beam, and keep it there. He had been flying very tentatively up to that point but now, at about 700 feet, he increased power a little until he heard the outer marker signal. Then he descended very carefully, listening intently for the inner marker signal.

This was hardly the way the crew wished to finish a successful operation and they all held their breaths during these nerve-wracking manoeuvres. Many pilots had crashed their aircraft at this point of a blind landing.

When John heard the inner marker signal, he descended until, to his profound relief, he could discern the beginning of the runway just beneath the aircraft. He touched down rather bumpily, further down the runway than he had hoped, with both wheels near the edge, but settled well enough and finally came to a halt right at the other end. Had he continued moving a few yards further, he would have been on the grass and close to the perimeter fence.

The crew tumbled out of their Lancaster a little faster than usual, Sam stretching his cramped limbs and wallowing in the sheer pleasure of being down and able to move. The others stamped their feet and walked about excitedly, fervently thankful that they were safely back after a battle with foul weather.

'John, that was a great piece of piloting,' Jack said, and the others added their congratulations.

'I'm pleased with the way T-Tommy performed,' John replied. 'With a new kite - or a new-old kite - ' he grinned, 'it's always a bit tricky. You never know how they're going to cope with a range of possible problems. Good old T-Tommy!'

Jack said, 'Yes, it's a good kite. But you still had to work wonders, John. We can all see the damage to the tailplane which must have made it the very devil to keep the kite on an even keel. But you've managed once again to bring us all safely back, after our seventh op., so I have a suggestion to make. When our de-briefing is over and we've put everything away, I propose we skip the usual meal and just have a quick snack in the NAAFI.'

'You can't be serious,' Sam protested. 'I'm ravenous! Eggs, bacon, fried bread and tomatoes are a life-saver for me after a long op.'

'I am serious,' Jack replied. 'You can eat as much as you like in the NAAFI but leave our main meal until the evening, until we've had a good long sleep. Later we can go to the Pig and Whistle. There's a good and varied menu there, and we'll be able to celebrate, with a nice bottle of wine, that we've just completed seven operations. True it's only part of a complete tour but I think it's a great achievement.'

'That's a marvellous idea,' Scotty put in, 'and there's a piano there, so perhaps we could have another sing song, Jack.'

'I second that,' Reg said. 'We managed to sing while sitting in damp clothes in the middle of the North Sea, so I'm sure we can improve on that in the comfort of a pub.'

'That's right,' John said. 'Let's celebrate, especially as we've always pressed on to the target whatever the damage to our kite, and we've never aborted an operation. '

'OK. I guess I'll survive,' Sam conceded with a grin.

***

They were in the Saloon Bar of The Pig and Whistle, enjoying a roast beef meal, with roast potatoes and parsnips, Yorkshire pudding, sprouts and what Freddie called 'lashings of gravy.'

'This is a smashing pub,' Reg remarked, 'but we never see some of our squadron crews here. I wonder where they are?'

'They're probably in The White Hart, getting drunk, and singing bawdy songs, ' Jack suggested.

'That's probably right,' John said. 'We all have to unwind after an op. Some do it one way; some another. Personally, I prefer to unwind here, in this very comfortable pub.'

'So do I,' Jack said, 'especially as it has a good piano.'

'And it's the pub the WAAFs go to,' Reg grinned.

They all laughed.

'What do you all think about today's op?' Sam asked.

'Well, cumulonimbus clouds and fog were big problems,' Reg replied. 'The weather dominated the flight back. It worried me more than Jerry's guns and fighters.'

'But it went well apart from the weather,' Freddie said. 'Our bombing destroyed some of the bunkers, and if we destroyed some U-Boats, too, that's a bonus.'

'Yes, the bombing went well,' John agreed, but the weather coming back was as dangerous as the enemy. I hate to think what would have happened if we'd got caught up in those cumulonimbus clouds. If T-Tommy's wings had been coated with several inches of ice, and her instruments had frozen up, I doubt if she we'd have remained airborne. Don't forget our damaged tailplane. '

'Yes,' Scotty said. 'I was scared stiff we'd be trapped in those clouds. If we had been caught in them, how would we have got out into the clear again?'

No-one was able to answer that question

'They were a real menace,' Jack said. 'They gave Reg difficult navigational problems and then John had to land in thick fog. That was very dicey, but he brought our Lanc down beautifully.'

'He did,' Sam agreed. 'In my turret I get really shaken up if the landing isn't reasonably smooth, but we landed in that thick fog with hardly a bump. I think John must have cat's eyes. I'm envious. If only I could spot Jerry fifty yards further away!'

Not for the first time, Scotty then drew attention to the odd life they were all leading.

'A little over fifteen hours ago,' he reflected, 'we were flying over Germany and our enemy was trying hard to blast us out of the sky, and now here we are, enjoying a nice meal in this cosy pub. It doesn't make sense, does it?'

'War doesn't make sense,' John put in. 'Except for a tiny number of people, no-one wants war. It's always a very nasty business.'

Sam was anxious to focus all their thoughts on pleasure and relaxation, not war.

'Agreed, but now it must be time for that singsong we were promised,' he suggested. 'Are you ready, Jack?' Jack grinned.

'I'm always ready to sing,' he said, 'and to play the piano.'

He strode quickly to the piano, and, without announcing a title, began to sing and play. After the first two or three notes, John's crew joined in, and before long all the other airmen and WAAFs in the saloon bar, both air and ground crews, were singing their hearts out.

Jack could sing and play a wide range of songs suitable for sing-songs. He chose pieces that most people knew, and had often sung at school, and which had plenty of repetition.

He played and sang –

> *Oh! My Darling Clementine,*
> *On Ilkla Moor Baht 'At.*
> *Who Were You With Last Night?*
> *Early One Morning*
> *Cockles and Mussels*

And then Jack stood up and announced that they would finish with -

If You Were the Only Girl In The World.

After that everyone clapped and cheered loudly and the conversation flowed freely, but especially between air and ground crews. John and his crew had enormous respect for the work such airmen as fitters, electricians and armourers put in to ensure that their Lancaster was able to fly with maximum safety and reliability.

This was an opportunity for them to express their appreciation and they took the opportunity to develop the warm and friendly relationship they already enjoyed.

CHAPTER 19

Sgt. Jack Rogers,

RAF Coningsby

April 3rd., 1945

Dear Maurice,

I was very interested to hear about your experience trying to produce as much food as possible. You're following the Government's request to GROW YOUR OWN. As German U-Boats are sinking so many of our merchant ships, including those bringing us food, it seems a very sound idea. What a response there has been! People are apparently digging up their lawns so they can plant potatoes, and sow vegetable and salad seeds. Some are even growing food on the roof of an Anderson air raid shelter.

Congratulations on your success growing carrots and spinach in your garden, but what a shame about the cauliflowers! You grew them, and the caterpillars ate them. I'm afraid there's always a battle with pests. Better luck next time!

Your parents, too, seem to have had mixed success. They reared a rabbit, planning several good meals, but your little sister was shocked when bunny's time drew near, and when he had been beautifully baked, she wouldn't eat a scrap of it. It might be an idea for your parents to keep several rabbits, but they'll have to insist they are definitely not pets!

Is everybody still putting all waste food into 'pig bins' supplied by the Local Authority? That always seemed to me a great idea. It keeps the pig farmers happy while helping to supply the bacon ration.

Sadly, it has been confirmed that Arthur's leg will have to be amputated below the knee. I know we must expect that kind of thing but we've all been in tears. Arthur has had to leave us and we've been such a close crew. We'll miss him tremendously, and I know he'll miss us.

The weather is sometimes our worst enemy on operations. Recently, coming home after a raid, the sky was so crowded with cumulonimbus clouds that there seemed to be no way to avoid getting iced up, tossed around by convection currents, and pummelled by hailstones. But we got through that OK, only to find that the UK was covered by dense fog — a real pea-souper, and the visibility was almost zero.

John got us down using what is called 'Standard Beam Approach,' which means listening and responding to radio signals. It was very tricky but we landed safely. I believe John could just about detect the runway when he was only a few yards above it. He's a really good pilot.

Well, that's all for today. Carry on growing those vegetables, and stop feeding fat caterpillars!

From your very good friend,

Jack

Soon after breakfast the next morning, John and his crew went to Dispersal to check the serviceability of T-Tommy. Though it had not suffered any major damage in the previous operation, it had been 'patched up' so many times previously that they thought there might be weaknesses.   An elderly aircraft, they thought, like elderly people, needed extra care and attention to ensure a good performance.

The tannoy announced the time for the operational meal.   It was always the same - egg, bacon, fried bread, tomatoes, etc.   It was generally welcomed, though for a few airmen, their inner tension might result in churning stomachs and no appetite for food.

In the late afternoon, briefing took place.

Tonight's attack would be in the Ruhr, the industrial heart of Germany, where many of her armaments were manufactured.   They included steel works and synthetic oil plants as well as tank and gun factories.   The whole of this industrial area had for years been a prime target for Bomber Command.

The specific target would be the Krupp armament works in the city of Essen.

At the briefing, the crews were given a great deal of information about how the Ruhr industrial area was different from any other region in Germany.   The combination of a smoky, industrial complex and a dense concentration of defences (anti-aircraft guns), creating even more smoke, produced an almost permanent 'smog.'   It hung about like a huge, dirty, dark grey cloud that never disappeared, and made it very difficult to identify a target, particularly in bad weather, so it hampered accurate bombing.

The concentration of anti-aircraft guns in the region, over 2,000, was denser than anywhere else in Germany, except Berlin, and comprised about one third of the total number in the country.

Essen had been attacked many times.   From a study of the grainy photographs taken over the target in 1943, it was clear that the raids had severely disrupted German steel production.   A proportion of the factories, though, had been moved to outlying plants, some in occupied countries, where the Nazis made extensive use of slave labour and sometimes even used inmates from concentration camps.

Outside the Briefing Room, some of John's crew sought clarification on some aspects of the operation.

'I've never heard of smog,' Sam admitted. 'I suppose it's a mixture of dirty smuts and the water vapour that is fog.'

'That's right,' Reg said, 'though I don't understand why it's not blown away by the wind.'

'I'm sure it is,' John broke in, 'but the factories and plants are working around the clock, belching out tons of dirty exhaust continuously. Not exactly a healthy place for people living and working there!'

'I'm worried about seeing the target through all that muck,' Freddie grumbled.

'There'll be Mosquito path-finders equipped with Oboe to help identify the target,' assured John, 'and they'll drop flares over it. If you can't see the target, you simply drop the bombs where you see the flares.'

'Fair enough, though I'd much prefer to see the target for myself, and watch the bombs crashing down on it,' Freddie replied. Then he had another thought.

'But will the flares be visible through the polluted air?'

'I expect so. ' John responded. 'It all depends on the weather. If there is no wind, the pollution would obviously build up a bit.'

'I'm glad we're going to attack the Krupp steel works,' Scotty said. 'Anything to shorten the war.'

'It should make a difference,' John agreed.

'I'm a bit worried about all those ack-acks guns,' Sam admitted. 'There are masses of them over the Ruhr.'

'But they are spread out over the whole area,' Scotty said, 'and we're not going to fly over the whole lot, are we?'

'No,' Reg answered.   'Most of our route is over the North Sea. We'll miss most of the cities of the Ruhr.'

Sam seemed satisfied with that.

Parachutes and Mae Wests were now picked up from lockers, and a number of other 'operational necessities' were collected, including 'snacks' for eating during the flight, and thermos flasks of hot tea or coffee.

At Dispersal, Freddie checked the bomb load.   Once inside the aircraft, he checked that the bomb sight and its control panel were working. If anything was found wrong with his equipment, the whole purpose of the operation would be null and void, and their lives put at risk for nothing.

Sitting at his table, Reg made sure everything was in the right place, especially his beloved sextant.

John and Terry went through all the pre-starting checks together. John missed Arthur, and often thought about him, but he was glad that he and Terry had developed an easy rapport and that Terry now had a warm relationship with all the crew.

They had already checked the undercarriage and tyres and other external features.   Now, they warmed up the engines, checked pitch control, and the number of revs at full throttle, etc.

Among other tasks, Jack tuned the wireless telephone and checked the direction-finding loop.

Having squeezed into the rear gunner's poky turret, Sam checked his machine guns and ammunition, and then spent some time protecting himself against the intense cold that was to come. He was always, at 20,000 feet, in a freezing cold environment. His removal of the front, eye-level panel to facilitate clear vision made it even colder.

Sam's hands were protected with three pairs of gloves, including gauntlets. His face was exposed except where the oxygen mask or helmet protected it. He covered those parts with a smear of vaseline.

He had two thermos flasks of hot coffee, one for himself, and the other in case his guns needed to be defrozen.

Scotty had noticed Sam filling his thermos flasks, and could not resist a little leg-pulling of his friend.

'Sam, you're a funny bloke. Shouldn't you fill one flask only with coffee and the other with hot water?' Sam had grinned and replied, 'It's now a habit, mate. I know I can defreeze with coffee, so I'm not likely to change. Besides, if I don't need to defreeze the guns then I'll have an extra flask of coffee that we can share.'

Scotty didn't have Sam's problem with the cold, but he was not much more comfortable, sitting on his suspended canvas strip with his head in the plastic bowl of his turret.

He was keen to ensure that both guns were ready to be fired, that all his ammunition was there, and that his turret swivelled easily round 360 degrees.

John now began to taxi T-Tommy round the perimeter track to reach the usual queue waiting for take-off. Once airborne, he set his compass on Reg's course, and turned on to it. Every operation, he mused, has not only the usual dangers, but also new and perilous hazards not previously encountered. What would they be on this op? Above all, would they all get back safely?

BATTLE ORDERS

***

Reg was dismayed to discover, when they were flying over the North Sea, that they had covered more miles than he had calculated.

The vagaries of winds were hardly his fault, but he always felt responsible if anything concerned with navigation didn't go according to plan. He spoke to John about it.

'Skip, navigator here, we're not getting the head wind that was forecast - actually we have a tail wind. We're in danger of arriving too early over the target. I suggest reducing our airspeed by 30 mph. so it will be 150mph.'

'If that will get us to the target on schedule, that's fine by me Reg. I'll cut back to 150 mph now,' John responded.

To find that his aircraft was first over the target area was the last thing John wanted. It would be the centre of attention. Searchlights for miles around would cone them. John's cabin would be flooded with light and it would be difficult to read his instruments. Dozens of anti-aircraft guns, all focused on the one aircraft, would open up, and they would be lucky to avoid being blown out of the sky.

When T-Tommy crossed the coast to fly over Germany they encountered only erratic anti-aircraft fire, but all the crew knew that their relatively peaceful flight would soon come to an end. Fierce ack-ack fire and night fighters would at some stage be ready to attack them.

Terry now moved down to the front of the Lancaster to begin dropping 'window.' in order to disrupt German radar. Each bundle of foil was sent down through a chute in the floor of the fuselage.

'Window' had been very effective in 'blinding' fighter pilots, though many German fighters now had a new radar device, called SN-2 that protected them from being jammed by the foil strips.

They were well into Germany, and flying in a southerly direction, over Bourtanger Moor, when they were coned by about thirty searchlights. John decided to climb and dive alternately to confuse the ack-ack. It seemed to work because the searchlights waved about tentatively, trying, without success, to focus on them once again, while the German gunners waited for them to do so.

A little later, T-Tommy was still slightly ahead of schedule, and only twenty miles from the target, with no other Lancasters in sight. John wondered what had happened to the others. Had they cut back their speeds more than he had? Had they modified the recommended route?

Alone in the sky, in a hostile environment, every member of the crew now expected the worst: a huge barrage of shells to be fired at them at any moment. However, the German gunners appeared to hesitate as if they were unsure of their foe. Perhaps they were expecting to see a stream of aircraft rather than a solitary one. After a few moments of thought, John decided on a ruse that he hoped might fool the enemy.

'Skip here for Wireless op. Were you given what may well be the German colours of the day?'

'Yes, Skip, we were told that they *might* be red and yellow.'

'Right, Jack, and do we have any red and yellow flares?'

'Yes, Skip, we have them.'

'Good, Jack, then fire them.'

Jack did so, and soon afterwards all the searchlights went out, and T-Tommy continued on her way unmolested towards the target area.

'Wow!' Scotty shouted. 'I don't think much of their aircraft recognition!'

'It's a mystery,' John chuckled . 'Though that trick has been used before, by others, I really didn't expect it to work quite so well.'

***

Near the target, the crew saw many Lancasters that must have taken a different route. Relieved, John spoke with a forced cheerfulness.

'Skip here for all crew. Cheers! The missing Lancs have turned up! At least the guns below won't all be taking a pot shot at us.'

In fact, John's jaunty tone disguised his primary concern. He was disconcerted to see so many aircraft in close proximity, most of which were trying desperately to evade ack-ack fire. The terrifying bombing of their aircraft by a Lancaster just above them was grafted on to his memory.

To make matters worse, while other Lancasters were constantly altering their height and direction, exploding shell bursts were producing hundreds of patches of black smoke which reduced visibility over a wide area.

Then John saw a Lancaster on fire and watched as four of the crew managed to bale out, and then another Lanc exploded into tiny fragments which rained down nearby. He'd seen similar scenes before, but he still turned pale.

'My God!' he shouted, 'it doesn't get any better, does it?' Sam's view from the rear was similar.

'No. All hell's breaking loose,' he agreed.

Debris from destroyed aircraft fell nearby and some of it rattled on the fuselage of T-Tommy, adding to the clang of those pieces of shrapnel from explosions nearby, which had not so far penetrated the interior. Suddenly, however, one red hot slither crashed through into the fuselage and penetrated Jack's leg. He was immediately in excruciating pain.

'I've been hit in the leg,' he shouted, and screamed with pain. 'A piece of shrapnel's cut into it!'

John arranged for Scotty to bandage Jack's wounds, give him morphine if necessary, and help him to the rest bed.

Explosions continued around the Lancaster and Terry was fairly certain that one had partially destroyed the hydraulic system. He was not sure how badly it was damaged but told John of his fears.

'Flight engineer for Skip. The hydraulic system has taken some flak. It controls the undercarriage, flaps and bomb doors among other things, any of which may have been affected.'

'OK, Terry. We'll soon see if the bomb doors are working.'

John now jigged the Lancaster continuously to avoid the flak as much as possible, but he knew they must keep moving steadily towards the target, and prayed that none of the shells would explode under the bomb bay. He decided to increase their height to 21,000 feet, a Lancaster's maximum. That would at least remove the danger of being under another aircraft's bombs.

Continuing towards the target at the new height, John saw a Lancaster below them, that was probably approaching the target area, as they were. There was an explosion just in front of its outer starboard engine, and when the smoke cleared he saw that the engine had completely disappeared. The aircraft shuddered but continued flying on the same course. John was full of admiration for the courage of its crew.

'We've flown on three engines, too,' he thought, *'on two of our ops.'* He hoped the other Lancaster would survive as they had, and tried to identify it. 'It's probably in another squadron,' he decided.

Freddie saw a Lancaster spiralling towards the earth about fifty yards in front of them, and noted that five airmen had got out in time. He was glad to see that their canopies were floating away from the inferno below and hoped that those airmen would survive, whatever was in store for them. The other two, he thought, must have perished. He wondered which two crew members had remained in that doomed aircraft.

'When an aircraft receives a direct hit and is fatally damaged it's difficult for all the crew to get out in time,' he thought. *'The Lancaster's a wonderful aircraft but it's easier to escape from some other kites.'*

Near the target, Freddie asked for the bomb doors to be opened. John signalled to Terry, and they opened without difficulty, John and Terry breathing a deep sigh of relief.

'Bomb doors open, Freddie,' John said.

Freddie, his eyes fixed on the bomb site, now guided John step by step towards the Krupp armament factories, which covered a huge area.

'Five degrees to starboard, Skip. That's good... Left, left, steady, steady... bombs gone!'

The crew's relief was profound. The last few miles to the target had been a nightmare, but now the job was done. Just as soon as a photograph was taken, they could get away from the maelstrom, and the quicker the better.

Most of them managed to look out to try to see the results of Freddie's bombing. About half the bombs had fallen within the target area; the rest had been scattered around its margins. It was not his most accurate bombing, they decided, but it had been effective, as the photographs would show.

Meanwhile, T-Tommy, divested of its huge burden, rose hundreds of feet in the air. Once it had settled, John banked the aircraft and turned on to the course that Reg had given him.

But the bombs hadn't all gone! T-Tommy was still over the target area when Freddie noticed that two bombs were still hanging under the fuselage. He reported to John, his voice full of despair.

'Skip, two bombs didn't drop. They're still hanging there.'

John couldn't help groaning. 'OK, Freddie. The hydraulics must be damaged after all, though the bomb doors opened alright. I'll try to shake the bombs off.'

He then moved T-Tommy about suddenly, switching from a steep climb to a dive, and vice versa. The bombs, however, remained stubbornly fixed in the bomb bay. Then he spoke to Freddie.

'Bomb-aimer, we must try to release those bombs manually. '

'Yes, Skip, but that doesn't seem to work.'

'I think we should try again when we are well away from this dangerous area. We'll have more time to do it, without so much risk. It's worth a try. We won't go back. Perhaps we can bomb a target that's on our way. Suggestions, Navigator.?'

'OK, Skip, we could target the marshalling yards at Recklinghausen. They've been bombed before. Any bombing of the

German transport system disrupts their ability to move troops and war materials.'

'Agreed. Thanks, Reg. We'll go for Recklinghausen.'

Reg gave Skip a new course, and after some minutes, Freddie identified the marshalling yards without difficulty and managed to drop the bombs manually

'Skip here to all crew. I'm glad we've got rid of them. I didn't fancy landing this kite at Coningsby with a couple of bombs hanging below It was bad enough landing with that 1.000 pounder after bombing the launching sites.'

There was a chorus of agreement. The nightmare of landing with a thousand-pounder hanging underneath them was still fresh in their minds.

CHAPTER 20

Reg's course now took them along a track similar, but not identical to, their incoming one, and for the next fifteen minutes, they met no night fighters and only occasional bursts of anti-aircraft fire.   Then Jack, whose wounds had been bound by Scotty, and who was feeling much more comfortable as the morphine took effect, decided to look out of the nearby astrodome. He and Scotty spotted the enemy at the same time, but he was the first to speak.

'Skip, Wireless operator here. There's a Junkers 88 some way above us and it's travelling in the same direction, but not yet moving to attack. Very odd.'

' OK, Jack. Skip to all crew. I suspect Jerry's going to light us up with a flare to make us an easy target for other fighters. We're not going to let him!' he shouted defiantly, while beginning a steep dive.

But several tracer bullets now penetrated the fuselage, most of them peppering with holes the rear half of the aircraft, and just missing Sam who was about to tell Skip about a new development.

'Skip, rear gunner here. I can see three Junkers coming at us from the rear - about a hundred yards away!   They're now diving down behind us.'

As he spoke, Sam fired a short burst at the nearest fighter and thought he had clipped it, but it continued to close the gap between them.   He and Scotty then fired short bursts at every opportunity, but with three fighters on their tail, the outlook looked desperate. As the tracer bullets tore through the fuselage, Sam considered their chance of survival very slim, and thought, without a trace of panic,

BATTLE ORDERS

'It may be our turn to get the chop.'

John, corkscrewing desperately, decided that they might have to bale out, and, in a hoarse voice, higher pitched than usual, warned-

'Skip to all crew. Check your parachutes. Prepare to abandon the aircraft!'

What happened next was beyond belief.

Reg felt under his desk for his parachute. Then he was horrified at what happened. The aircraft lurched, Reg slipped, and he accidently operated the parachute's ripchord, causing his life-saving device to billow out in the aircraft. He was distraught. If Skip finally instructed the crew to abandon T-Tommy, he could no longer do so. He would have to remain.

Sam, in his rear turret was also a victim of the violent evasive manoeuvres. He noticed that the last dive was the steepest one he had experienced, and following John's warning to check parachutes, was convinced that the Lancaster was about to go down for good. He was desperately anxious to retrieve his parachute in good time, and took off his gloves to open the turret door to get it. As he held on to the metal to pull himself out, his hands became severely frost-bitten and the skin on his palms and fingers was largely torn away. He was in agony and shouted through the intercom for help.

Jack, in spite of his own injury, hobbled down the fuselage and escorted Sam to the rest bed that he himself had recently occupied, and Sam was given morphine to ease his pain. The poor fellow spent the remainder of the flight on the bed holding up his injured hands. Their Lancaster had lost its main defence from rear attacks.

The three Junkers were closing in and firing at every opportunity, and John was considering if and when to give the order to bale out, when he noticed the proximity of some extensive cloud, and immediately steered T-Tommy into it. Blanketed thus, he could no longer see the enemy aircraft; nor could they see T-Tommy.

Tremendously relieved, he decided to stay there as long as possible. Their Lancaster was travelling through large cumulus clouds which almost touched one another, so he flew from one to the next. After some minutes, when none of the crew could see any sign of the fighters, he resumed the course on which they had been flying. As T-Tommy finally emerged from the clouds, there was no sign of the enemy.

***

John now took stock of the situation. T-Tommy was very badly damaged. Its fuselage was full of holes of various sizes, and there was freezing cold air rushing through. Soon, they would all feel the cold penetrate every part of their bodies.

There were several holes, too, in the wings. One of the port fuel tanks had been punctured and petrol was leaking steadily. Terry hurriedly transferred the fuel it contained to another tank to reduce the loss as much as possible.

He and John now knew that the undercarriage was damaged and the flaps were probably useless, following earlier damage to the hydraulics. Terry thought there was probably other damage that would become manifest when they reached their base and attempted to land. *'At least,'* he thought *'we still have four working engines.'*

Returning through Germany, the crew encountered no more enemy activity except for some occasional anti-aircraft fire. And once they were well over the North Sea, they continued unmolested back to RAF Coningsby.

Fortunately, there were only a few aircraft waiting to land, and, without much delay, John was soon able to discuss the condition of T-Tommy with Flying Control. They were given some bad news, though much of it was known to them and the rest was not entirely unexpected.

'T-Tommy's damage is considerable. We can see much of it quite clearly. You have only one leg down (undercarriage half down), your hydraulics are largely destroyed, and the aircraft is full of holes, including both wings and fuselage. It is likely that there is some other serious damage that we can't identify from here. Only a crash landing is possible. It would probably be better if most of your crew could bale out, leaving only yourself and your navigator to attempt a crash landing.'

John immediately consulted the crew.

'Skip to all crew. Control thinks that we can only crash land. You'll stand a better chance if you bale out over the airfield. Reg can't because he hasn't a parachute, so he and I will have to take our chance.'

Scotty was the first to protest.

'Skip, we've been through all this before, and we're still of the same mind. We all know that a crash landing is dangerous, but this crew always sticks together. I vote we stay put.'

But John wasn't at all sure that he could crash land a second time without causing serious injury or death to one or more crew members, especially as he was sure there was damage of which he was unaware.

'Yes, Scotty, it's great that we all stick together, but this is a real emergency. Flying Control can see damage that we can't. They have only our safety in mind. I think we should take their advice.'

The crew would have none of it. They were unanimous that at all costs the crew must remain. If Skip proposed to crash land, they would stay put and get ready for that.

'In any case, Skip, poor old Sam and Jack are hardly fit enough to bale out,' Scotty pointed out.

John hadn't forgotten about Sam and Jack. Scotty was right, though in fact, neither of them was fit enough either to bale out or to survive a crash landing. However, it had to be one way or the other and the crew had made their choice.

John informed Flying Control of their decision. It was accepted, with warnings about how dangerous it was likely to be.

John now spoke to all the crew.

'Skip here. Take up positions for crash landing. Get yourselves behind a bulkhead, and get right down, protecting your head under your arms. Good luck!'

The crew positioned themselves for a crash-landing, while insisting that Sam and Jack must be protected as much as possible.

John flew a circuit round the airfield while he considered how he would proceed. At first, it would be like a normal landing approach, but when they touched down, only one wheel of the undercarriage would hit the deck. It would be much better with no undercarriage at all.

As one leg touched the tarmac, the opposite wing would collapse, and the aircraft would scrape along the tarmac, wildly out of control and stagger madly in all directions. Anything could then happen.

John's notion of the crash landing was largely correct, except that the reality seemed much worse.

He brought the aircraft down very carefully, but, to his dismay, found that he was too far down the runway. He'd been fully occupied trying to keep T-Tommy straight and level. There was not enough runway left on which the aircraft could come to a halt.

As the single leg touched the runway, the Lancaster's unsupported half crashed heavily on the tarmac, and there was an ear-piercing scraping sound as the single leg collapsed and the belly of the fuselage was dragged along at 90 mph, with sparks flying. Then it careered off the runway, and bumped wildly over the grass before crashing through the perimeter fence of the airfield.

Finally, its momentum spent, it slithered towards a farm building, and shuddered to a halt.

There was then an uncanny period of silence, and it was as if no-one had survived, as an ambulance and fire wagon sped as fast as they could to the scene of the crash landing.

But one by one the crew managed to emerge - all of them. Everyone was badly shaken up, ashen-faced and with hearts thumping madly. Miraculously, however, they had only minor injuries such as bruises and cuts. Sam was the last to leave, still holding up his hands and in severe pain. The effect of the morphine seemed to have worn off. Jenny, who had been watching the drama unfold with bated breath, rushed forward to speak to him, and joined him in the ambulance. Had he been in his usual rear turret, he might not have survived, as the whole rear part of the aircraft had broken up as the Lancaster collapsed on the tarmac.

Sam and Jack were quickly placed on stretchers, and carried carefully to the waiting ambulance. They were transported to the hospital for immediate treatment by doctors and nurses.

John was still breathing heavily. It had been a nightmare followed by a miracle that his crew were all safe. Altogether, they had now somehow managed to survive eight operations during which they had faced a multitude of dangers. There were still twenty-two ops to go. Could their 'luck' continue? Why not, he thought; some airmen had completed two tours. He had a wonderful crew and they were learning by experience to survive the most dangerous activity of the war.

***

The five members of crew who were relatively unscathed were given first-aid, had a short rest, and then, still dirty, dishevelled and thoroughly exhausted, dragged their tired feet into the Debriefing Room to report on salient features of the operation to the Intelligence Officer. Once seated there, they related what information they could, about their experiences during the flight and the bombing.

Group Captain Bannister entered, and listened intently. At the end he turned in his seat to speak to the crew. He began by congratulating them on another successful sortie, and continued:

'And now two of your crew are in the sick bay. I've just been there to visit all the wounded. There were some serious injuries, including one airman whose leg may have to be amputated. The news about Jack Rogers, who is quite comfortable, is good. It's expected the shrapnel in his leg can be removed without difficulty and he will not need to stay there for more than 48 hours. Sam Bunting has severe frostbite but I'm told his skin should largely heal in a few weeks, though a new skin will remain tender for some time. The hospital is very experienced in dealing with frostbite cases and will give him some ointment for regular use during the next few weeks.

Now, you are all due for a fortnight's leave - the survival leave you've had doesn't count. I suggest you have your meal as soon as you've cleaned up and returned all your gear, and then take a long, well-earned rest. You can begin your leave tomorrow. Jack and Sam should be going on leave only a few days later.'

BATTLE ORDERS

John thanked the Group Captain, and then five weary airmen left the De-briefing Room to return parachutes, Mae Wests, and all their other operation-related gear. They then sat down to a generous-sized fried breakfast before having a shower and flopping into their beds. Tomorrow they would catch trains to take them to their homes in England or Scotland, and they would experience a short period of normal life with families and friends. A stress-free environment would help to heal both their bodies and their minds.

But it was still early in the morning and they would probably get up soon after mid-day. So, five exhausted, aching, nerve-shattered airmen - faces and hands covered in plasters or bandages - agreed, before collapsing on to their beds, that in the evening they would once again relax in The Pig and Whistle. They would miss Sam and Jack, but the pub was such a pleasant world away from the ghastliness of war that they wouldn't give it a miss just because they had been badly shaken up and very close to death. The atmosphere there helped them to recover, and become normal human beings once again.

The publican's welcome was especially friendly. He could hardly help noticing the array of bandages and plasters but avoided asking any questions. If they wanted to talk about what had happened - fine. But he would never probe out of sheer curiosity. His job, he felt, was to help them to forget; to let them get away from it all and enjoy themselves in The Pig and Whistle. They were good lads and he was proud to have them in his pub.

John, Terry, Scotty, Reg and Freddie settled themselves in armchairs, and were soon sipping their drinks and feeling comfortable and completely relaxed. It had been a particularly awful op. Jack's shrapnel injury and Sam's frost-bitten hand had again brought home to them the ever-present hazards of flying in Bomber Command, and the crash landing had been a terrifying experience for them all. Yet they appreciated that it could all have been so much worse.

John had a vivid memory of the explosion which removed an engine completely from the Lancaster flying behind them on the bombing run and told the others about it.

'With only three engines,' he emphasized, 'they pressed on towards the target. That took a hell of a lot of courage. The Lancaster performs amazingly well with three engines, but to keep it steady enough during the bombing run, especially when you're getting all the turbulence from explosions, and the slipstream from the aircraft in front, is almost impossible. But let's hope they got back safely.'

'That Essen op. was the worst we've had by far,' Reg said, 'and I was amazed we all survived both the tracers that crashed into almost every part of the fuselage, and the crash landing. Honestly, that crash landing terrified me. There was the great thump as the Lanc toppled over, and then the screaming and scraping as we skidded along the runway. The tarmac was being churned up, with a flurry of sparks. The fuselage could have broken up, and then we'd have had it.'

'Part of the fuselage did break up,' Reg pointed out. 'The rear turret was completely destroyed. Had Sam been there he'd certainly have got the chop.'

'Poor old T-Tommy must be a write-off,' Freddie suggested, and we haven't had it long. That will mean that we'll have to get used to another kite just after becoming confident in T-Tommy, and getting quite fond of him,'

John decided it was time to move the conversation right away from ops and aircraft, towards a more bantering mode.

'Right,' he said, grinning widely, 'we've got the Essen op off our chests, so let's now think about our leave. Scotty, what about this marriage of yours that we've been expecting for a long time. We'll all be getting you a wedding present, of course. When are you going to take the plunge?'

Scotty grinned too. 'Quite soon, he replied'. Probably while I'm on leave, perhaps the week after next. Don't forget that I've had to save up. Weddings don't come cheap.'

'We never hear about women in your life, John,' Reg said, and, turning towards Skip, smiled as he asked, 'Are there any, apart from your Mum?'

'You've never asked me before,' John replied, his eyes twinkling. 'Yes, I've been engaged to Mary for a couple of years. We hope to get married as soon as the war has ended and I am demobbed. I'll be back at university soon after that.'

'But Scotty will be getting married very soon,' Terry reminded the others, 'so we should celebrate it now, especially as he's going to be married in Ayrshire...which I believe is somewhere on the edge of the world. I'd like to get us all another drink so that we can wish him all the best and toast the happy couple.'

CHAPTER 21

Sgt. Jack Rogers,

RAF Coningsby

April 7th, 1945

Dear Maurice,

Congratulations on your promotion to Senior Scientific Officer, and you're only twenty-one! Terrific. You're obviously very good at your job and the promotion is well-deserved. Your work is essential to all the armed Services.

Women at home are also making a tremendous contribution to the War effort, aren't they? As well as the Women's Land Army there are thousands of women assembling RAF fighters and bombers.

Did you read that a group of women in Wales broke a record in assembling a Wellington bomber in the fastest time ever? Then there are the lady pilots of the Air Transport Auxiliary who pilot aircraft of every kind to wherever they're needed in

Britain. There are thousands of women in factories producing the weapons of war. One could go on!

All such civilians, including you, help to keep the Armed Forces well-equipped, and you're all just as essential to the War as we in the Services are.

There is some good news here. The shrapnel embedded in my leg was removed and it's recovering well, and Sam's frost-bitten hands, which were extremely painful, are slowly improving.

Poor old T-Tommy was badly damaged and won't fly any more operations.

As a crew we've had a pretty rough time on our ops so far, but we're all working well together and I wouldn't want to be in any other crew.

From your very good friend,

Jack

Scotty took his wife Lucy to the Odeon cinema to see Fred Astaire in *The Sky's the Limit*. As planned, they had married during his leave. Interested much more in each other than in the film, they relaxed in the back row and held hands, cuddled and kissed throughout the programme. No-one would have guessed they were married!

Afterwards, they boarded a double-decker bus, sat in the back seats on the upper deck, and fell into each other's arms. They had no home of their own, but Lucy's parents had agreed to put them up during Scotty's leave.

Back at RAF Coningsby, Scotty had to confront the grimmer aspects of his life. He thought about how often he had spent long hours scanning the sky searching for enemy night fighters until his heavy-lidded eyes ached with fatigue, and about how many times all the crew had faced death.

'It's a funny old world. We try to lead a normal life for part of the time. Then we are off to bomb a German target and might well be one of those who get the chop.

It's always so sad to see on the notice board the following day the names of friends in the squadron whose Lancasters have failed to return, to watch an officer emptying their lockers, and to see the empty beds. Those empty beds are a really moving sight. They bring tears to your eyes because as you look at them you can almost hear the words and laughter of the missing airmen. They remind you of the ever-present dangers in Bomber Command.'

***

All the crew had just sat down to enjoy a cup of coffee in the NAAFI. Sam was excited and bursting to impart his news.

'At last I've got some news about my friend Bill Irons,' he began, breathlessly.

The others turned to face him. They knew that Sam and Bill were very close friends, and that Sam had been very concerned since Bill's Lancaster had been shot down and he had been taken prisoner.

'His letter has just arrived. He was taken to Heydekrug, in East Prussia and the POW Camp is called Stalag Luft VI. It's a pretty spartan life, and the food is awful, but he has received a Red Cross parcel, which contained, besides food, some very welcome things such as a sweater, a tooth brush, handkerchiefs and soap. Apparently, it's becoming chaotic there because the Russians are advancing from the East and in front of them are thousands of refugees. At the same time, the Allied armies are advancing from the West. Bill thinks the Germans don't want their POWs to be rescued by advancing armies and that they may soon be moved.

I'm worried that, with all the confusion out there, some prisoners may try to escape. I can't forget the terrible fate of most of the airmen involved in The Great Escape on March 25th last year. You'll remember that 76 airmen broke out and that all but three were soon recaptured. Hitler was so enraged by the attempted escape that he ordered the Gestapo to shoot fifty airmen, and that was carried out soon afterwards. It was sheer murder and a massive war crime. I know that it is the duty of every POW to try to escape but I fervently hope that Bill doesn't make the attempt'

'I don't suppose he, or any other POWs will attempt an escape now that the war is nearing its end,' John said, 'but it's great that you've heard from Bill. You now know that he is OK and it's good that he is receiving Red Cross parcels. I'm not surprised to hear about the poor food there. I expect the Germans themselves are not getting much food at present.'

'Yes, I'm very pleased to have Bill's letter. At least I now know that he is alive and well, and hopefully the war will end soon and we'll see him back here.'

BATTLE ORDERS

***

They were on 'Battle Orders' that evening, and discovered they were going to Berlin again, this time to bomb its railway system. Scotty shared with his fellow-airmen both a dislike and a dread of any Berlin operation, because eight hours was such a long time, and with flight preparations and after-flight activities, it took up all the night and a good part of the morning. Then there was having to face the fearsome array of anti-aircraft guns.

Berlin was Germany's most vital railway centre, where twelve lines converged. It was also a key focal point for the railways of the whole of Europe. Thousands of soldiers and vast quantities of war materials passed through 'The Big City' as the RAF referred to it. It also contained important railway workshops.

If key parts of Berlin's railway system could be largely destroyed, it would have an almost immediate impact on the effectiveness of the German war machine. Bombing the nucleus of Germany's railway system would benefit our allies as well as our own army.

Jack had made a rapid recovery following the removal of a slither of shrapnel from his leg and had been able to enjoy almost all his leave. Sam's hands had taken longer to heal than he had expected, but the ointment that the Medical Officer had given him proved to be very effective.

John was amazed at how quickly T-Tommy had been largely repaired in a mere forty-eight hours, but it would only be used now for training.

The Lancaster in which they were flying tonight, a permanent replacement for T-Tommy, was another P-Peter, which pleased all the crew. They retained fond memories of the first Lancaster in which they had begun their tour.

But just after their briefing, John's crew, like many others, grumbled about having to go on another operation to Berlin.

'I'd rather go almost anywhere else,' Sam said. 'The ack-ack fire was terrible - the worst we'd ever had.'

'It was tough,' Scotty agreed, 'and then we had more aircraft over the target than we'd had before, and a bomb went right through our port wing. If it had struck one of our wing fuel tanks, we'd have had our chips!'

Reg said, 'For me, those Arctic conditions in the aircraft were a blessed nuisance. I had a layer of ice on my chart. Though that was nothing to do with Berlin, it helped to make that night one of our worst.'

'The only good thing about that op,' Scotty said, was that I got my first Jerry, a Messerschmitt.'

'And for me, it was that some of our bombs fell right in the middle of the factory complex,' Freddie added.

'Yes, they did,' John agreed, 'Let's not forget it was a very successful operation, and we all learnt a lot from it.'

He turned to Jack.

'Has your leg wound completely healed?' They were collecting their gear.

'I think so. I was surprised how soon it felt quite normal. The medics did a good job. I can't feel anything now. It was only a narrow splinter and could have been much more serious, but I had an awful pain at first. It was hot, sharp and excruciating.'

'I'm sure it was,' John said, 'but thank God it doesn't worry you now. What about your hands, Sam? Are they healing?'

Sam grinned. 'I think they are. They're better than they were. Before I had the morphine, I was in agony, John. The treatment I had at the hospital was very effective, though, and I was given some pain killers. I used them on leave - otherwise I wouldn't have had any sleep - also some ointment the nurses had given me which did wonders.'

'So how are your hands, now, Sam?'

'They're improving steadily, John. The new skin is still tender, though. The silk gloves help to protect them.'

'Tonight's op is sure to be different from the last time we were over Berlin.' Scotty said. 'The weather won't be the same, for one thing.'

'And the route will be slightly different,' Reg said. 'We'll go over the North Sea again. Then cross Denmark, fly over part of the Baltic Sea, and then head straight for Berlin.'

' It should help that there'll be diversionary raids to both Hanover and Frankfurt to cause more confusion for the Luftwaffe', Scotty added.

'They should help,' John replied, 'but Jerry isn't always fooled by them.'

They all knew that every operation was different. What kind of hazards would they face this time?

***

It was a clear night. They were flying at the Lancaster's normal operational height of 20,000 feet, with pollution-free air enabling the stars to sparkle brightly, presenting a night sky of impressive beauty.

Scotty thought that Reg would probably use astronavigation on such an evening. Spending so much time gazing around in his mid-upper turret at night, he himself had learned a little about the night sky. He could identify many stars within their constellations, such as Betelgeuse and Rigel in Orion, Antares in Scorpius, and Regulus in Leo. He knew that while the Plough and the Square of Pegasus constellations are always visible in the Northern Hemisphere, Sirius, the brightest star in the heavens, can be seen only in a short period during the Winter. Scotty liked to spot it during its relatively rare appearances.

'Yes, he thought, *'I like star-gazing. A plus among many minuses.'*

They were flying over the North Sea, and were now about a hundred miles from their base. Scotty swivelled his turret for the umpteenth time from one side to the other. He would become dog-tired during the long operation, but fatigue, like fear, had to be overcome. It mustn't be allowed to obstruct his high level of alertness.

And then his perseverance was rewarded. He just managed to spot two Focke-Wulf 190 fighters, to starboard, at approximately their own height. They were still about 800 yards away but moving rapidly towards them. He reported his sighting immediately.

'Skip, two Focke-Wulf 190s...approaching to starboard, level with us and about 750 yards away. The gap's closing fast.'

'OK, Scotty.'

'Skip to all crew, prepare for a corkscrew, an extended one.

John was anxious to keep below the attackers. Recently the Germans had been using their upward-firing Schlage Musik guns to shoot between two engines, with the aim of setting fire to a petrol tank. They had often succeeded, sometimes leading to the complete destruction of the bomber.

John's dive, the first part of his corkscrew, was one of the fastest he had ever flown a Lancaster, and his Air Speed Indicator showed the speed as nearly 400 mph. He was sure that his new P-Peter had never before been flown so fast and hoped he wasn't putting too much strain on an aircraft of which his experience was limited. As the Lancaster dived, John slowly turned it to port.

Sam always felt he was in the worst place when the Lancaster was plunged into a very steep diving turn, followed by an equally steep climb. The wings would drop and he would find himself looking upward at the stars. Then, as the aircraft swiftly pulled out of the dive and turned skywards, he would suddenly be swung round and find himself looking earthwards. The G force pressures felt as if a great weight was pressing in his head. But he still had to be prepared to fire his four machine guns whenever there was a reasonable chance of hitting a fighter.

Scotty, sitting in his sling seat, hated watching the wings actually bend, such was the violence of the movement. In spite of that, he usually managed to stay put, but dropping almost vertically at an unaccustomed speed proved to be too much for him this time. He was tipped out of the canvas strip and tumbled onto the floor of the aircraft. He continued sitting there stunned and breathless for a few moments, checking that he was uninjured, except for some minor bruises, and then, recovering, and realising that he might yet be able to fight off the Focke-Wulfs, he scrambled back into his sling, which he always struggled to do, rotated his turret and re-focused his machine gun on the enemy aircraft as they flashed by.

Then Scotty saw his chance and fired a short burst at the nearest Focke-Wulf, clipping its starboard wing. Before the next diving turn, Sam fired at the other Focke-Wulf, and shot away part of its tailplane. Although both enemy aircraft were now damaged, neither pilot showed any sign of giving up the contest.

Nor were the gunners likely to give up.

John was completing a climb when Sam had a rare opportunity to complete his attack on the Focke-Wulf 190 he had damaged. He fired immediately, and was both startled and pleased to see a stream of his bullets rip holes in its fuselage. He shouted with triumph. A few minutes later, he cried out again when he saw that it was on fire. It then exploded and began to fall earthwards, turning over and over, with a stream of smoke and flames trailing behind. Sam hoped that the pilot had managed to get out in time, and was relieved to see his parachute billowing out and swinging from side to side as it drifted earthwards. It was his intention primarily to destroy aircraft; not to kill their pilots. But then the truth suddenly hit him. The parachutist was falling into the freezing North Sea and would certainly perish very soon. 'Poor devil,' he thought.

John had seen it all.

'Sam, that was great!' he shouted. 'A definite kill. And Scotty, you've done well, too. I think the other Jerry has slunk away. Can anyone see it?'

No-one could. The pilot of the surviving Focke-Wulf may have decided that P-Peter had two deadly gunners and that he didn't want to share the fate of his friend.

They reached the coast of Denmark, and crossed it without meeting any more enemy aircraft. Then they turned to fly over the Baltic Sea. Some of the German-occupied islands had heavy concentrations of anti-aircraft guns. John had been warned about them during the briefing. Where possible he skirted them.

After flying for so long with his Lancaster completely blacked out, John's cabin was suddenly illuminated by beams of intense light, coming from many directions. Coning was always a frightening experience and this was no exception. However, the follow-up was only desultory anti-aircraft fire, and after a few more minutes, John left the Baltic Sea behind by turning to fly directly to Berlin.

None of the crew spoke very much during an operation, except when they were being attacked or when communication was essential. As P-Peter roared towards Berlin there was silence except for the deafening sound of the four Rolls Royce engines. However, each crew member was occupied by his own thoughts.

Scotty reflected that although they had managed to shoot down some fighters, four-engined bombers were always disadvantaged in their combat with fighter planes.

'They are specially designed to attack and destroy us, and they're faster and more manoeuvrable than we are. They also have the advantage of being able to spot us before we can spot them.'

Terry was thinking how glad he was that they were flying in a Lancaster rather than any other four-engined bomber. He loved the aircraft because it performed so well, even when badly damaged.

'Halifaxes have some good features, its Mark 3 especially, but there are always flames flowing out of their rear exhaust ports, which can be seen by Luftwaffe fighter pilots a long way away.'

Sam was straining his eyes as he looked through the opening at eye level where the panel of Perspex had been removed. He swept his eyes in all directions as he searched for the first sign of an attacking aircraft.

Reg was checking their progress as they approached the target, and considering whether any small changes to their course or speed would be necessary to ensure that they would arrive over the target within the time frame given to them at the briefing.

BATTLE ORDERS

Freddie was feverishly preparing to play his crucial role at the climax of the operation: bombing the central core of Berlin's railway complex.

Those crew members free to do so looked out as P-Peter approached the city.

Ahead of them, they could see the fantastic pyrotechnic display produced by the white probes of searchlights, the yellow/red bursts of flak, lines of yellow tracer bullets, the green and red target flares fired by the pathfinder aircraft, and the explosions as two aircraft received direct hits from very accurate anti-aircraft guns. Altogether it was both fascinating and intensely frightening. And through it all were some parachutes, slowly drifting earthwards, the canopy of one drifting past them being full of holes, and smouldering, but still functioning. Sam hoped the airman would be OK. He knew that he would have an uncertain future once he landed on enemy soil.

Some airmen parachuting over cities had been set upon by local people and beaten up before being rescued by someone in authority.

It was getting increasingly cloudy. While the sky was clear, the searchlights had easily focused on the Lancasters flying over the city. As the cloud increased, they still managed to be effective as their beams shone on the cloud base so that the bombers above were silhouetted, and again became fairly easy targets. Anti-aircraft crews also fired flares above the clouds to guide the Luftwaffe night fighters.

The target area was now only a few miles away. Freddie was ready and as alert as usual. His excited voice now announced the nearness of their objective.

'Skip, it's getting cloudy, but there's a clear gap. I can see where the twelve railway lines converge, and there's a complex system of lines, railway buildings and numerous platforms. It's a very extensive target. Open bomb doors.'

John nodded to Terry who carried out the request.

'Bomb doors open, Freddie.'

Freddie had matured during the past few months while honing his skills as a bomb-aimer. Like the other crew members, he had now left behind his boyishness and become a man.

'Five degrees to right...steady...more right...steady...steady...little right...steady...Bombs gone... Keep steady for the photo...'

The bombs struck many parts of the railway complex below, hitting railway goods yards, platforms and stations, rolling stock, converging lines, railway offices and repair yards.

As P-Peter, freed from her massive bomb load, responded by shooting upward many hundreds of feet, all the crew felt the upward pressure.

Now for home.

CHAPTER 22

John had received from Reg the first course for the homeward journey, and, at 20,000 feet, he increased their speed to 230 mph., which P-Peter could now manage easily, having dropped its huge bomb load and used half its fuel.

He looked out anxiously, watching the frequent puffs of exploding shells all around them. There was one bomber in flames, with some of its crew baling out. A few parachute canopies drifted quite close to their Lancaster. John fervently hoped that those airmen would not be caught in the ack-ack fire, and killed before they reached the ground.

A few miles away from the target area, the anti-aircraft guns were silent, and the puffs of smoke, already in the sky, spread and faded. Almost immediately afterwards, Sam spotted two Focke-Wulf 190s.

'Skip,' he almost shouted, 'Two Focke-Wulf 190s approaching from the rear. They're slightly lower than us. About 500 yards away.'

'OK, Sam,' John replied.

'Skip to all crew. Prepare for corkscrews. Hold tight!'

He then began to corkscrew in the manner in which his crew were now familiar, beginning with a steep, fast, dive.

Scotty didn't have much to hold on to but, determined not to be tumbled out of his sling this time, he gripped the metal frame of his turret and shifted his position slightly in accordance with the Lancaster's movements.

Both Sam and Scotty now prepared to continue the battle of attrition in which they had been engaged many times. The Focke- Wulf pilots were now very near and firing their canon at every opportunity.

Then Sam had an opportunity to aim broadside at one of the fighters as it swept past, and he wasted no time, firing his four machine guns at just the right moment. It was a very brief burst but its bullets crashed into at least one petrol tank. Fire broke out immediately and after flying a short distance, the Focke-Wulf was a ball of fire, hurtling to the ground while it disintegrated, pieces of the aircraft falling close to their Lancaster.

All the crew cheered. The other Focke-Wulf pilot tried one more attack, but then broke away while. John was in the middle of a corkscrew.

Sam reported its retreat from the battle, and John congratulated him on his success. Like his crew, John was delighted with the gunner's victories over German fighters, but he was also worried. They were still surrounded by too many other Lancasters that were also involved in evasion manoeuvres of one sort or another and there was the constant risk of collisions. When pilots were concentrating on survival, it was difficult for them to keep an eye on all the other aircraft hurtling around them, turning, diving and climbing.

About ten minutes later, his worst fears were realised. There was a thunderous, juddering crash and the aircraft shook violently. They had collided with another Lancaster. It was not a head-on collision, which would have been fatal for both aircraft and crews, but it was serious enough.

Scotty reported that part of the elevators had been ripped off and he believed also that both port engines had been hit and were damaged.

The Lancaster now went into a very steep dive, hurtling towards the ground, and spinning slowly as it did so, to the alarm of all the crew.

It took John by surprise. He pulled back the control column as hard as he could, but the aircraft continued on its almost vertical descent.

'Help me move this blessed thing forward,' he shouted to Terry.

Terry moved across to help John, and together they pulled the control column forwards, with all their strength. But it was not until they had descended several thousand feet that they succeeded in flattening out the Lancaster, and straight and level flight was achieved, though the aircraft was still inclined to dip towards the ground, and the two airmen had to maintain their pressure on the control column. Finally they managed to tie it with some rope, in a position which kept the aircraft fairly level, but John found that he could maintain a straight course only with one rudder fully on.

Terry soon realised the reason for that. He reported that the two port engines, one of which had been partly torn away, were not working at all. He used the cross-feed cock to transfer fuel to the starboard tanks.

Suddenly, Sam shouted out,

'Skip, my turret won't move. It's useless.'

'Sam,' Terry pointed out, 'the port outer engine is kaput. It drives a pump which operates your turret.'

'O my God.' Sam was distraught. Unable to swivel his turret he felt quite useless. John tried to cheer him up.

'Skip here, Sam. It's a blow for you, and for all of us. We now have no sting in our tail. But you destroyed a Focke-Wulf 190 and that was great.'

They were now in a seriously vulnerable state. For the remainder of the flight, they would be dependent on the two starboard engines, and one rudder would have to be fully on, to counter the tendency to turn to port. John was not at all confident that he would be able to get his crew home safely. In addition to the damage they had sustained, they had lost their main defence against attack. Sam's four machine guns, normally protecting them from rear attacks, were now trapped in an immovable turret, making them virtually useless.

Jack asked John whether he thought they could fly back on the two remaining engines and a broken elevator.

'Yes, Jack, I hope we can'...he gave a short laugh. 'With two engines, we can maintain height, but only below 10,000 feet - so soon you'll be able to take off your oxygen masks. With no bombs, less fuel and two engines we can stay at about 10,000 feet and our speed will be down to barely 125mph. That's right, isn't it, Terry?'

'Yes, Skip, we've used just over half our fuel.'

Sam asked about the damage to the elevators.

'That'll be a nuisance, Sam, especially when we want to land. I'll test the elevators on our way. We'll know how well they're working by the time we land.'

Following that exchange, silence reigned; each airman was left to his own thoughts. They all knew the dangers of flying at a reduced speed and at a much lower height. They had done that before, but with three engines, not two, and they were still flying over Germany. They would also be without Sam's four guns in the rear turret. They all hoped that they would not meet any more fighters and not too much flak before they reached the Baltic Sea.

The plan was to return largely the way they had come. That meant that after flying north to the Baltic, they would turn westwards, before cutting across Denmark. John had already decided that he would bypass those German-occupied islands in the Baltic, in which there were heavy concentrations of guns.

Meanwhile, they had a long way to go over Germany. Fortunately, there was only moderate anti-aircraft activity over most of the German leg.

It was very different when they were flying near Greifswald, where there was a large cluster of guns in a wooded area. Here the anti-aircraft fire was both dense and accurate, and a loud explosion occurred just under the damaged outer port engine. Terry had seen it happen and reported to Skip, with a rueful smile.

'Skip, no need to worry. That shell would have shattered the outer port engine, but as it's already out of action, it makes no difference to our progress.'

'OK, Terry. Let's hope Jerry will leave us alone for a while.'

They reached the Baltic without further attacks of any kind. Turning west, John consulted Terry about their fuel reserves. Rather than fly across Denmark, he now wanted to fly straight out to the North Sea and further west than planned. He was sure that would be safer for them than flying over any more German-occupied territory. Over some parts of Denmark they would probably face more night fighters as well as ack-ack guns. However, the problem might be a shortage of fuel. The last thing he wanted was to have to ditch in the North Sea again, if they were to run out of fuel, or had insufficient to complete the journey home.

'Skip for flight engineer. Have we enough fuel for a diversion round the top of Denmark, before flying straight home?'

'Yes, Skip, we have, but that will not leave us much in reserve when we're over Coningsby, especially if we have to mess around stacking.'

'OK, Terry, I think we'll take our chance.'

When they were flying over the North Sea, John had time to think about the problem of landing P-Peter with only the two starboard engines and damaged elevators. His foot had remained on the rudder pedal since the engines had been put out of action and his extended leg was aching with the strain. He was relieved, though, that he was able to fly P-Peter on only two engines, and that they had been unmolested for a large part of the journey home. And he was pleased that once again they had completed their bombing task successfully, and that no crew member had been wounded or worse.

'In this game, one has to be grateful for small mercies,' he mused.

Approaching Coningsby, he received the good news that there were very few aircraft waiting to land, so that they would not have to face a formidable wait in a stacking queue.

***

John's two surviving engines were both on one side of the aircraft - the starboard. He knew that the one-sided pull of those engines would make his landing very difficult, so when his turn came to begin the landing procedure, he was not surprised to be told to fly a circuit with starboard engines on the inside of the turn. He was also advised to leave the undercarriage and flaps as late as practicable and to keep extra height in hand.

He lowered the undercarriage and had it locked down just before the final approach.

'*So far so good,*' he said under his breath, but the critical phase, the landing, was ahead. He was not very confident about that, but he carefully followed the advice from Flying Control.

He had to work very hard to keep the Lancaster straight and level, as there was the constant pull towards the port side, but by making full use of the rudder he managed it, albeit with occasional jerks and wobbles.

He made the final approach at 100 mph. When he thought that he was reasonably well positioned for landing, he lowered the aircraft's flaps. The runway now opened up before him and he found that he had travelled too far without getting low enough. His concentration on flying P-Peter straight and level had caused him to neglect wider considerations, such as the need to keep an eye on both the surrounding area and the runway.

He finally touched down at 90 mph and was tremendously relieved to be running along the tarmac, although he was already more than half way along it. His efforts were now focused on trying to keep the aircraft in the centre of the runway, and that was very difficult.

Finally, P-Peter, which had already veered to the extreme left of the runway, ran off the end of it, careered over the grass and the perimeter track, crashed through the boundary fence and didn't stop until it had run over part of a field of potatoes. The last twenty yards or so were very bumpy, and when the aircraft finally settled, it was, quite suddenly, completely and eerily silent, and none of the crew spoke or moved. They were in shock and very tense.

Fortunately, although all seven of them, especially Sam, were badly shaken by the landing, no-one was injured and the damage to P-Peter was negligible, though the fuselage was splashed with mud and looked a sorry sight.

The first one to speak was Jack, who quickly assessed that, in spite of their justified fears of a calamitous crash, they were finally at rest, following yet another 'very dicey op;' that all seven of them, though stressed and drained, were uninjured except perhaps for a few cuts and bruises; and that P-Peter was intact.

He decided to snap everyone into life by injecting a little boisterous humour into their present situation.

'Welcome,' he began, loudly and portentously, 'to John Mason's potato patch!'

John had had a nerve-wracking time over much of the flight and had been particularly tense over the past few minutes. His relief was such that he was ready to laugh at almost anything. He guffawed loudly and the rest of the crew followed.

Then Jack shouted out, 'We've got a great skipper!' and began to sing 'For He's a Jolly Good Fellow' and, weary and battered though they were, the others joined in. Their Skip had brought them back safely once again in spite of all the difficulties and dangers they had experienced.

Before anyone could then think about climbing out of the Lancaster, a Land Rover bumped over the field and stopped near them. Out of it stepped Group Captain Bannister, their Commanding Officer, wearing rubber boots. John stepped down to meet him. Their CO was grinning from ear to ear.

'Well done, John. I was told about the damage to your kite and watched your approach. You're a damn good pilot. Landing with two dud engines on the same side is very tricky.'

'Yes, sir, I was a bit anxious,' John said. 'We didn't touch down until the kite was half way along the runway. I hope P-Peter is OK. She's our third regular kite, and she's now proved her worth.'

By this time all the crew had stumbled out of the Lancaster and were forming a circle round the speakers. The Group Captain had a word with each of them. He told them that transport was on the way to take them to de-briefing, and then returned to the Land Rover and was driven back to the airfield.

'We should consider ourselves highly honoured by all the attention we're getting from our CO.' John commented as the Land Rover disappeared. 'I think he's quite taken with us.'

'I agree,' Scotty said. 'I think he's a good old stick.'

Jack laughed. 'A good old stick he is, though I would think he's no older than about forty.'

A little leg-pulling now helped the crew to unwind.

'John,' Sam began, grinning mischievously, 'I hope you won't land us in a potato patch again. It's much more comfortable if you stick to the runway.'

'Yes, it is,' Freddie agreed, 'but I don't think John finds the runway long enough.' His fellow airmen grinned.

'Nor is it wide enough,' put in Scotty.'

John smiled. 'Well, there are times when runways aren't long enough, and even not wide enough. I'm sorry I gave you all an uncomfortable time among the potatoes, but at least none of us *had our chips!'* They all enjoyed that one!

***

All the crew were once again in the saloon bar of The Pig and Whistle,' and seated in their usual corner, in plush armchairs. Jack decided the time was ripe to put in a serious word about their Skipper.

'I think we've had more than our fair share of death-defying experiences,' he said, 'and our survival owes a lot to John. Landing on two engines with a broken elevator was a great achievement, as was the ditching in the North Sea.'

Several of the others added their warm agreement, and gave more examples of his achievements. John responded by emphasising that it was all a matter of team effort.

'Our aircraft has been navigated successfully to targets because of Reg's great work, especially his astro-navigation. We've been defended by those amazing sharp-shooters Sam and Scotty. First Arthur and then Terry have nursed our engines and got the best out of them. Freddie has pin-pointed our targets with enormous care so that we have a high reputation for bombing accuracy, and last, but by no means least, we have Jack, who is a wonderful asset in any emergency. Personally, I'm proud to have you all in my crew.'

Then John decided it was his turn to have a little fun. He turned to face his mid-upper gunner.

'Scotty, isn't it time you told us something about your married life?' he asked. 'You got married during the leave following the Ruhr op, so now you're an old married man and we're all lonely bachelors, dying to learn something about the marital state.'

'Actually, though I've just had my twentieth birthday,' Scotty replied, 'I think I'm still fairly young.'

"True, but enlighten us about married life.' John tried hard to maintain a serious expression and a matching voice.

'After all, we may be married some time. Just give us a few intimate details that we might find useful if and when we take the plunge.'

'You should really ask me about married life in twenty years' time,' Scotty began, 'but as you're all so curious, I can give you a brief account which I hope you'll find of some interest.'

'That'll do nicely,' John said.   The others leaned forward and appeared to be hanging on his words, though laughter was bubbling just below the surface.

'Well, marriage is absolutely wonderful,' he responded, ' but... - his listeners sat motionless, with baited breath, leaning forward and waiting for Scotty to continue,

'It'll be a helluva lot better when Lucy and I can live together, all the time, in our own little cottage.'

CHAPTER 23

Sgt. Jack Rogers,

RAF Coningsby

April 11th., 1945

Dear Maurice,

I'm sorry to hear that more V2 rockets have been falling near you, and many houses have been destroyed. That monster Hitler sees the V2s as his last hope of victory. I'm glad your young sister Sylvia has been evacuated again, and to the same farm in Derbyshire where she was so happy before.

Do you remember early in the War, when we were still at school, we had to carry gas masks everywhere with us? We carried them around in cardboard boxes, some of which were decorated by us or our parents. Thank heaven gas was never used by the Germans. I suppose one reason for that is that Britain would have retaliated in kind.

Have I told you how well John has mastered the corkscrew? When we're attacked by a fighter, he often uses it. He begins by putting the aircraft into a terrifyingly steep dive and we all have to hold on for dear life. Last time, poor old Scotty tumbled out of his mid-upper sling on to the floor, but he was soon back in action.

During out last op, we collided with another bomber over Germany, and we lost two engines and part of our rudder. Fortunately, there wasn't the full impact that would have destroyed both aircraft, but we had to fly back at a slower speed and a lower height. That made us much more vulnerable to enemy attacks. Somehow, we got back safely, but our landing was rather unorthodox, and we finally came to a halt in a field of potatoes!

From your very good friend,

Jack

In the Eperlecques Forest in Northern France, the Germans had built an enormous bunker, to assemble, store, prime and launch V2 rockets which would fall on England, mainly around the London area, at any time in the day or night, without warning, causing much destruction and loss of life.

Hitler believed that the V2s, which had an operational range of 200 miles, could turn the tide of the war in his favour. He regarded them as terror weapons, but he wanted the number produced to be increased to help to ensure a German victory.

John's crew learnt at a briefing that the rockets were transported southwards from Peenamünde - a place they had twice bombed- and launched towards England from a number of launch pads in the north west corner of France and from Holland.

The Eperlecques bunker, near the Calais-St.Omer Road and the Calais canal, was of central importance in this German enterprise. That was where the liquid oxygen to fuel the rockets was manufactured, and where they were made ready for launching. In addition, the bunker had the required transport links, including a rail line to Peenamünde, and was out of the range of warship's guns. A railway station, considered by the Germans to be bomb-proof, was built where the rockets would be received and unloaded.

Launch pads for V2 s had been constructed in other parts of northern France, and there were also mobile launch pads (*Meillerwagen*), but the bunker in the Eperlecques Forest was by far the most important factor in Hitler's V2 plans.

To launch one rocket required 4.7 tons of liquid oxygen (LOX), so the production of huge quantities of it in the bunker was vitally important. Enough was produced for 10 launches a day, but 36 launches were planned. 100 V2s, could be stored there. Built in 1943, the bunker had already been bombed by USAAF Flying Fortresses in a daytime raid that had inflicted enormous on it, but the Germans had invested a tremendous amount of time and money in the bunker. It now had a new reinforced concrete roof which was several feet thick and much of the damage had been repaired. 150 tons of LOX was stored on the site. One problem was that LOX evaporated very easily so its production had to be near where the rockets were waiting.

BATTLE ORDERS

Following their briefing, John and his crew discussed some details of the coming operation. It was to be another daytime one.

'How is it,' Sam wanted to know, 'that although we've occupied almost all of France, 'this bunker is still in German hands?'

'I don't really know,' John answered, 'but it's very strongly guarded, and it's in the middle of a forest, which tanks would find difficult to penetrate. I suppose it was bypassed and left to the RAF and the USAAF to deal with.'

'What about poor old P-Peter?' Reg asked. Have the ground staff managed to make it airworthy again?'

'I believe so,' John answered. 'It's fairly easy to replace damaged engines, and also the broken tailplane section. The ground staff are wonderful. But Terry and I will take no chances. We'll give P-Peter every possible test of airworthiness, and the two replaced engines will have our special attention.'

'Hooray!' Sam said, grinning, 'and I hope that with the replacement of the port outer engine, my turret will spin from side to side as easily as it did before.'

'If it doesn't, Sam,' John assured him, 'we won't take to the air!'
'Fair enough,' Sam responded.

Scotty wanted to talk about the operation.

'This bunker in France is huge,' he began, 'and it's well protected with walls that are several feet thick, with a massive roof of reinforced concrete.'

'Yes,' John said, 'and it would be impossible to destroy it with normal bombs. '

'And we won't have normal bombs?' Reg asked.

'No,' John replied. 'We're going to carry a Tallboy, again - 12,000 pounds of high explosive. It's designed to penetrate and destroy massive constructions, like reinforced concrete that's several feet thick. You'll remember, we used one on the U-Boat bunkers in Hamburg.'

'It should smash it,' Jack said. 'It's known as an earthquake bomb.'

'This will be our second daylight op over France,' Scotty said.

'And are we going to have a fighter escort?' asked Freddie.

'Yes, we'll be flying near enough to England for that.' John replied, 'so we'll have fighter escorts for the first time. But some of our fighters are based in France now that the allies have captured a number of airfields further south. They are probably the ones that will escort us. '

'So we'll have Spitfires and Hurricanes,' Jack said.

'Or perhaps Mosquitos,' John added. 'The Mosquitoes won't be carrying any bombs, so they'll be able to fly as fast as most fighters.'

'I bet there'll be some fierce air battles,' Scotty said. I've never seen a dog fight.'

'If you'd lived in the south of England in 1940, you'd have seen plenty of dogfights during the Battle of Britain, ' Jack said.

'With a fighter escort, shouldn't this be the easy op we've been hoping for?' Freddie asked.

'Well, we've been warned that this op may not be an easy one,' John cautioned. 'To the Germans, the bunker is extremely important so they've got masses of anti-aircraft batteries in the area. I expect they'll be as concentrated as those we've already experienced.'

Sam laughed. 'We haven't had an easy op yet,' he said,' though I think we deserve to have one.'

'True,' John agreed, 'but it's a probably best if we never expect an op to be easy. We've got to be ready for everything Jerry throws at us.'

***

John's crew arrived at the locker room to change. Then there was the collection of Mae Wests, parachutes, food and drink, maps and escape kits. Terry carried his bag of tools, and Reg, all his navigational equipment. It was soon time to be driven by a waiting WAAF to dispersal.

John was anxious to test P-Peter for airworthiness, and worked closely with Terry. Outside, their examination included the tyres, undercarriage, and all moving parts, which had been lubricated with grease guns. Inside they carried out all the pre-starting checks together.

The two new Rolls Royce engines and the fuel gauges had particular attention. The engines were warmed up to 3,000 revs per minute, at full throttle.

When both John and Terry had completed their checks, John went across to the ground crew hut to sign form 700, the aircraft maintenance form, to agree that he was satisfied with the airworthiness of P-Peter.

The two gunners checked the swinging movement of their turrets and their guns and ammunition. Jack checked all his wireless channels and transmission facilities. Reg spread out his Mercator chart on which he had drawn the track to be followed to the target.

When it was time to taxi round the perimeter track, John moved off steadily, using the outer engines for steering, keeping a good interval behind the aircraft in front and watching out for any other vehicles. An aircraft fully loaded with bombs must always be handled with care while on the ground, and carrying a bomb weighing 12,000 pounds, he felt, was an awesome responsibility.

There was a small queue of Lancasters waiting near the threshold of the 2,000-yard-long runway, and P-Peter took its place behind them.

As John watched the aircraft ahead of him take off, he could not avoid thinking about incidents that could be extremely dangerous every time a Lancaster loaded with hundreds of gallons of fuel and several tons of high explosive, accelerated along the runway.

Bombs were arranged in the thirty-three- foot long bomb bay, which was being carried at an increasing speed just a few feet above the tarmac. And this time there was the awesome Tallboy. With such loads there would always be risks.

What could go wrong? Tyres sometimes burst, and that could cause an aircraft to career wildly off the runway and possibly crash into another aircraft not far away, with calamitous results. Or an engine could cut. Or an Air Speed Indicator could malfunction. There were many possibilities and each one could be dangerous. All a pilot and his crew could do was to ensure that all relevant checks were thoroughly carried out before the aircraft left Dispersal.

Standing nearby was a group of WAAFs and ground staff ready to wave off P-Peter. Jenny was there at the rear of P-Peter, where she could see Sam clearly. She waved enthusiastically, and Sam waved back.

On the runway threshold, John flashed his Lancaster's letter name and received back from the runway controller's caravan a steady green. It was time to go. The little group standing on the grass now waved more vigorously, and crew members who could look out, Sam, Scotty, Freddie, Terry and John, waved back once again.

BATTLE ORDERS

They were soon on their way to their tenth operation.

***

The tail plane having been raised, and the control column eased back, at about 110 mph, P-Peter rose steadily from the middle of the runway. As it gained speed and power, John kept his eyes on the aircraft in front. He had previously experienced the power of the slipstream behind a heavy bomber. It could cause the aircraft behind to rock about alarmingly and there was nothing a pilot could do about that.

The flaps were raised by degrees, Terry carrying out this task, reporting to John as he did so. P-Peter responded well to all the controls and John was satisfied with its performance so far.

In the air, there were further checks and actions to be performed. Jack tuned the wireless telephone receiver and switched on the identification for friend or foe. Throughout the flight he would be listening.

Once P-Peter had passed London, the crew knew that they were less than eighty miles from the target.

'At least,' Sam told himself, *'this is going to be a fairly short trip.'*

His cheeks were well greased, and he assured himself that tonight they would not fly quite as high as usual, so perhaps the temperature in the turret would not fall too low. But even at 15,000 feet the temperature was 45 degrees Fahrenheit below that at sea-level, and Sam's breath soon formed icicles.

Jack, listened almost continuously for the transmission of any new messages. There could be several messages between base and aircraft.   He gave Reg new wind velocities and the latest weather forecast when they were about half way across the English Channel.

A little later, he turned on VHF so that they would be able to listen to the master bomber for his instructions to the crews, and later still he would give Freddie the 'bombing wind' to be set on his bombsight.

Scotty had no doubt that this op would be much less dangerous than previous ones.

'It's not only a short one, ' he reflected.   *'We'll be over France where I don't suppose the ack-ack will be as accurate as over Germany. And we'll have a fighter escort. Marvellous! Let's get on with it.'*

But given the importance the Germans attached to the Eperlecques bunker, wouldn't they defend it to the death, with both guns and fighters?

CHAPTER 24

It was a pleasant day, with a blue sky, patterned with small, white cumulus clouds; and the visibility was good. As usual the gunners swivelled their turrets almost continuously, always searching the sky for the first signs of enemy fighters.

Since the Allied invasion of France on June 6th., 1944, the invasion forces had spread out across France. In spite of determined defence by the Germans, especially in and around Caen, Allied armies had been making good progress, and several airfields had been captured. Those now being used by RAF fighters could give close support to Allied Armies and RAF bombing aircraft.

The plan for the V2 Bunker attack was that fighters would *rendezvous* with the Lancasters just before they reached the French coast, and then escort them towards the target area.

It did not, however, work out precisely as planned. P-Peter was still five miles from the French coast when two Heinkel 190 fighters appeared ahead, about half a mile away. Scotty saw them first.

'Skip, Mid-upper gunner here. There are two Heinkel 190's ahead and flying rapidly towards us.

'Right, Scotty. Let me know when they are about 500 yards away.' A little later he had Scotty's response.

'Mid-upper gunner for Skip. The two fighters are now about 500 yards away. They're starting to descend. Do you think they're planning to attack us from below with their Schlage Musik guns?'

'Could be, Scotty. We must be prepared for that.'

John was concerned about taking evasive action while carrying the Tallboy bomb. He decided he would nevertheless try a modified corkscrew. Pulling out after a dive, while carrying that enormous bomb, would be difficult.

'Skip here to all crew. I'm going to turn and fly towards them while diving and turning slowly

Most of the crew held on tightly during the first, almost vertical dive, but Reg, immersed in his navigational tasks, found himself rising up, as before, and, as he put it, 'stuck to the roof .'

Both gunners began firing at about the same time as the fighters. It wasn't easy for the latter, with their fixed guns, to focus them on an aircraft that was diving rapidly and turning at the same time.

Sam managed to train his guns on one of them when it was well in his sights and the short burst from his four machine guns severely damaged the fighter by removing part of its tail plane. The pilot was obviously finding it difficult to control his aircraft, and it turned back towards the French coast.

The other Heinkel continued its attack, and at the top of one of John's corkscrews, it succeeded in spraying the fuselage with canon shells, which hit it like a sledgehammer. The shells ripped through the metal sides of the fuselage, in a series of loud, frightening crashes, leaving a line of ragged holes. Sam's heart was pumping fast, as he was sure that the shells were getting ever nearer to his turret, but he continued to swivel it and to fire short bursts whenever he had the enemy in his sights.

Scotty, too, swivelled his turret to focus his guns on the Heinkel. He was sure that he must have damaged it, but while he looked for evidence of that, it abandoned the combat and turned away towards the coast. He was both relieved and disappointed.

The other crew members, however, expressed only relief and they now enjoyed a few miles of peace. John was anxious to know to what extent P-Peter had been damaged by the canon shells.

'Skip here. We're now holed like a colander,' he said, 'but what's the damage otherwise?'

'Well,' Terry began, 'I'm afraid we have a broken fuel line on the starboard side. I think the outer port engine may also have been damaged. It appears to be working, though the prop. is bent a little.'

'I can still swivel my turret, so the outer port engine seems to be OK.,' Sam put in.

'And we're still maintaining our speed so perhaps the engine damage is not serious,' John added.

They were now approaching the French coast and anti-aircraft guns began firing. The shell bursts were not very near and John continued to fly towards the target. Freddie had switched on his bombsight gyros which needed about half an hour to settle.

The anti-aircraft fire died down and suddenly Scotty cried out excitedly-

'Look to the right. There's a dog-fight, the first one we've seen.'

'Yes, I can see it, Terry said. 'There are three Messerschmitt 109s and two Spitfires.'

'You're right,' Scotty added. 'But one Spitfire has just been shot down and the pilot has bailed out. It looks as if the wind might float him towards Allied-occupied territory. Good!'

'And look, one Messerschmitt has just been damaged,' Sam said. 'It's burning from end to end, and dropping like a stone, but again the pilot has bailed out. He laughed. 'I wonder if the two pilots will meet after they've landed.'

As they approached Eperlecques Forest, Freddie reported on the scene spread out before him.

' I can now see most of the forest; it's enormous.'

John took the Lancaster down to a lower altitude so they could study the area in detail. As he did so, Terry could see that there was a surprising amount of activity below.

'I didn't expect to see so many people here,' he said.

'Most of them are moving about and look as if they might be working in the bunker,' John said.

'I wonder how many of them are slave labourers or Prisoners of War,' Terry wondered.

'Quite a number I would think,' John said. ' Perhaps they are also working inside, assembling and priming the V2s, and even launching them. ' Suddenly Freddie spotted their target and shouted,

'There's the bunker, about a mile ahead of us.'

Flying over the forest, the enormous area that had been deforested to create an area suitable for the bunker could clearly be seen, and groups of anti-aircraft guns had been deployed on the edge of the forest, which partly hid them.

Several ack-ack guns now began firing simultaneously. There was then a very loud rattling of shrapnel against the fuselage, but at first none penetrated it. Then one shell exploded just under their tail plane, part of which was destroyed. That made John's control of the aircraft difficult but he continued flying towards the target.

Sam spotted a Lancaster about fifty feet behind and below them. He was concerned about the possibility of a collision.

There was a renewed burst of gunfire from the ground and explosive puffs appeared between the two aircraft. Sam stiffened. Then he saw one shell bursting very close to the following Lancaster, which blew out all of its windows. He reported the incident to Skip.

'Thanks, Sam,' Skip replied. 'but we must just carry on as we are because we're very near to the target.'

He continued to fly straight and level, and there were several shell bursts nearby. Falling shrapnel again clanged against the fuselage.

A pilot in the Master Bomber, flying in a Mosquito, and at a higher altitude than P -Peter, now began giving bombing instructions in a quiet, authoritative voice, which was heard distinctly.

Freddie, listening carefully to the Master Bomber, was ready to begin the lead-in to the bombing. He was very conscious of his huge responsibility at this crucial juncture. He had to see that the 12,000-pound bomb landed right in the centre of the bunker where it might eliminate, or at least seriously damage, the vital liquid oxygen plant, and hopefully also V2s in storage or being assembled. It was now time for him to assume centre stage.

'Skip, bomb-aimer here. I can now see the whole layout of the bunker beautifully. Bomb doors open.'

'OK Freddie,' John responded

Terry switched on the bomb bay lever and John confirmed,

'Bomb doors open.'

'A little to port, Skip. More to left... that's it...steady...couple of degrees starboard..good...steady..steady.. steady.. bomb gone! Now, we have to wait for the photograph.'

The photograph was now taken automatically a short period after 'Bombs gone.'

Those crew members who could, tried to see the result of dropping what had been dubbed 'the earthquake bomb.' Even Reg left his table to move forward to look through the bomb-aimer's turret.

They watched the Tallboy penetrate the massive roof and then huge, dense clouds of cement dust and debris rose up to create a massive grey cloud that soon covered the entire site, and rose rapidly, preventing further observation.

'Well done, Freddie,' John applauded. 'I'm sure that under all that debris lie the remains of at least part of the liquid oxygen production plant.'

Reg was jubilant. ' I'm glad I went forward to see the result just before the cloud of dust rose up', he said. 'The Eperlecques Forest Bunker has been massively damaged.'

John thought that perhaps they were both getting carried away, and being too optimistic so he sounded a note of caution.

'The bunker has been bombed many times,' he reminded the crew, 'and it will be bombed again and again. The Germans are determined to repair any damage, and we're just as determined that they'll never finish it. Now...let's get on our way. Can I have a course, navigator?'

Reg gave John a course for the first homeward leg, and they were soon on their way.

Behind them was another Lancaster which was not the one that had followed them over the target. Sam was watching it and noting that it was not in their squadron. He was estimating its distance from them, when an anti-aircraft shell struck the middle section of its fuselage and another the petrol tank in one of its wings. Immediately, a fire quickly engulfed the aircraft. For a few minutes only the Lancaster continued on its course. Then Sam saw four airmen tumble out, one after the other, and was glad to see their parachutes open.

Shortly afterwards. the aircraft blew up and hundreds of pieces of red-hot debris fell to the earth. Evidently three crew members had not managed to save themselves.

Although Sam had witnessed such scenes before, they always affected him deeply. Like themselves, those three airmen were aged perhaps nineteen or twenty...and, in a moment they were no more. Sam blinked back his tears.

Over the French coast John's crew met the same somewhat ineffectual anti-aircraft fire as before.

'I wonder whether some Frenchmen have been forced to man the guns here, and their hearts aren't in it,' suggested Terry

'Yes. We've never had such half-hearted ack-ack fire,' John agreed.

Soon clear of the ground attacks, they would soon be challenged by fighters as there were many in the neighbourhood.

They were only a few miles from the coast when two Messerschmitt 110s descended through some cloud and began diving towards them.

'Skip, two Messerschmitt 110s are diving towards us to starboard. They're only a hundred yards away!'

John had spotted them almost at the same time and made a sudden decision which he hoped would upset the plans of the attackers. He turned towards them and went into a very steep dive. There had been no time to warn the crew, and it was Reg, again, who suddenly found himself floating upwards in the fuselage.

Sam suddenly found both Messerschmitts in his sights, as P-Peter dipped towards the earth, and he prepared to fire. He fired a short burst at one of them and swivelled his turret to fire at the other. The first burst was well directed for the fighter's petrol tank exploded, and soon afterwards the aircraft disintegrated in a ball of fire. His second burst, following a very hurried movement, missed the second Messerschmitt completely. Nevertheless, John's crew were jubilant and Sam smiled with satisfaction.

The surviving fighter now turned and dived towards P-Peter, which was by now well below it, and raked it with canon fire. Some of its shells destroyed the Lancaster's inner port engine and were quite close to the propeller of its inner starboard one.

Scotty meanwhile had trained his guns on the Messerschmitt and fired a burst as it levelled out after its dive. Some of his bullets cut away part of the fighter's elevators. It then turned and dived away, towards the French coast.

'Well done, both Sam and Scotty,' John said. 'One Messerschmitt 110 completely destroyed and another with its elevators partly cut away. And before that, one Heinkel's tailplane completely removed and another Heinkel probably damaged.'

The crew cheered loudly, and then Jack asked, 'Skip, what about our damage? There's not much left of our inner port engine as far as I can see from the astrodome, and it's pretty draughty in this kite since it's been turned into a sieve!'

Terry had assessed the damage.

'Yes, the inner port engine has gone completely, and there is other damage. The inner starboard propeller is bent, but it seems to be turning pretty well. I'm especially worried about the undercarriage which is damaged.'

'Thanks,' Skip said. 'I think that pretty well sums up the situation. We're flying with three engines, and getting along well. Terry's transfer of fuel means that we are unlikely to run out of gas. I'll worry about the undercarriage when we're getting ready to land

'Skip here for Wireless Op. Jack, would you take a look at all those holes in our fuselage?'

Jack reported back within a few minutes. 'There are dozens of holes, Skip, all jagged and two or three inches in diameter. I don't think we can do anything about them.'

'OK, Jack.'

'Skip here to all crew. Keep warm in any way you can.'

John now kept P-Peter at about 10,000 feet with a speed of 145mph. With only three engines, and without a bomb load, that height and speed could be managed comfortably. Fortunately, they soon crossed the English coast and were well on their way to RAF Coningsby. It was a relatively short journey, but with the fuselage peppered with holes, all the crew were feeling the cold as they approached their station.

There were only two aircraft already waiting to land, and only a brief period was spent stacking. John informed Flying Control of their damage, and began flying a circuit. He told Terry to lower the flaps. The undercarriage had been severely damaged and it was clear that they had to land without it. Terry informed John.

'Flight engineer to Skip. Whatever is left of our undercarriage won't budge.

'OK Terry. Skip to all crew. We're going to have to crash land again. Brace yourselves behind bulkheads wherever you can!'

CHAPTER 25

John began the final approach at 115mph, told Terry to lower the flaps further, and then cut the Lancaster's speed to the minimum.

He lowered the aircraft a little earlier than usual and with a loud bump, they plopped down near the beginning of the runway, and the bottom of the fuselage began scraping over the tarmac with a frightening, ear-splitting scream as it surged along.

John couldn't control it at all. Half way along the runway, it moved away and churned up the nearby grass, until it crashed into a petrol bowser. Fortunately, the bowser was empty and P-Peter had by this time lost its momentum and shuddered to a halt.

Sam was badly shaken.

'My God!' he gasped, 'I thought my turret was going to break off. Every time it bounced, my head hit its roof.'

'Sorry, Sam,' John said, 'I'm afraid I just couldn't control the kite.'

He, too, was pale and shaking, and anxious to hear from the others.

'Is everyone more or less OK?,' he asked them.

They had all had yet another frightening experience, but all assured John that they were alright.

After a few minutes, they tumbled out, one by one. Sam had a deep cut in his forehead, blood was running down Reg's face, and all the crew had bruises.

The crew sat on the grass or stood, stretched their legs, and chatted, while awaiting the bus to drive them to debriefing. They had just completed their shortest op. but so much had happened that they were as exhausted as if they had just finished a much longer one. The gunners, especially, had tired, aching limbs. But they were all relieved to be back, although shivering with cold, after an extremely draughty return journey.

A WAAF-driven bus arrived to take the crew to debriefing but first she diverted to the sick bay so that all the minor cuts and bruises could be inspected and treated. Sam's injured head was the worst injury. Once the blood was cleaned from Reg's face, only a minor cut was revealed, and none of the other crew members had any injury that required more than a plaster.

The Intelligence Officer at the debriefing was very interested in the extent of the damage to the bunker that they were able to report. Their visual evidence was especially valuable because the photograph taken shortly after the bomb dropped was merely a picture of the huge cloud of dust which billowed out shortly after the explosion.

'I had an excellent view when the bomb landed,' Freddie said. 'I can tell you that it landed squarely on the bunker and I believe it destroyed a part of it.'

'Yes, and from my rear-gunner position I had a pretty good view,' Sam added. 'I saw the bomb falling. I hadn't realised before how enormous it was. And then it struck the bunker and there was the biggest explosion I've ever seen. After that there was such a massive cloud of dust and debris that it was impossible to see very much.'

'Good,' the IO commented. 'Our reconnaissance aircraft will probably fly over the area tomorrow, when the dust has settled, to take photographs of the scene and that will provide detailed information about the scope of the damage and the success of your operation. It seems to have gone very well.'

Later, the crew were very happy to learn that P-Peter's damage was repairable. Damaged sections of the fuselage were replaced and a new inner port engine fitted.

***

***

After a much longer sleep than usual, the crew had made their way to *The Pig and Whistle*. They had been sitting in the Saloon Bar for about half an hour, sipping their beers and chatting.

'This is a great way to relax,' Scotty said, stretching his limbs and settling deeper into the plush armchair. 'I still wonder why we don't see more members of our squadron here?'

'Especially since this is where the WAAFs go,' Reg said. 'Perhaps they come here because we're here.'

'Wishful thinking,' Sam commented, and they all laughed.

As if on cue, some WAAFs entered the bar. Sam immediately noticed that Jenny was among them.

'Jenny's here with her friends,' he said. 'I think I'll go over and have a word with her.'

'But we don't want to lose you, Sam,' Reg said, and added, with a grin, 'let's all go and ask if we can join them. I expect we know most of them anyway. Maybe, I'll be able to find a girl friend. I'm a bit envious of you, Sam.'

'I'm not surprised,' Sam said, with a grin, 'especially as I've got the best-looking one!'

'But let's do as Reg suggests,' John said. 'Of course, they may not want us to join them, but I rather think they will.'

He was right. The WAAFs welcomed the airmen with smiles, and were very happy to chat. The conversation gradually increased in volume, and there was much hilarity, as a warm, party atmosphere developed among the group, most of whom had seen the others around the station.

At one point, however, Jack thought he detected some flagging of the conversation, and he decided to introduce something new. Quite unobtrusively, he settled himself at the piano and before anyone really noticed him, began to play *Chopin's Revolutionary Study*. The effect was dramatic. Almost immediately there was silence and his audience listened spellbound as Jack's fingers sped over the scalic passages that characterise the music, one of the most inspiring, exciting and uplifting pieces ever written. To his fellow airmen it was as if Jack was expressing all the emotions that engulfed them on every bombing operation.

As the music was concluded, there was a hush, followed by loud and enthusiastic applause. Jack stood up and acknowledged the ovation, which was accompanied by calls for more pieces to be played. He had, of course, anticipated that. Nothing, he thought, expressed the crew's experiences better than *The Revolutionary Study*, but he would play one other piece, also by Chopin. It, too, would be fast and furious in part, but it would have its slow and reflective section, and that, too, could be related to their situation as an RAF bomber crew.

He played *Fantasie Impromptu*. The reflective part is in the middle, and the piece ends, as it begins, with an *allegro*.

Again, there was loud applause, and before that ended, Jack produced his next surprise. He began to play and sing *The White Cliffs of Dover,* and almost from the first note, his audience joined in by singing the words. At the end, there were calls for more, and this time Jack obliged in full measure - choosing only wartime songs - with

Don't Sit Under the Apple Tree, often played by Glenn Miller and his Orchestra.

Comin' In on a Wing and a Prayer, which Jack thought was entirely appropriate to their return from bombing operations!

In the Mood. Another piece played by Glenn Miller.

A Nightingale Sang in Berkeley Square.

Take the World Exactly as You Find It.

The sing-song ended with,

We'll Meet Again. Everyone knew all the words to that.

There was more clapping as everyone prepared to leave. On the way out, Sam and Jennie noticed that Reg, too, was accompanying a WAAF, whom he introduced as 'My friend Sarah.'

***

John's crew had now completed ten operations. Senior staff had noted that each one had been successfully carried out in spite of the many dangers and difficulties they had faced. With their Lancaster often seriously damaged and malfunctioning on the way, they had always pressed on to the target regardless. Many crews in similar situations might, quite reasonably, have aborted an operation and returned to base.

The success of the gunners in destroying, or seriously damaging, enemy aircraft had also been recognised, as had also the outstanding activities of the Wireless Op., particularly when Jack had dived into the icy North Sea to free the dinghy, which had somehow been caught up under the doomed Lancaster. Without his efforts all the crew might have drowned. Later, when the crew had spent many hours waiting to be rescued, and their morale was low, he kept up their spirits by starting a sing-song.

Sam, Scotty and Jack were all awarded the Distinguished Flying Medal (DFM) and John was awarded the Distinguished Flying Cross (DFC) for his outstanding leadership. All the Sergeants had by this time been promoted to Flight Sergeants and John had become a Pilot Officer, and joined Terry in the Officers' Mess.

The division of the crew between an Officer and Flight Sergeants made no difference whatever to the relationships and camaraderie in the crew. Had the pilot been a Sergeant and some of his crew Officers, he would remain captain of the aircraft and the acknowledged leader.

While all the crew were delighted with these awards, Scotty put forward a view that they all shared to a degree.

'I'm very pleased about the DFMs and so is Sam; and Jack deserves it as much as anyone. But what we've achieved as a crew has been the result of all of us working together as a team. As a crew we have lashings of good old 'esprit de corps.' I think we should all be treated the same - have the same awards.'

'I agree,' John said, 'that it all comes down to team work, but the senior staff who make these decisions have to take into account specific actions. Sam and you have brought down or damaged many more aircraft than any other crew that I know about, while Jack risked his life to save us all by jumping into the North Sea and freeing the dinghy.

Reg has been wonderfully successful in navigating us to various targets and then guiding us back, while Freddie has had great success as a bomb-aimer. I would expect their work will be acknowledged another time. And aren't we lucky to have Terry as Flight Engineer, carrying on the good work of Arthur.

By the way, these awards have come early, and that's because we've had a particularly tough time with both ack-ack fire and fighter bombers, and because we've been one of the most consistent crews in successfully carrying out each operation. Well done, all of you.'

CHAPTER 26

April 15th, 1945   Flight Sgt. Jack Rogers,

                             RAF Coningsby

Dear Maurice,

Greetings! I read your views about food rationing with a lot of sympathy. I don't blame you for a good old grumble. My special moan when I was at home was about the weekly rations of 2 ounces of butter, 2 ounces of cheese and 4 ounces of bacon or ham. Cheer up! Rationing won't last for ever. Of the food that's left after the U-Boats have sunk many of our merchant ships, the lion's share now goes to us in the Armed Services, I'm afraid.

World War One was called the War to end all wars, and nineteen years later we had another one. Now, I see that delegates from 45 countries will meet in San Francisco to plan a United Nations that will try to prevent another war. I hope it proves more effective than the old League of Nations.

BATTLE ORDERS

During a recent daylight raid, when our Lancaster was attacked by fighters an engine was destroyed and a propeller bent, but there were no casualties. John was marvellous, as usual, and brought us back safely, but then the undercarriage budged, so we had to crash land. There was a piercing, screeching sound of metal on tarmac as our plane touched down at 100 mph. But though shaken up, we were all OK.

We still go to our local pub, The Pig and Whistle, in the evening when we can. We unwind there and try to forget about the horrors of war. We're lucky to have such a cosy, comfortable pub so near to Coningsby.

By the way, you mustn't worry about not being in the Armed Services. You are a scientist, and in a 'reserved occupation.' You're just as essential to the War effort as any sailor, soldier or airman.

Write soon. Your very good friend,

Jack

'What's it all mean?' Sam asked. 'We're on 'Battle Orders' for today, but there's something different about it.'

'Yes,' John replied, 'we're certainly going to fly an op today, but it's clearly something special. I don't know what it is. I'm intrigued.'

John was right. It was something special. Instead of carrying and dropping bombs they were going to carry and drop food to people who were in great need. A genuinely humanitarian operation.

They were going to take part in *OPERATION MANNA*. The name related to the food miraculously provided to the Israelites in the book of Exodus.

It was April, 1945. The European war against Germany was coming to an end but for the people in the north of Holland there was a serious crisis. This was a part of the country that had not yet been liberated. Thousands of its population of three million had already died of starvation while thousands of others were in serious danger of suffering the same fate.

There was no doubt about the urgent need for help. Prince Bernhard had appealed to General Eisenhower and then to both Winston Churchill and President Roosevelt. Both British and American Governments were fully cooperative, and after arranging with the German authorities that participating aircraft would not be fired on, provided they flew within specified corridors, the RAF and the USA Air Force were instructed to draw up plans.

Apart from the British and American participation in this humanitarian food drop, Canadian, New Zealand and Polish squadrons would be involved with the RAF.

At the briefing, the Station Commander at RAF Coningsby emphasized several key points for the crews to bear in mind.

'This, chaps, is something very different. Instead of flying at around 20,000 feet and dropping bombs from that height, you will fly as low as 300 to 400 feet once you are over Holland. That's because, the food you will be dropping is not in boxes, or otherwise protected. It won't be dangling from parachutes, either. It will be in sacks in specially made panniers in your bomb bays - 70 sacks in each pannier

'You will need to carry out this task with the greatest care to ensure that the food is dropped in precisely the right spots and at recommended low heights. The Dutch people will know where and when the food should be dropped. Some of them are in danger of starving so they need food supplies urgently. Over 6,000 tons will be provided altogether. You'll all be flying grocers.'

There was a ripple of amusement among the crews. The C.O. continued,

'The food will include tinned and dried food, chocolate, spam, dried eggs, flour, yeast, milk powder, cheese and dehydrated meat. It is thought that if you fly as low as we have said, then the food should not be spoiled or damaged.

'The sites earmarked for dropping the food will each be well marked with a large cross. There are several sites, so that the food will be well distributed. Make sure that your aircraft drops its food in the place allocated for your drop.

'Some of you will drop over the Duindig race course in The Hague; some over the Volkenburg airfield; others over Ypenburg airfield; or Rotterdam's Waalhaven airfield or to Kralingse Plas, which is also in Rotterdam; some will drop over Gouda.' He grinned. 'I can't guarantee, by the way, that I'm pronouncing all these Dutch places correctly.'

That drew a laugh from his audience, not one of whom had any idea how the language should be spoken.

'Your Lancasters will be completely unarmed so no ammunition will be taken for the guns.' With those words, except for his final 'Good luck, chaps,' the Station Commander ended his briefing.

The section leaders, as usual, added their own words of instruction or guidance. It was going to be a very different operation, but fundamentals such as flying conditions and potential low-flying problems had to be discussed.

As they left, John's crew were bubbling with enthusiasm for the venture, and also had a question or two.

'What a great idea!' Scotty said. 'We'll be taking part in a wonderful, humanitarian act.'

'And apart from the British, they'll be Australian, Canadian, New Zealand and Polish squadrons of the RAF taking part,' Terry added.

'The Americans have their own operation dropping food over Holland, ' John said. 'I expect they'll be using Flying Fortresses.'

'And what a change from our usual op,' Sam observed. 'We won't have to worry about fighters or ack-ack. Instead of getting sore eyes peering into the darkness to try to spot a Jerry fighter, we'll actually be able to relax.'

'That's right,' Scotty agreed, 'and it sounds as if we'll be sent back several times because Bomber Command is committed to deliver over 6,000 tons of food. I think you and I, Sam, will really enjoy this op.'

'It sounds fine,' Sam said. 'but what has happened to cause the problem? Why are so many people in this part of Holland on the verge of starvation?'

'I'm not sure.' John answered. 'Last year the RAF bombed the dykes on the island of Walcheren which were breached. Evidently the free Dutch approved the bombing because the island was German-occupied and it controlled the approach to Antwerp. It caused hardship among people living on the island, especially the farmers. It would have ruined their crops. '

'But John... Antwerp is in the south of Holland and we're going to help people in the north,' Reg pointed out.

'That's right,' John responded. 'I just wondered if that dam breaching had a serious effect on total Dutch food supplies.'

'I don't think so,' Terry began, 'because it's only in the north of Holland that there's a food crisis. The Germans are retreating and have an urgent need to bring in more troops and arms, so they need the railways. But Dutch transport workers have refused to co-operate with them and have been on strike so Germany punished the population by holding back food supplies.'

'I'm not too worried about how the situation has come about,' Jack said. 'The important thing is, we're going to help these hungry people in the best possible way. I'm very pleased we're involved.'

'So are we all,' Freddie smiled.

'We're doing it before the war has ended, which makes it really remarkable,' Jack pointed out. 'The Allies and the Germans have been negotiating the details of this op, and obviously they have put their skates on and reached an agreement quickly.'

'That's right,' Terry said. 'Now the war is coming to an end, the power of the Nazis is waning and some sensible senior officers are free to make decisions like this one.'

'Yes. I can't imagine Hitler approving a scheme of this kind,' John said.

'There's just one point I'm not really confident about,' Sam said. 'We're not going to carry any ammo., and the war isn't over yet. The

Germans have said that they won't fire at our aircraft if we keep within agreed channels, but I wonder if that will work. I mean, will all the gunners and pilots obey? If they don't, we're in trouble.'

'Yes. I'm a bit doubtful about that, too,' Scotty said. 'Even if the Germans have agreed to leave us alone, we could be fired on by gunners that haven't got the message or want to take a pot shot at us, anyway.'

'I think we'll have to take that chance,' John replied. 'I think it's very likely that the Germans will keep to the truce. They've already punished the Dutch, but probably don't want an even bigger tragedy than they've got already.'

***

Preparations for Operation Manna were similar to those for a normal operation. P-Peter had to be tested in the usual way, but Sam and Scotty, having no activity to carry out with their guns or ammunition, could relax, while Freddie examined all the food sacks in the bomb bay. Releasing them from a very low height would be entirely different from dropping bombs with the aid of a bomb sight. For him, it posed a new challenge.

'No amphetamine tablets needed this time,' chortled Scotty, to no-one in particular.

'No, I'm sure you'll be on full alert throughout this op without them,' John grinned.

John, Terry, and Jack worked as usual to try to ensure that their Lancaster was fully prepared for the flight and that it would be as trouble-free as possible, while Reg prepared his Flight Plan as for a normal operation.

BATTLE ORDERS

P-Peter left RAF Coningsby with hundreds of other Lancasters. The weather was excellent, with a clear blue sky. They flew over the North Sea and chatted in a much more relaxed manner than they did usually on an op.

'I hope the sacks don't fall on anyone's head,' Scotty said, not too seriously.

'I'm sure Freddie will make sure of that, and place them in a clear space in the middle of the crowd,' Reg joked. 'You know how accurately he can drop bombs.'

Scotty wondered whether they would find a large crowd at the dropping point.

'I bet we will,' Terry said. 'Some of the Dutch are starving and they know where we're going to drop the food. Believe me, they'll be there in huge numbers - men, women and children.'

'I reckon you're right,' Jack agreed. 'I think we're going to have quite a reception!'

'I think so, too,' John said. 'My one concern is they'll be many aircraft flying over a small area at a much lower height than usual. We'll all be looking down to see what happens when we drop the food, but we must keep a sharp eye on all the other Lancasters clustered around. A collision over, say, the racecourse at The Hague crowded with men, women and children would be ghastly. So, Sam, Freddy and Scotty, please keep your eyes skinned!'

' Yes, Skip,' Scotty assured him. ' We'll all do that.'

The crew had to trust that the Germans would not fire on them, and that was in their minds as they crossed the Dutch border at a much lower altitude than usual. Flying over enemy-held territory with no defence whatsoever gave them an uneasy feeling.

In general, they were left alone. They were not confronted by German fighters, but a few isolated anti-aircraft guns opened up here and there. It was only random fire and didn't trouble the crew, though they wondered whether there would be more intense gunfire as they got nearer to the dropping zone.

'I think we may be OK,' John assured his crew. I'm going to go down lower than I've ever been before and that will surely confuse any would-be gunners.'

John's crew had been told to drop their food on the racecourse in The Hague, and Reg saw to it that P-Peter approached it without a hitch.

Most of the crew now looked down as they flew over it, and wondered,

What kind of reception would they have?

CHAPTER 27

Freddie shouted with excitement.

'Look. There are people everywhere. They're waving - Dutch flags or Union Jacks...they look really excited as if they're very pleased to see us.'

'I'm sure they are,' John said. ' We're helping to save their lives and I'm sure they'll be very grateful.' He checked the aircraft's altitude and spoke again.

'We're still much too high. I'm going to fly a circuit round the racecourse and lose height. That'll give you all a chance to see the people. It's an amazing sight. There are thousands of men, women and children. They're so excited. I'm really pleased we're doing this.'

'So are we all,' Scotty said, and there were murmurs of agreement from other crew members.'

'Look,' Sam shouted! 'There are messages laid out in tulips in a field near the racecourse. 'I can read one which says *THANK YOU BOYS.'*

'I can see another message in tulips which says, *WELL DONE RAF,*' said Scotty, 'and now we're getting lower you can almost see the expressions on people's faces. Look, there's a large group just below us, looking up and waving madly. There are people of all ages. Many of them look like families.'

'There are supposed to be German soldiers here, though I can't see any,' John said. 'They should ensure that the food is distributed in an orderly way. Perhaps, now the war's coming to an end some of them are getting rather 'bolshie.'

'Freddie,' he continued, 'we can release the food at any time. No, hold it! We 're now flying at 400 feet but I'll go even lower because at this height those bags are going to burst open and scatter the food too much, and perhaps spoil some of it... Yes, I'm going down to about 200 feet, but not for long, Freddie, so I leave it to you to release the food when we're at our lowest altitude. I don't want to find that we're heading straight for a skyscraper or some other tall building.'

'Understood, Skip,' Freddie replied.

John went lower, and the excitement on the faces of people below was a very moving sight for all the crew, most of whom were looking out of the aircraft's windows and waving back. Freddie released the sacks of food and they watched it fall to the ground.

It didn't happen exactly as planned because a few of the bags burst open on impact, and the crowd rushed forward to pick up as much food as possible. There was quite a scramble for it, though no fighting. Most of the people walked off carrying cans or packets of food, but a few began eating as soon as they laid their hands on the food. Everywhere there were people cheering and waving.

'It's a bit chaotic down there,' Freddie commented.

'It is,' John agreed, 'but at least we've delivered the food, and the Dutch have received it. There is, of course the possibility that some of the really hungry ones will eat too much too soon, and that won't do them any good at all.'

'Yes, I've just seen someone wolfing down the food, but I'm sure that most of them will just have a good meal at home,' Jack said.

'Did you see that?' Sam shouted excitedly. 'There was a very old man who tried several times to bend down to pick up a sack. He just couldn't get down, but he was very determined and kept on trying. And then, when he'd almost succeeded, he fell over, flat on his face. A woman with two young children, standing nearby, then picked up the sack and handed it to him.'

'I'm sure that most of them will be helping one another like that,' Reg said.

'Yes,' Sam agreed. 'One very able-bodied man has just picked up a number of sacks and is giving them to a group of elderly people on the fringe of the crowd, and furthest away from the drop. It's great to see the way they are helping one another.'

Unlike his carefree crew-mates, John was beginning to feel uncharacteristically edgy. He was very conscious of the potential dangers in an area in which there were several aircraft flying fairly low. The danger of a collision was obvious.

'We must turn back, now,' he said. 'I'll keep fairly low over Holland and climb to about 10,000 feet after we've crossed the coast.'

'Do you think we'll have another sortie today?' Scotty asked.

'I don't know,' John answered. ' We'll certainly have a rest when we get back, and another sortie today is possible. And we may also find ourselves back again tomorrow. I hope so.'

'So do I. It's been very moving,' Jack said. 'I'll never forget this day.'

Before they reached the coast, a few anti-aircraft guns, as before, produced some desultory fire. Perhaps their crews had not received the message; or they were just defying orders. The gunfire was, in any case, ineffectual and did not worry the battle-hardened crew.

***

'Today was unforgettable,' Freddie said.

Scotty agreed. 'I couldn't see as much as some of you from my position, but it was wonderful to drop so much food to starving people and it's extraordinary that this has happened before the war has ended.'

All the crew were in their usual corner in *The Pig and Whistle,* and sipping their beers.

'The Dutch were really pleased to see us,' Freddie said. 'I had a perfect view of the scene below. There was so much cheering and waving. They were really excited.'

'It was all heart-warming stuff,' John said.

'It was just a pity, though, that it was a bit of a scramble, ' Reg thought. 'The Germans were supposed to see that the food was distributed in an orderly way, to make sure it was distributed fairly.'

John agreed. 'Ideally that would have been the best way, but I expect most of the people got a good share. Also, there are going to be further drops so if anyone missed out, they'll get some food another time.'

'It was also great to be involved in an operation where our lives were not threatened by either ack-ack guns or night fighters,' Scotty said.

'Yes,' Terry agreed, 'it was almost relaxing - rather different from flying to the Ruhr valley!'

'I think we're lucky to have been involved in *Operation Manna*,' Sam said. It was wonderful. I hope we'll be back tomorrow.'

In fact, they did not have the opportunity to return. Some Lancasters did repeat the operation, but with Allied armies advancing well into Germany, Britain had control of the air, and there were plenty of aircraft and crews available. RAF losses were now comparatively low.

It had been the long-awaited 'easy op.' But the next operation for John's crew would bring them face to face with a life-threatening danger they had never previously experienced.

CHAPTER 28

Flt. Sgt. Jack Rogers, DFM.

RAF Coningsby

April 19th, 1945

Dear Maurice,

I 'm very sad and sorry to hear about your bomb damage from a V2 Rocket. You are very unlucky to suffer damage to your home at this stage of the war.

Thank goodness that at least the 'doodlebug' menace is over. Our Army has captured almost all of the launching pad sites in Northern France, but some of the V2 rockets are launched from Holland, which has not yet been fully liberated. There's no defence against them. They travel high, at over 3,000 mph and can travel about 200 miles. But Allied armies will soon capture the sites.

Anyway, I'm relieved that your house didn't have a direct hit, that you and your family are OK, and that the house can be repaired. But you are still living there. Have emergency repairs been carried out?

Our crew has just had a wonderful experience. We, and hundreds of other RAF crews, dropped food over Northern Holland, where many thousands of people are starving. You've probably seen it on the News.

I'm amazed it could happen before the war has ended. The Germans apparently allowed us to fly on this mercy mission provided we flew in a given air corridor. I'm sure Hitler wouldn't have agreed to it, but I suspect that his generals are now making many of the top decisions.

The Dutch people welcomed us in their thousands – cheering, waving flags, sending messages in tulips set out in the fields, etc, and how glad they were to get the food! We flew very low so we could look down and see it all. It was heart-warming. We'd love to do it all again.

By the way, Sam, Scotty and I have been awarded the Distinguished Flying Medal (DFM) and we've all been promoted to Flight Sergeant, except John, who is now a Pilot Officer, and has been awarded the Distinguished Flying Cross (DFC). But we'll just carry on working together as always.

I look forward to receiving your next letter,

Your good friend,

Jack

A ll the crew met for coffee in the NAAFI.

'Sam, have you any more news of Bill Irons?' John asked.

'I have. In fact, I've just received a second letter from him.'

'Then spill the beans,' Scotty said, with a grin. 'We're all agog!'

Sam looked around. All his fellow crew-members were clearly anxious to hear news about his friend.

'Well, the chaos around POW camps seems to have continued… As the Allies advance, the Germans seem determined to prevent their prisoners being rescued. You'll remember that Bill was in Heydekrug, in East Prussia. He was then transported, sometimes in dirty cattle trucks, or in the filthy hold of a ship, but also, after a long march, without much food or water, to Stalag Luft IV, at Grossetychow, but airmen weren't there very long before continuing the march. They sometimes had to sleep in the open. *Sam was finding it hard to hold back his tears.* They crossed the river Elbe and slept in a barn. The barn was bombed. Some POWs were killed; Bill was wounded by a small shell splinter in his back. He was treated for that at a POW camp near Schwerin, where I suppose he is now, though with all the confusion of army advances, refugee movements and some deserters moving around it's difficult to know what will happen next.'

'It sounds as if the Germans just don't know what to do with their prisoners now,' John said. 'Their armies are retreating on every front and they are demoralised.'

'That's about it,' Scotty agreed.

'I'm glad you've had another letter, Sam,' John continued. 'At least you now know that Bill is surviving amidst the chaos, and you can be sure that it won't be long before British, American and Russian armies meet and all the POWs will be freed.'

'Yes,' Sam said. 'And I must hope that day will soon come, but I'm just a bit concerned, John, about Bill surviving in such a confused situation. Demoralised soldiers, including some German deserters will be carrying their guns and some Russian soldiers might want to settle scores with them, especially if members of their families were killed during the German advance.

'I understand that, Sam, but Bill is alive -which is great. I expect he'll soon be rescued and we'll get more news about him quite soon. Meanwhile we're on 'Battle Orders' for tonight's op.

***

'Skip, skip, are you alright?' Terry was almost shouting. 'Skip! Skip! Becoming increasingly desperate, he began to tug the lapels of John's flying jacket. 'Skip, wake up!'

John's complexion was pale, his lips and nails were blue, and he looked, thought Terry, like a drug addict who has recently overdosed. His eyes were still half open, and the aircraft was flying normally, but his expression showed that he was by no means his normally alert self.

'Anything the matter, Terry?' he said, his words slurred and indistinct. He turned his head slowly towards his flight engineer.

'Afraid so, Skip,' Terry replied, relieved at having got a response. 'Look at your fingers; your nails are blue. Your lips are turning blue as well. We're not getting any oxygen. The supply must have been cut off when we were hit by the ack-ack. We 're all getting sleepy. Some of the crew may already be unconscious. You must get the kite down. Now. It's urgent!'

It was a few moments before his message began to sink in. Terry was becoming increasingly concerned. Then John replied, still slurring his words.

'OK, Terry. Thanks. I'll get us down to below ten thousand feet. We'll be OK then.'

He then turned to peer sleepily at Terry.

'My God. I can see that you 're affected, too. Blue lips and blue finger nails. Can't we restore the oxygen supply?'

'Afraid not. I think the line's broken.'

They still hadn't yet even begun to descend, and every minute counted. Terry was becoming increasingly worried. John's response hardly matched the gravity of their situation. He spoke again, a new sense of urgency in his raised voice.

'Skip, you need to get a move on. Get the kite down before we're all unconscious or dead!'

John turned his head towards Terry, patted him reassuringly on the back and answered,

'OK, Terry, I've got the message,' but to Terry he still looked and sounded complacent and relaxed.

In fact, John was now doing his best to concentrate as he fully realised the imminent danger to all his crew. He pushed the control column forward, and the Lancaster dipped its nose and began to descend. Terry hoped it was not too late.

When people don't have enough oxygen, they are often unaware that anything is wrong. The effect is similar to that of mild intoxication. John and his crew were feeling very relaxed and pleasantly drowsy while the dangers were increasing. They could no longer see properly and the loud Rolls Royce engines could hardly be heard. While their lips and finger nails turned blue, their breathing was becoming laboured and their hearts were beating rapidly. They were becoming less able to think clearly and to co-ordinate effectively.

That no crew member could do his work effectively was dangerous enough; but the danger was much greater than that. Without an oxygen supply, at an altitude of 20,000 feet, their sleepy condition would soon lead to unconsciousness, and, shortly afterwards, death.

The Lancaster was now descending rapidly, and Terry remained by John's side. John then had a further thought, which he expressed in the same slow, slurred speech as before.

'We've got some bottled oxygen in the aircraft, haven't we Terry? Would you check the state of the other crew members. If it's necessary, give them some of that? And poor old Sam has that nasty leg injury, so see how he is getting on.'

'I'll do that right away,' Terry replied. He was immensely relieved to see that John was slowly recovering, and beginning to act like his normal self, in spite of his slurred speech. His skipper grinned.

'And thanks, Terry, for waking me up to the danger. You seem to have managed to stay more alert than I was.'

'Well, lack of oxygen does affect people differently, but I'm sure I'd have been sleepy pretty soon.'

Most of the crew were not affected much more than Terry, but both Jack and Scotty were almost unconscious and in urgent need of oxygen. Scotty, in particular, was slumped in his sling in the mid-upper turret, and would obviously have been of no use had an enemy fighter appeared. Sam had been given morphine and his leg injury was not now troubling him as much as before. He had become a little sleepy but Terry found him cheerful and more alert than most of the crew.

Both Jack and Scotty began to recover soon after the bottled supply of oxygen was brought to them.

'Thanks, Terry,' Scotty said. 'I was out for the count. Without that oxygen it would have been curtains for me. And my God- Jerry might have attacked us while we were nodding off!'

Jack was still finding it difficult to think clearly, but after a while, he was as sharp as usual.

Meanwhile, John had brought the Lancaster down to 9,500 feet, and everyone soon recovered completely, although one or two still had a slight headache.

John now spoke to all the crew.

'I hope you're all feeling better now. I'll keep the kite at this altitude so we'll have enough oxygen. Had we remained at 20,000 feet we might all have had our chips by now. The bottled oxygen was a life-saver, and thank God Terry alerted me to what was happening. Like some of you, I was nearly out cold! You've just saved the lives of all of us, Terry. I can't thank you enough.'

'I was just lucky,' Terry responded. 'The lack of oxygen hadn't got to me too much. I noticed that you appeared to be dozing. Then I saw your blue lips and I realised what was happening. Somehow you managed to get back to piloting without taking anything from the bottle of oxygen.'

'Well, I thought some of the others might be in a worse state than I was. I was right, wasn't I? '

Terry laughed. 'Yes, you were, Skip, but you're the bloke whose driving us home so you've got to be looked after all the way!'

***

The crew had been on a daylight operation over Frankfurt, with the support, for part of the way, of Spitfires. The operation was in support of the Allied armies advancing northwards and eastwards.

The Normandy landings had taken place from June 8th. to the 25th., 1944, and by September most of France, Belgium, Luxembourg and Holland had been liberated. Allied forces were soon pressing towards Nancy, Metz, Trier, Aachen, Maastricht and Antwerp.

But the front was fluid. While the Allied armies were advancing, the Germans often fought back desperately.

Following the capture of a number of French airfields, Hurricanes and Spitfires had been based there, and so were able to both give some support to Allied armies and also escort RAF bombers. Command of the air was seen as essential.

BATTLE ORDERS

Bomber Command had also set up radar transmission stations in occupied France, so that Gee and H2S radar could be used deeper into Germany. That made possible more accurate navigation, and therefore more accurate bombing.

Today's target for John's crew had been the central railway system of Frankfurt, Germany's fifth biggest city.

The crew had been glad to have the Spitfire escort for at least some of the time, and, as they approached the target, John had wondered whether, at last, they were going to have a reasonably easy operation, though his instinct had told him that easy operations almost never happened, at least for his crew.

The accompanying Spitfires were soon engaged in dogfights with German aircraft, so they had to abandon their escort role temporarily. As P-Peter roared on towards its target in broad daylight, its escort was nowhere to be seen. The crew felt very vulnerable.

Near the city, P-Peter was subjected to barrage after barrage of fierce anti-aircraft fire, so John had to work hard to make the Lancaster as difficult a target as possible. The crew were naturally apprehensive, but because it was a daytime raid it did not seem to any of them to be quite as frightening as a typical night time operation, with all its horrors illuminated in the blackness of the night: exploding ack-ack shells, aircraft on fire, and lines of tracer bullets or canon fire.

However, two shells which had exploded just outside Sam's turret had given him a scare.

'Whew!' he cried out. 'That was a very near miss!'

'OK, Sam,' John said, 'the gunners seem to be well trained on us. I'll try to move about a bit more.'

The shells continued to explode very close to their fuselage, and shrapnel clanged against it on all sides. Terry became concerned that some of the shells must have seriously damaged P-Peter in some way. He had no means of knowing that the oxygen system had been damaged.

As they ploughed through the dense mass of exploding shells, it had seemed to Scotty that it was only a matter of time before they would be hit.

'It seems they're all aiming at us'. With his head above the roof of the aircraft, and seeing shells exploding in all directions around him, he felt particularly vulnerable. So did Sam, who felt more isolated than ever in the rear of the aircraft.

'This is not the easy op I'd hoped for,' he reflected. *'And no wonder they all seem to be having a go at us because I can't see any other Lancs at the moment.'*

Another shell exploded very close to his turret, rocking the Lancaster violently, and this time some pieces of shrapnel crashed through the turret's perspex. One piece penetrated Sam's left flying boot and became embedded in his leg. He screamed with pain.

'Skip, rear gunner here. God, it hurts. A piece of shrapnel has cut into my leg. The pain's awful and it's bleeding!'

Immediately, John asked Terry to go to Sam, to give him first aid, and morphine, if needed, and then take him to the sick bed. He then spoke to the injured rear gunner.

'OK, Sam, help is on the way. We'll do all we can.'

Terry tended to Sam's injuries, gave him some morphine and stemmed the flow of blood as much as he could. The embedded piece of shrapnel would not be removed until Sam was treated in the sick bay at Coningsby. Meanwhile, they had to fly on to their target and get the job done without their vitally important rear gunner.

CHAPTER 29

Their target was only a few miles away, and several Lancasters could now be seen nearby, also heading towards it.

Scotty, swivelling round as usual, saw a Lancaster just behind them receive a direct hit under its bomb bay, and the aircraft seem to disappear in a huge cloud of dust and debris. None of its crew would have known anything about it. He had seen similar scenes before, but this time the tears rolled down his cheeks uncontrollably. It was, for him inexpressibly sad. He dabbed his cheeks with a handkerchief.

Freddie, looking for signs that they were approaching the target, could not help observing the overall scene. Though every bombing operation was different in terms of visibility, the number of aircraft, the intensity of the anti-aircraft fire, etc, there were always familiar features: explosions in every direction: aircraft climbing, diving and turning as they sought to escape destruction and here and there a few floating parachutes.

Those airmen, swinging from side to side erratically, through the chaos, were especially in Freddie's thoughts. They had somehow managed to bail out of aircraft that may have been on fire, or were fatally damaged. He was anxious that they would reach the earth safely, after floating through a scene of such chaos and destruction. Then, he thought, they might succeed in reaching the liberated areas of France.

Freddie then took his eyes off the surrounding battle-scene, and focused them strictly ahead. A few minutes later, he saw the target a few miles away.

'Bomb aimer to Skip. I can see the central railway system clearly,' he announced, excitedly. 'There are a number of lines quite close together, and I can place our bombs in the middle of them. The station buildings, platforms and signals are also nearby.'

'That's fine, Freddie,' John responded, 'and well done, Reg, for some great navigation, once again.'

Freddie's bombsight, set with the latest wind velocity, provided by Jack, was now made ready, with all the settings complete and he requested John to open the bomb doors.

However, before that could be carried out, several anti-aircraft shells exploded so close to the aircraft that slivers of shrapnel penetrated the fuselage in several places. John immediately spoke through the intercom, in a louder voice than usual as there was some noisy interference, and he was very concerned

'Skip here to all crew. Sam's now as comfortable as we can make him. Is everyone else OK?'

Five of the crew responded that they were OK, though Jack reported that a large splinter of shrapnel had penetrated the fuselage just above his head. John continued -

'We've had a real battering. I'm going to carry on towards the target. The bomb doors are open, Freddie; over to you.'

Freddie lost no time in beginning his guidance as the target was now very near.

'Left a little, Skip... A little more...Steady... Still a little more to the left...That' s it...Steady...Steady...Bombs gone. Hold the course, Skip, and keep it steady for the photo…OK, that's done.'

'Skip to navigator. I want to fly to the nearest area known to be liberated. It might be more peaceful than around here. Can you give me a course for that?'

'Navigator here, Skip. 190 degrees.'

'Thanks, Reg. Our Spitfire escort should meet us soon after we cross the German border, and then perhaps we'll enjoy a spell of flying with less danger from fighters or ack-ack.'

'Skip, you're an optimist!' Terry said. 'We're still over enemy territory and unescorted, and poor old Sam is on the sick bed.'

'Yes, I *am* an optimist,' John replied. 'I have to be.'

'Mid-upper gunner here, Skip. I'm quite close to Jack, and I can tell you that one splinter of shrapnel nearly parted his hair. Another six inches lower, and he would have been decapitated.'

'Thanks, Scotty. You know what Jack's like. He never says much about his own narrow escapes.'

Terry had been speculating about the potential damage caused by the shelling.

'Skip, I'm wondering whether the hydraulics have been damaged or perhaps something else,' he said. 'We'll soon find out.'

But they didn't for a while. The severed oxygen line had stopped the flow into their oxygen masks. They had not been flying very long, following the bombing, and were still over Germany when the oxygen deficiency began to affect them. But in the very relaxed state that caused, they were completely unaware that anything was wrong. For a time, the crew were anything but alert and their Lancaster could have been attacked without risk to the fighter pilots.

Now, flying at 9,500 feet, the awful prospect of dying through lack of oxygen was behind them, and all the crew were fully recovered.

Though Sam's injury meant there was no defence from rear attacks, most of the crew felt unusually relaxed and happy. Their Lancaster would soon be flying over a liberated part of France, and then they would be flying home steadily, powered by all four engines, and not two or three as on some earlier operations. Soon they expected to have their Spitfire escorts once again.

They were a little too relaxed, as events proved.

***

P-Peter had not flown very far from the German/French border when two Messerschmitt 109 fighters swooped down on the starboard side. The crew were taken by surprise. Though over most of the liberated part of France, Allied air forces dominated the skies, near the German/French border the Luftwaffe was very active, as the Spitfires had discovered.

Scotty saw the enemy aircraft first.

'Two Messerschmitts 109s to starboard, diving towards us, at three hundred yards. '

John put P-Peter into a steep dive, turning it to begin a corkscrew, while Scotty waited for an opportunity to fire back. He was very aware that with Sam on the sick bed, their defence was his responsibility, though Freddie would be helping in the forward turret.

During the dive, Jack was concerned about the safety of Sam, so he stayed with him, bending over him and keeping him firmly in position during violent movements.

Scotty happened to have his guns turned towards the port side when one Messerschmitt flashed past, and he fired a short burst. From that moment the enemy aircraft, though largely undamaged, seemed to meander aimlessly across the sky. The pilot was dead. The Messerschmitt would not stay airborne for long.

Freddie, Terry and John had seen it happen and cheered loudly. 'Great shooting, Scotty,' John said.

The other Messerschmitt was now some distance away, and seemed about to make another attack. Then it suddenly turned towards the German border and flew away. It was Freddie, looking out from his forward canopy, who saw the reason for the change of plan.

'Skip, bomb aimer here. Our Spitfire escort is back!'

'That's great. Better late than never!' John said.

Both Spitfires were a little late because they had been involved in other bouts of combat with enemy aircraft. Dogfights near the Franco-German border were still frequent at this time. The Spitfires stayed with them until they turned towards the French coast, and then flew back to their bases in France.

Over the English Channel, P-Peter met no fighter opposition.

Arriving at RAF Coningsby, John had to join about ten other Lancasters waiting to land. This time, he accepted the need for stacking philosophically. At least, he would land on four good engines, he thought, and on a very pleasant evening with excellent visibility.

In fact, because of Sam's wound, P- Peter had a high degree of priority, and all the crew were in good spirits and not unduly tired when they finally touched down.

An ambulance was waiting to take Sam to the airfield's hospital, and Jenny was there to accompany him.

BATTLE ORDERS

***

Following debriefing, the crew received a message to go to a meeting in the afternoon, when they had eaten, showered and rested.

There were five other crews there and they were addressed by their CO, Group Captain Bannister. No-one had the slightest idea of the purpose of the meeting and all the airmen were rather bewildered. Their bewilderment veered towards dismay when their CO had completed his explanation, which was as follows:

'Now that much of France and many other European countries have been liberated, it's anticipated that the European war will not last much longer. Bomber Command has been planning ahead.'

You may know that Winston Churchill and President Roosevelt had a meeting in Quebec, Canada - the Quebec Conference - about ending the Pacific war. It was agreed that the RAF would help to finish off the Japs by providing Lancasters and Lincolns. These bombers and their crews would join crews from Canada, Australia and New Zealand, to form a formidable group, to be known as *Tiger Force*. From the island of Okinawa, recently captured by the Americans, *Tiger Force* will attack targets on the mainland of Japan.' He paused...

John and his crew remained perplexed, as did many other crews, and that probably showed on their faces.

'What on earth,' they were thinking, *'has Tiger Force got to do with us? We're in a squadron of Bomber Command.'*

The Group Captain appeared to read their minds.

'You are among the most successful crews in the Group. We now want you to serve the RAF, and your country, in a new way. We want you to join a training course to equip you for operations in the Pacific, as a part of *Tiger Force.'* He paused.

'Before beginning your training for *Tiger Force,* you will all have two weeks' leave.'

'May we ask questions, sir?' asked John.

'Of course. Go ahead.'

'The war in Europe isn't yet over.' John began, 'and there seems to be plenty of work for us yet. Why can't we carry on as we are? We've learnt a lot. We're much better than we were. And all our experience has been in Europe.'

'I understand all that, John,' replied the Group Captain, 'but we must begin planning now, and it is imperative that we begin with a highly efficient nucleus of experienced crews, as you all are.'

'I am giving you advance notice of *Tiger Force.* As you said, John, the war in Europe isn't yet over, though I don't suppose the Germans can hold out much longer. When Germany capitulates, we'll be able to concentrate fully on Japan. In the meantime, most of you will certainly be needed in Europe for more ops or perhaps diversionary flights.'

'What kind of special training do we need for the Pacific, sir?' Jack asked. The Group Captain smiled.

'Frankly, I don't know what exactly is being planned. Obviously, you are going to be flying over much longer distances, you'll have a different enemy who has different aircraft and techniques from Jerry, the terrain will be different, the climate will be different, and so on.'

'And apart from the differences you've mentioned, sir,' Scotty said, 'will each of us still have the same basic job in the crew?'

'In general, yes,' was the reply, 'although there may well be a requirement that you overlap a little more. Each one of you should be very competent in performing the work of another crew member. You have only one pilot, for example, so it is essential that someone, probably the Flight Engineer, is able to take over should anything happen to him. Your bomb-aimer already helps the navigator with map reading, and he will probably be trained in more of the arts of navigation. And, of course, you'll all need instruction in the recognition of Japanese aircraft. Your gunners, especially, will need to identify the silhouettes of aircraft such as the Mitsubishi Zero and the Kawanishi Shiden, after an exposure of a second or so.'

The Group Captain then gave the crews the latest information about their wounded comrades. In regard to Sam, he said,

'Sam Rogers has had a piece of shrapnel removed from his leg. I'm glad to say that no bones were broken, the leg has been well bandaged and he is comfortable and quite cheerful. He should be discharged from the hospital in a couple of days. He'll be fully informed about *Tiger Force*.'

'Now, I must go. Enjoy your leave.'

When the CO had gone there was a bubble of conversation.

'Do you think we've just been soft-soaped?' Freddie asked, with a grin.

'Or, to put it another way, given a load of bull?' another airmen added.

'Yes, perhaps we have, ' Jack said, 'but it's the CO's job to help to organise this *Tiger Force,* and there's a huge war in the Pacific. He's just doing his job.'

'But what a funny time to tell us about it,' Freddie expostulated. 'We've only recently landed after an op.'

'I suppose the CO decided to speak about it at the first opportunity so that he could tell us about our leave without any delay,' Reg said.

'That's probably true,' John said. 'I must say that I'm pleased to hear about the leave.'

'Yes, that bit is good anyway,' Scotty conceded, and grinned. 'Perhaps Lucy and I will manage to have our postponed honeymoon, then.'

CHAPTER 30

Flt.Sgt. Jack Rogers, DFM

RAF Coningsby

April 23rd, 1945

Dear Maurice,

Thanks for a newsy and welcome letter. So much is happening now and it's good to talk about it.

Congratulations to you on cycling twenty five miles to a farm, to pick up some eggs. Only one fresh egg a week is a bit much. When I was home, I got used to powdered eggs but there is nothing like a fresh one.

I was pleased to hear that the British Army has almost reached Rangoon. The 14th. is often called 'The Forgotten Army' isn't it, because our minds have been filled with the German war and we haven't thought enough about fighting in The Far

East? Those poor soldiers have been fighting in the tropical, humid heat of the Burmese jungle for years. Many have died from dysentery, malaria and various other fevers, and the Japanese have been fierce, and often cruel fighters. I hope those soldiers can soon be brought home.

We have a casualty. Poor old Sam was struck in the leg by a piece of shrapnel. He was in great pain, but he's in good hands now and will be OK.

We've been flying during the daytime. Quite a change! I think Reg, our wonderful navigator, prefers night flights, when he can navigate by the stars, which he loves.

We had a difficult time when our oxygen system was damaged. We were at 20,000 feet, where you don't last long without oxygen, but before we all passed out, John took our Lancaster down to below 10,000 feet where we don't need our oxygen masks anyway. We're lucky to have such a great skipper.

Keep your letters flowing, Maurice. I like to hear about all your family news.

BATTLE ORDERS

From your very good friend, Jack

***

In the Pig and Whistle that evening there was only one topic. Scotty expressed his reservations about the prospect of joining Tiger Force.

'It's great about the leave, ' he said, 'but I'm not really happy about going to the Far East. We've had twelve dicey ops over Europe, and now we're going to start doing it all over again with a different enemy, just when European ops have probably started to get easier.'

'I agree,' Jack said, 'but it may not be as bad as it sounds. I reckon both wars will soon end and we may not have to do much in the Far East. The Japanese are retreating in Burma, and in the Pacific; the Americans are capturing more and more islands.'

John nodded. 'I think Jack could be right, though I, too, understand Scotty's reservations. It's true we may find ourselves preparing for something that never happens. By the time our 'Tiger Force' training ends, the Pacific war may be over. Anyway, we're staying together as a crew. For me, that's important. We work together very well and we get on marvellously.'

There were murmurs of wholehearted agreement from all the others. John continued. 'Of course, we can't be certain about the future, but we're going on leave. Let's enjoy it!'

John's words seemed to lift the mood of all his crew, and lighten the atmosphere. Lively conversation, anecdotal exchanges and bursts of laughter began to fill the room.

Then a group of ground staff, including WAAFs entered the Saloon Bar. Jenny was among them, and she made her way immediately towards the crew. She told them that she had visited

Sam in the hospital, that he had proposed to her, and that she had accepted.

'That's great news,' John said. Congratulations. How is Sam feeling.'

'I think he's very happy,' Jenny replied. He's not in pain and we're both pleased about being engaged. And by the way, he has been told about *Tiger Force*, and I don't think he's very keen on that.'

'Of course not, ' Scotty exclaimed. 'You and Sam must have been hoping that the war against Germany will soon end, and that you could then look forward to spending your lives together, and living like normal human beings.'

Jenny nodded her head vigorously.

'That's absolutely right, Scotty.'

'We all sympathise with you,' John assured Jenny. 'This is going to affect us all in different ways. But we wish you and Sam every happiness. We'll visit Sam, of course, before we go on leave, to congratulate him on the engagement, and to wish him all the best. Now, you'll have a drink with us, won't you, so that we can toast you both.'

'That would be nice,' Jenny replied, 'but after that I must join my WAAF friends. Will you join us?'

'We'd all like that,' Reg said.

At the end of the evening, John, Arthur, Freddie, Scotty, Jack and Reg returned to their Nissen hut. Tomorrow they would have few opportunities to talk together as they would be visiting Sam before hurrying away to catch their various trains, so they had a brief chat before dropping into their beds.

They discussed their operational experiences over Germany. They had faced death many times, laughed together, pulled one another's legs, and all the time generated a unique camaraderie. All their experiences, they felt, had welded them into a very special crew, and drawn them ever closer together.

BATTLE ORDERS

Whatever the future held, they were glad that they would face it together.

***

John's crew had their fortnight of leave. It was a wonderful opportunity for Scotty and Lucy to have their long-postponed honeymoon, and Sam's leg healed quickly, so he was able to spend most of the time with Jenny.

On their return, the crew began their month-long training for *Tiger Force*. Sometimes they were together on long flights on new routes, which gave Reg, assisted by Freddie, an opportunity to hone his astro-navigational skills, and posed new challenges for all the crew. At other times, they had separate skill training, as when Sam and Scotty increased their knowledge of the appearance and capabilities of the most modern Japanese aircraft, and learned to identify them from short exposures of silhouettes, at various distances, and at various angles.

The crew were also called upon to take part in a number of diversionary flights, but had no more operational flights over Europe.

***

The crew met one morning in the NAAFI for coffee, and were chatting about their experiences, when they saw someone hurrying towards them.

It was a WAAF some of them knew. She looked excited and was out of breath when she reached them. She had some momentous news. It was May 8th, 1945. They looked up as she gasped out loudly.

'Have you heard? The Germans have signed an Unconditional Surrender Agreement. They've had to agree to our terms. We've won the War! Isn't it marvellous?'

Everyone in the room heard the news and there was a thunderous outburst of cheering, with happy smiles all round. Six years of death and destruction in Europe had ended. It was almost unbelievable.

'Wonderful news,' John said.

'The best,' Reg agreed. 'You know, we were kids of thirteen when this ghastly war began. It's dominated our lives. Some of us have lost family members and close friends. As a crew, we've managed to survive attacks by anti-aircraft guns and night fighters, but many of our friends in the squadron haven't been so lucky. My God, let's for heaven's sake start living a normal life when we get the chance!'

'Yes, as soon as possible,' Terry said.

'But that can't happen for some time because we've got to help to defeat the Japs,' Jack reminded the others.

Before anyone could respond, however, the crew became aware that there was a rising commotion in various parts of the Station - a buzz of voices, rising in tone, and punctuated by shouts, cheers and laughter. Aircrews and ground staff, including WAAFS, were all celebrating what was to be known as VE Day, Victory in Europe Day. Several groups were making for the bars; others talked excitedly in small groups. A gramophone appeared on a trestle table, someone wound it up and put on a record, and dance music flooded the Station. Some airmen and WAAFs began to dance. Many airmen abandoned whatever they were doing to talk about what had happened, and to speculate how they might be affected. Excitement and euphoria spread like wildfire.

BATTLE ORDERS

John's crew left their table to join in the celebrations with other crews and with friends among the ground staff, and to dance with the WAAFs. It was a time of uninhibited celebration, when everything else was temporarily forgotten, or pushed into the background, as the full implications of peace in Europe began to be realised. For the moment, no-one gave a thought to the other war, yet to be won. They cheered, drank, sang and danced. Everybody was caught up in the same overwhelming relief, excitement and joy.

***

John knew his crew would soon be affected by Germany's capitulation. Preparations for the Pacific War would be accelerated. Some crew-members did not have long to wait.

Reg was told the very next day that the radar aids, H2S and Gee would be removed immediately from P-Peter, because he must now use only astro-navigation on every flight. He didn't mind that, for he had not used radar for some time. He knew that for the War against Japan, radar would be of little use. The range of Gee was only about 400 miles. All bomber aircraft destined for Okinawa, and the *Tiger Force,* would use astro-navigation, because the distances to be covered were enormous and there was no alternative to the stars.

John asked Reg how he felt about navigating their Lancaster over India, Burma, Thailand, French Indo-China, and a long stretch of the Pacific Ocean. ' Have you any special worries about that?'

'Yes and no,' Reg answered. 'I'm happy about the astro-navigation side, but much of the route covers poorly-mapped areas, there are long flights over mountains, and we may have to pass through typhoons or monsoons. I suppose I am a bit unsure about what to expect flying over an area we've never experienced before.'

'Yes,' John said, 'but you've never been in any doubt about our position and always got us back safely.'

'Thanks, John,' Reg responded, and grinned. 'With a little help from the pilot.'

John laughed. 'But I'm only the bus driver who steers whatever course you give me.' He then spoke more seriously and almost confidentially.

'We all have our special concerns, Reg. Mine is that the Lancaster might not be well adapted to flying in tropical conditions. No-one knows how it will perform in Asia.'

It was true all crew members had concerns. Scotty and Sam remained uneasy about possible attacks by *kamikazi* fighter planes.

'They won't fire at us,' Sam said to Scotty, 'they'll just try to crash their aircraft into ours.'

'Yes, we'll just have to hope that we can destroy them before that happens,' Scotty replied.

Terry was concerned about carrying sufficient fuel for the long flights planned. If any of the targets in Japan were in the northern island of Hokkaido, they would have to fly further north than Vladivostok, while even Tokyo was 800 miles from Okinawa.

John wondered how long the Japanese could continue the war. The British 14th. Army had pushed back the Japanese in the Burmese jungle, and the Americans and Australians had captured some parts of New Guinea, and several islands of the Dutch East Indies. The Americans had leapfrogged many islands to capture Okinawa. Clearly the end could not be so far away, he thought. But the Japanese always fought desperately and they had occupied such an extensive area of the Far East that the War seemed never-ending.

One day he chatted to Jack, who raised the question of invading Japan. John shuddered to think how that could turn out. His view, he told Jack, was that it would be even more dangerous than the invasion of Normandy.

'Why do you think that, John?'

'Because the sea distance is greater, the Allies would not have the command in the air that they had in Europe, and there would be the *kamikazi* pilots ready to fly their aircraft straight into ours.'

It was a horrifying prospect.

'Do you really think the Allies will invade mainland Japan, John?'

'I do. Unless something entirely unexpected takes place, it must surely happen before long,' John replied.

***

There had been some tremendous naval battles between the United States and the Japanese Navies. Losses were heavy on both sides, but there was a general feeling that a good proportion of the Japanese Navy had been destroyed.

John discussed the various developments with his crew in the Pig and Whistle one evening. All the crew were sitting comfortably in a circle, holding their pints of mild and bitter.

'I think Japan may be on its knees,' he suggested.

'Yes, I agree,' Terry said, 'but we have no idea how long it will be before it surrenders. There are still several islands where they are holding out. They fight to the death because they regard it as a disgrace to be taken prisoner. And it is one thing to fight them successfully in lands they have occupied, but invading the Japanese mainland is quite a different matter. This war could drag on for months ... even years.'

'You're probably right,' Jack said, 'and it might not end until the Allies have invaded and conquered all four main islands.'

'Well, you know what I think about that,' John responded. 'I believe that if and when we invade the Japanese mainland - irrespective of which island we attack - the casualties will be horrendous!'

'And what about 'Tiger Force?' asked Scotty. 'When are we going to fly to Okinawa to play our part in finishing off the Japs?'

'I haven't a clue,' John admitted. 'I'm afraid we just have to wait. One day we'll have orders to fly out there, but I don't think the island is ready yet. We're having to build a new airfield there.'

'I'm in no hurry,' Sam admitted. 'I'm not worried about going on normal operations, but those *kamikazi* suicide pilots do worry me a bit.'

'Me, too,' Scotty said,

'I don't like the present uncertainty, ' Reg said. 'Surely we'll hear something soon?'

They did, but it was not what they were expecting.

CHAPTER 31

Flt Sgt .Jack Rogers, DFM

RAF Coningsby.

May 12th, 1945,

Dear Maurice,

At last the long nightmare is over! I believe the war against Germany finally ended on May 8th, following Hitler's suicide on May 1st. I've just seen the newsreel at an Odeon cinema. What excitement! The whole country seemed to burst into joyful life, with bonfires, church bells ringing, flag waving, dancing and singing, and lights everywhere, instead of the dismal wartime blackout we've all got used to. People were packed along Whitehall and in front of Buckingham Palace, and the Royal Family appeared on the balcony again and again, sometimes with Churchill. Britain still knows how to celebrate!

We were tremendously excited here, too. We cheered, danced to a Glenn Miller record (with WAAFs), drank, and had a very noisy party!

Well, you won't have any more doodlebugs or rockets, but it looks as if rationing is going to last for some time yet. And you'll have to wait a while before you can enjoy a really good steak again.

Now we have to finish off the Japs. Some of our crew don't want to fly out to Okinawa to join Tiger Force. Scotty is married and naturally wants to stay in the UK, and Sam and Jenny want to get hitched. Also, they're not at all sure how they'll cope with Japanese kamikaze (suicide) pilots. I suppose we all feel we've already done our bit. But when we're told the time has come to go East, I'm sure we'll all be happy enough to go. I think we've got a lot of what the RAF calls 'esprit de corps.' And we're happy to be together.

It's always good to hear from you. I hope we can keep in touch when I'm in the Far East.

Your very good friend, Jack

BATTLE ORDERS

There was a glint of excitement in Sam's eyes as he spoke to other members of the crew. He suggested that they should meet as soon as possible in the NAAFI canteen. He said he had a wonderful surprise for them; something none of them could have expected.

They responded with alacrity and were soon sitting round a table in the NAAFI, clutching cups of coffee. All eyes, full of anticipation and curiosity were turned towards Sam. Scotty was probably the least patient.

'Come on then, Sam. Spill the beans. We can't wait. My guess is that you and Jenny have been secretly married. If that's so...'

'That's a lousy guess, Scotty,' Sam interrupted, with a grin. 'Very wide of the mark. Actually, I'm expecting the subject of my surprise to walk through the NAAFI door any minute now.'

All eyes swivelled towards the door. Some airmen and WAAFs entered, but Sam didn't react so they were not the surprise.

By this time, other airmen and WAAFs in the NAAFI knew that someone quite unexpected was about to enter, and there was a hush as all eyes focused on the door.

John's crew had no more idea than others in the room, who might be about to come in.

Then, to the amazement of most of the crew, in walked ex-Prisoner-Of-War Bill Irons! He was not well known to everyone, but they all knew him by sight, and as soon as they set eyes on him, cheers and a resounding roar arose from all corners of the room, along with expressions of astonishment and delight. He was the first POW to return to the Station since the German capitulation.

Bill made a beeline for Sam as he approached the table and all John's crew gathered round him to shake his hand, pound his back and welcome him back with unbounded enthusiasm. Scotty brought another chair while Jack fetched an extra cup of coffee. John smiled.

'Bill, Sam has told us about recent experiences of POWs, some of which were pretty awful, I think, and it's marvellous that you've managed to get back safe and sound.'

'Yes, there have been some dicey moments, but I've also had some luck, too.'

'So, what happened, Bill,' Sam asked. 'You'd written to me about all the chaos as the war was drawing to a close, with refugees, German deserters and wounded, and Russian soldiers, all milling about near your POW Camp.'

'Yes, and when were you released?' Scotty said.

'Well, in fact we prisoners weren't actually released. On May 2nd the German guards just disappeared, leaving us free. That sounds fine, but with all the movement around us, we were very uncertain what to do, which way to turn. We wondered how far away were the British and American armies. We weren't too keen to be rescued by the Russians.

'Then, hooray! Six American jeeps and two lorries suddenly appeared, the troops spilled out and gave us more food than we'd seen for months. I can't tell you how grateful we were. Our food had been getting worse as the Camp became increasingly disorganised.'

'Thank God for the Yanks!' Sam breathed.

'After a while, they took us to Lüneburg, where we stayed in some German barracks for a few days. The Yanks continued to provide us with plenty of food until the time came for us to fly back to England. We flew back in a Lancaster and landed somewhere in the Midlands. There were dozens of WAAFs waiting to welcome us there. They took us to a hangar decked out with bunting, where there were tables laid with tea, cakes and sandwiches. There was a small RAF band, and afterwards we danced with the WAAFs. The whole of the welcome once we set foot in the UK was overwhelming, really quite wonderful.'

Sam had listened very attentively and seemed close to tears. Finally, he said. 'It's great to see you again, Bill. You've had some nasty experiences and I'm so glad it's all over.' Sam and Bill turned and hugged each other.

'It sounds as if you were very lucky that the Americans were the first soldiers to reach your Camp,' Jack said. 'They looked after you well and obviously co-ordinated their rescue with the British so that you were brought home as soon as possible.'

Bill agreed. 'Yes, we were very lucky. Had the Russian Army arrived first I don't know where we'd have finished up. It might have been alright, but there would have been more uncertainty.'

'I have a suggestion to make, ' John said. 'Let's have a drink just before lunch to celebrate Bill's return, and tonight we'll all have a meal together, and celebrate Bill's return properly, in the Pig and Whistle.'

'That's would be great, ' Bill said. 'Later today I must meet some other friends, and there are one or two senior officers who would like to see me, and Sam and I will have a long chat. Then tomorrow I'll begin the leave we ex-POWs are entitled to have.'

'And well deserve,' John added.

***

Preparations for going to the island of Okinawa were now intensified. There were new courses for each member of the crew, and longer flights to discover any new problems for aircraft or crew they might reveal.

The aircraft to be used by Tiger Force were Lancasters and a larger version of them called Lincolns. Unfortunately, neither aircraft could carry enough fuel for the enormous distances to be covered from Okinawa to potential targets in Tokyo, Yokohama, and the island of Hokkaido.

Early ideas to solve the fuel problem had envisaged 580 -gallon tanks in the wings, and a 680-gallon tank in the bomb bay. There had also been tentative discussions about a so-called *saddle tank* replacing the mid-upper gunner, though that would have seriously reduced the fire-power of the aircraft.

It was evident that every conceivable solution to the fuel problem had serious disadvantages.

There were also training problems. The astro-navigational skills of some navigators had been described by one senior officer as 'rusty as hell. '

Reg Atkins was exceptional in that regard. He always loved looking at the night sky at 20,000 feet because, well above the Earth's electric light and smoky pollution, they shone with a radiant beauty. He was therefore quite relaxed about using the stars throughout every night flight.

Most other navigators had a different view. Astronavigation involved much more effort than working with radar or simply using radio beacons, and it was less accurate, so they had used the stars only as a last resort.

But now, astro-navigation was to be practised by all navigators. There was, quite simply, no alternative. Rusty skills had to be polished; and they were.

BATTLE ORDERS

Within a few weeks, every member of all the crews earmarked for Tiger Force was fully trained and ready for the new challenges.

But when would they fly to the Far East?

How long would they have to stay on the island of Okinawa?

Which parts of Japan would they attack?

CHAPTER 32

Flt. Sgt Jack Rogers,

July 28th, 1945   RAF Coningsby.

Dear Maurice,

I'm glad to hear that you and your family are well. How are you all finding life after six years of war? I would think that the most important change is that you can go out and about, visit cinemas and theatres, etc. without the risk of being bombed. And wasn't it dreary having a black-out – no lights anywhere – for six years. I know there's a terrible shortage of houses and just about everything else, as most of our factories have been geared to war-work for so long, but it can only get better!

I think the most important news recently has been the landslide victory of the Labour Party on July 26th. Many people thought that the Conservatives might win because Winston Churchill proved to be such a great war leader.

He is still very popular, but perhaps not seen as well suited to be a peacetime Prime Minister.

Anyway, the new Labour Government now has to cope with the war against Japan as well as dealing with all the problems following the long war against Germany. Then there are plans to nationalise many major industries, including railways, coal mines, airlines, electricity, gas, transport and water. That will all cost a lot of money, and after six year of war there isn't much of that left! But I expect the country will give the new Government a fair chance to see how it manages.

Our crew is still very busy but we have no idea when we'll fly out to join Tiger Force. We all feel that we've had quite enough training for our new tasks, but it just goes on day after day. Perhaps the new airfield that is being built in Okinawa is not yet finished.

I really look forward to receiving your letters. Keep writing!

BATTLE ORDERS

Every good wish, from your good friend,

Jack

Jack heard it first on the radio, and he could hardly wait to tell the others. It was August 7th and all the crew were meeting after lunch. Jack was the last to arrive. He flopped into a chair. The others could see that he had something of significance to tell them, and leaned forward expectantly.

'An atomic bomb has been dropped on Hiroshima,' he announced breathlessly. ' It has almost wiped out the city and there are thousands of casualties. It happened yesterday, August 6th at 8:30 in the morning.'

For a few moments, Jack's fellow-crewmen were stunned. This was an entirely unexpected development. Their thoughts had been on *Tiger Force,* and taking part in normal bombing operations against the Japanese mainland. They knew nothing about nuclear war. Then Scotty broke the silence.

'Well, perhaps that will help to shorten the war, but what a terrible death toll.'

'It may shorten the war,' John responded, 'but I'm not so sure. London and Berlin have been heavily bombed, but in neither capital did the morale of the people collapse.'

'No, it probably stiffened resistance in London,' Jack reflected.

'In any case,' Terry pointed out, 'Hiroshima is an important port, not the capital. Tokyo is where the big decisions are made about war and peace.'

The others were silent. All they knew about atom bombs was that they were obviously horrible weapons, and that the war had clearly entered a new and grimmer phase.   They didn't know what to make of it.

John sensed their mood.

'Tomorrow,' he said, 'we've all got a busy day with our specialist departments.   Let's meet in The Pig and Whistle in the evening.   I suppose the atom bombing of Hiroshima might affect us in some way. I really don't know.   Let's talk about it then.'

***

The crew sat in their favourite corner of the Saloon Bar in The Pig and Whistle, each lounging comfortably in the same easy chair he had occupied dozens of times previously.   They sipped their beers in contented relaxation.

'Well, what do you think about Hiroshima now you've had time to mull over it?' John asked.

Terry responded immediately.

'I'm not really happy that the war has now entered such a terrible stage, and that we can never put the clock back. What on earth will the next stage bring?   I mean, we know that Japan has suffered a long string of defeats on land, sea and in the air, and that her total defeat can't be long delayed. Was it really necessary to take this awful step into the unknown?   In any case, as you said yesterday, John, the bombing of cities sometimes stiffens resistance.   The atom bombing of Hiroshima won't necessarily shorten the war.'

'But it might,' Sam countered, 'and if it helps to bring about the end of this terrible war, then I think it was justified.'

Scotty concurred.

'This war looks as if it could drag on for years. The Japs are well dug in over a huge expanse of South East Asia and the Pacific. Any way we can shorten the war is to be welcomed.'

John had been listening intently to the different views. *'This is the first time,'* he thought, *'that opinion among the crew on any matter of importance, has been so deeply divided.'* Finally, he said,

'I must admit, I'm not at all sure about it. There are arguments for and against. The use of atomic weapons is highly controversial. It's ghastly; but so is war. I expect dropping an atom bomb on Hiroshima will be argued about for many years by historians, politicians and others.'

'I'm sure you're right, John,' Reg said, and smiled as he added, 'but it's happened, and there's nothing we can do about it.'

'That's right,' Jack said, 'but I agree with John that what's happened will be controversial for a very long time. I, too, don't know whether the use of an atomic bomb is justified at the present time. When we seem to be winning the war, is this huge step into the unknown justifed?'

'I don't think we can make up our minds about the bombing at the present time,' Sam suggested. 'Let us wait and see what happens next. If it does bring about the ending of the war in a fairly short time, then I, for one, will say it was fully justified.'

'Can't we leave it at that then?' Freddie asked... 'Listen to the music...Someone's just put on a Glen Miller record - my favourite band - and if you don't mind, I'd like to ask that attractive WAAF sitting near the bar to join me in a quickstep.'

'Go ahead, Freddie,' John said. 'We can carry on this discussion another time. Let's just enjoy this evening.'

CHAPTER 33

Flight Sergeant Jack Rogers

RAF Coningsby,

August 8th, 1945

Dear Maurice,

I am sending this letter as soon as I can because I'd like to know what you think about the dropping of an atom bomb on Hiroshima.

Our crew is split on the issue. The gunners, Sam and Scotty, feel that it is fully justified and that it must shorten a war which has been dragging on with a huge number of casualties. They think that in the end it will save many lives.

Then there is the view of our flight engineer, Terry. He feels that the Allies are well on the way to winning the war and that atomic warfare at this stage is not necessary and therefore unjustified.

Most of the crew are undecided because the final outcome is not yet clear, but I cannot remember any issue on which they have differed so clearly or on which they feel so strongly.

We understand that the atom bomb has flattened Hiroshima and caused an enormous number of casualties, and that there will be many more as radiation takes its toll over the coming years.

You said that peace in Europe hasn't brought much joy to many people. I'm sure there must be a feeling of anti-climax and disappointment that life is not much better at the moment.

I imagine that the war has been so costly that the country is virtually bankrupt. And beating the Japs will add to the country's debts.

Rationing has to continue and I know that many items of food that were never actually rationed, including bananas and oranges, are still not available. Then there's the shortage of houses when many service people are being demobbed and returning to Britain hoping to get married and start a family.

But cheer up, Maurice. You and your family have survived the war, and, as I said before, things can only get better, but it will take time.

Nil desperandum!

Your very good friend,

Jack

It was August 9th. Scotty, who had been listening to the latest news bulletin. rushed to join the others, who were sitting on deckchairs outside the Sergeants' Mess.

'Another atom bomb has been dropped,' he announced, breathlessly. 'This time on Nagasaki, a port on Japan's southern island of Kyushu. The destruction is widespread and there have been thousands of deaths. A huge mushroom cloud formed over the city.'

Most of his listeners were stunned into silence, but Terry was immediately indignant.

'One was bad enough, ' he said, 'but dropping another one can't be necessary. This war is going to end very soon anyway. It makes me wonder whether atom bombs are now being dropped because they have just been perfected as weapons of war, and ready to be tried out. Perhaps their designers and manufacturers, as well as the politicians, were anxious to discover how effective they are.'

Terry's last suggestion shocked the others into silence. They had learnt quite a lot in the last twenty-four hours about the terribly destructive power of nuclear bombs, about the number of expected deaths through radiation, and the likely incidence of cancer deaths over many years.

'Terry,' John said, in a tone of mock reproof, 'I've never before heard you sound so cynical.'

'Sorry, John, but I feel very strongly about it.'

Jack sought to find common ground.

'As I see it, there could be some truth in Terry's suggestion. Obviously, many years of research have led to the perfection of the atom bomb as a weapon of war. Once it was ready for use, and the war seemed to be dragging on, the leaders of the Free World decided to use it. In the middle of a war, it is winning it that matters above all, and I'm afraid moral considerations take a back seat.'

'That's a fair summary of what usually happens,' Scotty agreed, 'but we still don't know whether dropping atom bombs will bring the war to an early end.'

'If it does, ' Sam said, 'It'll be wonderful! We all want a peaceful world as soon as possible, don't we?'

***

Several days went by without any further news, and the crew wondered whether the dropping of atomic bombs had really made any difference. Then, on August 15th came further epoch-making news. It was what everyone had been hoping to hear.

Emperor Hirohito broadcast to the Japanese nation and announced that his country was surrendering unconditionally to the Allied forces from that date.

Whatever the crew felt about the atomic bombs, they were jubilant about Japan's capitulation, and their relief was profound. At first, they found it difficult to accept that the world was now at peace and they would no longer have to take part in attacks on Japan. They heard that all aircraft were to be grounded and that they would shortly be sent on indefinite leave. A weight had been taken off their minds, the prospect of resuming a normal life dawned, and they felt suddenly, for the first time in many years, happy and carefree.

As the news of peace travelled around the Station, cheers erupted everywhere, and as on VE Day, airmen and WAAFs, air crews and ground staff, celebrated by singing and dancing to war-time songs, played on their gramophone perched on a trestle table. Work stopped everywhere, and some airmen made a rush for the bar in both the Sergeants' Mess and the Officers' Mess. This would be known as VJ Day (Victory against Japan Day). Everywhere there was an overwhelming feeling of happiness and relief that at long last both terrible wars were in the past. At last every airman could think about the future, about careers in *civvy street*, and about families and home life.

John's crew made their way that evening to the Pig and Whistle and joined their friends among the ground crews and the WAAFs, who included Sarah and Jenny.

No-one was now concerned with any news from overseas. It was their own news that was of paramount interest.

'I'm really glad that we're not going to the Pacific, ' Scotty told the others, 'especially as Lucy is expecting a baby and of course I want to be with them both.'

'That's marvellous,' John beamed. 'Congratulations.' He addressed the others. 'Let's drink to Scotty, Lucy and the baby!'

Before they could respond to that, Sam said that he had some news he wanted them all to hear. He held Jenny's hand and they both smiled.

'Jenny and I have now fixed a date for our marriage. We'd like to invite you all to come. It will be during our leave. We very much hope you'll all be there.'

'I'm sure we'd all love to be with you on that very special day, ' John said.

'It's great news, ' Jack said, 'and do you have somewhere to live?'

'No, we don't. There must be a massive housing shortage as so many houses were destroyed by bombing and there has been very little building for some time. Perhaps we'll be able to have a couple of rooms in my parents' house. That's our only hope. My sister will be moving out shortly as she is going to a Teachers' Training College so that should help.'

'Well, good luck to your sister, and the very best of luck to you, Sam,' Jack added.

'It's good to hear everyone's news,' John said, 'but bear in mind that none of us will be demobbed for some time.'

'Why not? ' Sam asked.

'Well, it's going to be a *First In, First Out* policy. Those who joined the Forces at the beginning of the War, and have served for six years, will be back to civvy street very soon. We're among the youngest and we joined the RAF in the last few years, so we'll be last out. That's very fair, isn't it?'

'It is, 'Sam conceded, 'so what will happen to us now? '

'I think we'll all have to do something else in the RAF for the next year or two,' John replied. 'But that shouldn't dampen our spirits. The great thing is that two wars, both against countries trying to dominate the World, have ended. We've helped to defeat both enemies. We have survived the most destructive war of all time and are now going on a period of indefinite leave!'

'Yes, that's great news, 'Scotty agreed. 'But why is it going to be indefinite?'

'Well, I imagine that the authorities need time to work out what to do with us, and to make plans for that.' John replied. 'And now, can we take up my suggestion and begin to celebrate the best news we've ever had, that we're at peace, and also drink to the happiness of our lucky couples?'

'Yes please,' Reg said.

'I can't wait, ' Sam grinned.

Jack raised his glass to propose a toast.

'To the happiness of the lucky couples.'

They all drank to that, and then someone suggested a sing song. Jack looked at all his fellow airmen and they all nodded in agreement.

He strode quickly to the piano and began to play a medley of war-time songs, and everyone in the room soon joined in the singing.

He began with one from the First World War –

'Keep the Home Fires Burning, ' and followed that with, 'We'll Meet Again'

'If You Were The Only Girl in the World, ' and 'Roll Out the Barrel. '

Jack then paused to find out whether his audience would like to carry on singing, and John seized the opportunity to say a few words.

'Jack, you've played and sung for us many times, and we are very grateful to you for that. 'Everyone in the room cheered loudly, and when it was quiet again, John continued,

'The first time we heard you sing, we were in a desperate situation. Our Lancaster had ditched in the North Sea. You had helped to launch our dinghy by diving into the freezing sea, a very brave act which may have saved all our lives. Then we sat for hours in wet flying kit while waves splashed over the sides. Later, we took our chance in a flimsy lifeboat that had been dropped to us by parachute, from an Air/Sea Rescue aircraft. We were very cold and the sea was getting rougher. I'm sure we all had similar thoughts.

'Would our little lifeboat break up?

'Would we die, one after the other, of exposure?

'We all felt that as time went by, our chance of being rescued was fading. Then, suddenly, something happened that was really astonishing. You began to sing some songs that we all knew, some of which we'd learnt at school. We soon joined in singing those songs and, for a while, they took our minds away from our desperate situation. It was quite amazing. Somehow, everything seemed better after that. We chatted more and talked about our hopes for the future.

'Finally, the launch sent to rescue us by the Air/Sea Rescue people, guided to us by two Hudson aircraft, came into view. A wonderful moment. We were saved. But you had kept up our spirits at a critical time. We'll always be grateful for that. Thank you, Jack.'

Everyone present then joined in singing 'For He's a Jolly Good Fellow,' and that was followed by loud applause. Then, with minds full of the news of Japan's surrender, the happy event announced by John's crew, and the graphic reminder of how the crew had survived ditching in the North Sea, the party dispersed.

BATTLE ORDERS

John's crew would face a future quite different from the one they had expected only a week ago.

**

www.ingramcontent.com/pod-product-compliance
Lightning Source LLC
Chambersburg PA
CBHW071905020726
47502CB00003B/910

* 9 781911 593775 *